BERTIE & THE CRIME OF PASSION

PETER LOVESEY
BERTIE & THE
CRIME OF PASSION

THE MYSTERIOUS PRESS

Published by Warner Books

A Time Warner Company

Mysterious Press books are published by Warner Books, Inc.,
1271 Avenue of the Americas, New York, NY 10020.

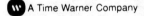 A Time Warner Company

The Mysterious Press name and logo are registered trademarks of Warner Books, Inc.

Printed in the United States of America
First published in Great Britain 1993 by Little, Brown & Company
First U.S. printing: January 1995

10 9 8 7 6 5 4 3 2 1

Library of Congress Cataloging-in-Publication Data

Lovesey, Peter.
    Bertie and the crime of passion / Peter Lovesey.
      p.   cm.
    ISBN 0-89296-550-9
    1. Edward VII, King of Great Britain, 1841–1910—Fiction.
    2. Bernhardt, Sarah, 1844–1923—Fiction. 3. Murder—France—Paris—Fiction.
    4. Paris (France)—Fiction. I. Title.
    PR6062.O86B45 1995
    823'.914—dc20   94-28274
                                                    CIP

Note to the Reader

Anyone coming freshly to this series of detective stories may be interested to know that in an earlier book, *Bertie and the Tinman*, reference was made to the detective memoirs of King Edward VII having been deposited in a sealed metal box in the Public Record Office. A hundred-year embargo was placed on publication. This might explain why biographies of the king published prior to 1987 contain no reference to his career as an amateur sleuth.

However, in an afternote from the editor, readers were advised that it was extremely unlikely whether Bertie, either as Prince of Wales or king, ever found the time or inclination to write a book. This publication of a third volume should dispose of all doubts.

BERTIE & THE CRIME OF PASSION

The start of the adventure is sharp in my memory. Picture me at breakfast in my suite at the Hotel Bristol in the rue du Faubourg-Saint-Honoré, where I arrived the previous evening with my faithful Irish terrier, Jack, and thirty-odd servants. Only the delights of Paris could tempt me year after year, each March, across the freezing Channel. It is the most enchanting of all cities. A surprising claim, you may think, from a future British sovereign, but I must be truthful. London is not in the business of enchantment, for it is the capital of the world, a masculine metropolis, soberly dressed, commanding respect, not adoration. I suppose of all our native cities, Edinburgh holds the most appeal, but for all its Caledonian charm, Edinburgh will never let you forget that it is built on granite. I definitely prefer Paris. I remember vividly toward the end of my first visit there, at thirteen, pleading with the Empress Eugénie (I adored her) to allow my sister and me to remain. She said she fancied that my mama and papa could not do without us, to which I retorted, "Not do without us? Don't fancy that, for there are six more of us at home, and they don't want *us*."

My secretary, Francis Knollys, ever the brake on my spirit of adventure, but a good fellow for all that, put his grizzled head around the door. His timing is uncanny, for I had just finished the last croissant in the basket.

"What is it, Francis?" I inquired as I shook the crumbs off the napkin.

"Your engagements for the day, sir."

"Not many, I trust?" One of the problems with Paris is that it's a honey pot for royal visitors, and if I don't watch out, I find myself doing nothing but visiting and receiving cousins and nephews.

"The Duc de Rheims will call at ten."

"That, I can endure, so long as he doesn't insist on standing beside me." (I should explain that the duc is a beanpole at least six feet six inches tall.)

Chapter 1

Paris.

Paris.

Paris.

No good at all. Do you notice how the pen twitches each time I form the word? I suppose not, if you are reading these memoirs of mine in print, but you can take it from me that in my own fair hand the effect is just as if a spider had walked through the ink.

It is hardly surprising.

I'll try once more.

Paris in 1891 was the setting for one of the most audacious adventures in my secret career as an amateur detective.

That, I think, is legible.

Eighteen ninety-one, the year I saved the Sûreté from obloquy. I must guard against embroidering the account, for these things sometimes grow in the telling, and I was so occupied in the drama that I kept no journal. Fortunately, certain other documents have survived, including several letters to my dear wife, Alexandra, the Princess of Wales (who was visiting her family in Copenhagen at the time), and I shall refer to these to curb excesses of the imagination.

"Madame Bernhardt is coming at eleven."

"Sarah! Now *she*'s in proportion, charmingly in proportion."

"And luncheon with the Comte d'Agincourt has, unfortunately, been canceled at his request."

"Canceled, Francis?" This news surprised me. I didn't have any objection to time in hand, so to speak, with the bewitching Bernhardt, but Jules d'Agincourt was an old friend who wouldn't lightly have broken a luncheon engagement. "Did he offer a reason?"

"He apologizes profusely, sir."

"Of course he does, but what is behind this?"

"He characterizes it as a family crisis."

"Is that all? My family is permanently in a state of crisis."

"That was all he said, sir."

The matter continued to exercise me until the lady known across Europe as the Divine Sarah arrived to pay her compliments, wrapped in a cloak of gray velvet. My friendship with this peerless scrap of flesh and bone goes back more years than I care to name, to a first night at the Odéon, when she played the Queen of Spain in Hugo's *Ruy Blas*, with an exquisite coronet of pearls and lace fastened high on her red hair. She mesmerized me. I think it was, above all, the voice, that incomparable sound that ranged from the purity of a blackbird's song to the power of the great bell of Notre Dame. You may think I exaggerate; that, I promise you, was the effect on me that night. I fell in love with Bernhardt. All Paris fell in love with her. Such is my devotion that one evening I actually joined her on the stage to play the part of the corpse of her murdered lover in Sardou's *Fédora*—a splendid lark that only the French could appreciate, Sarah weeping over me as I lay in my shroud longing for a cigar and trying not to cough.

"Sarah, my dear!"

"Bertie." We embraced. The French are terribly demonstrative, so don't let your imagination run riot over a bear hug from Sarah. For some unfathomable reason, she had never entirely capitulated to my charms. Being French, she didn't mind everyone believing she had—which made my situation all the more frustrating. But I still adored her and looked to the future with confidence.

"So kind, so kind." I spoke in French, of course. I have spoken the language since my youth.

"What is it you are saying?" she asked.

"You are so kind."

"Ah—but why?"

"Why, your coming to see me here. You know I'm not too comfortable visiting your house."

She waved her hand dismissively. "In Paris, it's no scandal. It's nothing."

"I know that, Sarah. There's another reason. The last time, if you remember, a monkey sat beside me on the sofa."

She threw back her head and laughed at the memory.

I inquired charitably, "Do you still have the little creature?"

"Darwin? Yes. He's very friendly."

"I would rather be friends with you. And is the lion cub still in residence?"

She shook her head. "Stupid people complained about the smell when he got large. He wasn't smelly. It was hardly noticeable. I donated him to the Jardin des Plantes. But I still keep a cheetah and the parrots."

The sure way to charm Sarah is to talk about her menagerie, all of which, believe it or not, is housed in domestic rooms at her house in the boulevard Pereire. I don't mind talking about our dumb friends (my wife, Alix, is dotty about them and keeps a cockatoo in her rooms), but I draw the line at sharing a sofa with a monkey.

With nice timing, Jack trotted in and sniffed La Bernhardt's boots. For this understandable curiosity, my terrier was snatched up and hauled to her bosom. He endured it philosophically.

"What is the gossip?" I asked, steering the conversation into more familiar waters.

"About you—or me?" asked Sarah.

"About everyone else, of course. Is there anything I should be told about the Agincourts?"

She gave me a penetrating stare with those Cleopatra eyes. "When did you arrive?"

"Last night."

"Haven't you heard about the man who was shot at the Moulin Rouge last week?"

"A man shot?" I spoke so sharply that Jack gave a yelp and leapt from Bernhardt's arms. "Not Jules d'Agincourt?"

"No, not Jules."

"Thank God for that. You'd better tell me, Sarah. Jules was due to call on me today and has canceled. There was some message about a family crisis."

"A family crisis!" This innocuous phrase caused a hoot of laughter. The refinements of polite conversation are quite foreign to Bernhardt.

"Come, come," I said. "If someone was shot and it concerns the Agincourts in some way, I demand to be told."

She said, "Do you remember Rosine?"

"The child?"

"A child no longer, Bertie."

"Little Rosine was the victim? That's dreadful! She used to sit on my knee and play with my watch chain."

"Stop leaping to conclusions, Bertie. I'm trying to tell you that Rosine blossomed into the most beautiful woman in Paris."

Coming from Bernhardt, this was uncommonly altruistic, and I told her so.

She angled her head in a pose that emphasized her flawless neck and said, "I'm a grandmother now."

I said—and meant it, "That, I refuse to believe, Sarah."

Having fished for her compliment and landed it, she returned to the sinister matter under discussion: "Rosine became engaged. It was her fiancé who was killed."

"At the Moulin Rouge?"

She nodded. "The papers are full of it. I'm surprised you haven't heard."

"I haven't looked at a paper since I got here. An accident?"

"Accident, my aunt! In a dance hall? It was cold-blooded murder, Bertie."

"My word. That would certainly explain why Jules felt unable to call on me." I stood up, my sleuthing sense alerted. "Have they arrested the assassin?"

"The Sûreté?" She rolled her eyes upward.

"Then I must find out whether I can be of assistance."

Sarah now introduced a note of caution. "It may not be exactly as I described it. You know what the newspapers are like."

"You don't have to tell me, of all people, about the newspapers, my dear."

"Everyone likes to dramatize a little."

"Speaking of drama," I said, my thoughts galloping ahead, "what are you playing at the moment?"

"Nothing."

"Resting—is that the expression?"

"Hardly. A week from today, I embark with the Bernhardt Troupe on a world tour, commencing in New York."

"Excellent!" I told her. "In that case, my turtledove, you may join me in unraveling this mystery." Momentous decisions are sometimes taken lightly. Bernhardt had never seen me in fearless pursuit of a murderer. Who could tell what effect Bertie the Detective might have on her? This could be the opportunity I had waited twenty years to grasp.

But she pursed her lips ominously.

"No, Bertie."

"No, Sarah?"

"I am insulted."

I stared at her. "But why?"

"I will not be likened to a turtle, even by a prince."

"A turtledove, my dear. That is something else—a pretty bird renowned for the purity of its note and the constancy of its affection."

"*Tourterelle.*"

"What did I say?"

"*Tortue.*"

A foolish error, particularly as I've consumed gallons of turtle soup in my time. "But you will accompany me?"

"Impossible. I have to pack for the world tour, Bertie."

"How many trunks?"

"Seventy-five."

I blinked in disbelief. "For the entire troupe?"

She opened her hands in a gesture of helplessness. "For my simple needs."

"You mean the costumes you wear in the plays?"

"No, no, the costumes travel separately, in fifty-six enormous crates. The trunks contain my personal clothes."

I resisted the impulse to comment; after all, it was her own fortune that funded this more-than-adequate wardrobe. "But you have a maid, surely. She'll do the packing. Trust her."

Without committing herself, Sarah asked, "Bertie, how exactly do you propose to investigate this mystery, as you term it?"

"I shall visit the Agincourts and offer my services. I am not without experience as a detective."

"A surprise visit?"

"Exactly."

"Royalty on the doorstep—is that fair, Bertie?"

"I shan't expect a fanfare, if that is what you mean. They're old friends, Sarah. I've known Jules for twenty years. Damn it all, he's not far short of royalty himself."

She clicked her tongue at my last remark and said, "We had a revolution, Bertie."

I refrained from pointing out that since 1789 France had crowned two emperors and three kings. "Well, am I to call a cab?"

"A cab?"

"I'm sure you don't approve of carriages in your republic."

She put her tongue out. She can be extremely vulgar on occasion.

I informed Knollys simply that I was going for a drive with Madame Bernhardt. Knollys doesn't regard my detective escapades with unqualified approval. Come to that, he didn't look overjoyed at the prospect of my sharing a carriage with Sarah. The poor fellow has more than enough worries, so I try not to add to them.

Montroger, the main residence of the Agincourt family, is a short drive out of the city, on the road to Versailles. We used a closed landau and Sarah prattled on so much about her forthcoming world tour that I was beginning to regret recruiting her as my assistant. I was mightily relieved when the main gates of the park came in view, because she had only reached Chicago and there remained at least eighteen months of the itinerary to discuss.

Montroger is probably smaller than Sandringham, but I wouldn't stake my inheritance on it. These Louis Quinze mansions, all shutters and balconies, can be deceptive. I must say, it looked strikingly like a house in a fairy story, with a glittering patina of frost on the gray slate roof.

Sarah insisted on remaining in the carriage while I went to the door. She was uneasy about our arriving unannounced, and I suppose she was right. The advent of the two of us, the Prince of Wales *and* the first lady of the French theater, might have been daunting. I took the view that, if nothing else, our arrival would succeed in distracting the family from their trouble.

When I announced myself, the girl who answered the bell behaved much as I expected, with a touch more Gallic hysteria than one experiences in England. I'm well used to it. I make more informal calls on my friends in France than is generally realized, and the domestics always act as if the Day of Judgment is at hand. It's to be expected, and I blame nobody, as I always make clear.

That first panic over, the girl admitted me to a reception room where there was a decent fire and a copy of *Le Monde*. I found nothing about the murder. I went to the window and waved the newspaper sociably to my companion, sitting chilled to the bone in the landau.

"Bertie, *mon ami!*"

I turned to greet my dear old friend Jules, immaculate as always in a morning suit and pale purple cravat. He crossed the room and embraced me in the French fashion, regardless that his cheeks got rasped in the process.

"You must forgive me for descending on you. I received your message that you have a family crisis," I explained, "but I couldn't allow that to prevent me from seeing my old friend."

His eyes moistened. They are a very emotional nation. He held on to my right hand with both of his. "Such grief!" Of course, I'm translating here. What he actually said was, "*Quelle douleur!*" and the way the French have of speaking the phrase makes it immeasurably more heartrending than the English equivalent.

How can I depict Jules in words? Unprepossessing in physical terms, slight in stature, with a long, lined face and a nose that preferred to hide behind a cigarette, and usually did, he nonetheless exuded charm. "But it is so uplifting to see you, Bertie. Let us drink champagne."

I mentioned to Jules that Bernhardt was freezing to death outside.

He gave a little gasp of amazement at the news, said that he was doubly honored, and insisted on going in person to

the carriage to invite her inside. It says much for his character that he could still be so hospitable.

The shivering Sarah was escorted in and given cognac in preference to the bubbly. Because she was so cold, she remained wrapped in the cloak and her fur bonnet, striking a Napoleonic pose in front of the fire. Jules knew her well; how well, one prefers not to inquire, but then, Sarah is such an institution that most of Paris behaves as if it knows her intimately.

In the circumstances, small talk about the family was going to be difficult, so once we had the glasses in our hands and had drunk one another's health, I trotted out the old maxim that a trouble shared is a trouble halved and asked Jules if he cared to speak about the matter.

He gave a slight sigh. "It is a tragedy, Bertie. I never dreamed that such a calamity could devastate my family. Rosine, my only daughter—do you remember Rosine?"

"The last time I saw her was at Biarritz. She must have been about thirteen."

"She's twenty now, a young woman. Exquisitely beautiful. I'm not expressing a father's biased opinion, Bertie; I'm quoting the *Figaro*. But *beautiful* isn't the word that would spring to mind if you saw my little Rosine now. She is racked with grief. I even begin to fear for her sanity, she has taken this so badly. And her mother, Juliette, of course, is in a state of profound shock. You must forgive us if neither of them comes to be presented."

"Jules, I wouldn't dream of disturbing them," I assured him, recalling Juliette as a domineering woman who wanted the family and everyone else to dance to her tune. Her state of profound shock was a happy escape for us.

Sarah added with more tact than I thought she possessed, "It is more than enough that you are willing to receive us."

In a low, expressionless tone that was so unlike his usual conversation, Jules gave us the salient facts. "Rosine became engaged two weeks ago to a young man called Maurice Letis-

sier. The Letissiers are well regarded, a family who have occupied the same château in the Loire for three centuries. I know the parents well, and—without being snobbish—they are the sort of people one hopes one's daughter will live among."

"They race horses," I remarked, to indicate that I'd heard of them.

"Yes, indeed. They have stables at Longchamp, just down the road. I don't think Maurice was actively involved in the racing. His sport was shooting."

"What did he shoot—grouse?"

"Waterfowl mainly, I believe."

"So what happened? Was it a loose gun?"

"No, no. I'm coming to that. All this is frightfully confidential, Bertie. There's been far too much in the newspapers already."

I assured him warmly, "You may depend on me. I've held the press at bay for most of my adult life. And I'll vouch for Sarah's discretion."

Jules nodded. "I can vouch for that myself."

Bernhardt turned her eyes up to the ceiling as if she were in direct communication with the Almighty. I'd seen her do it before, when playing Jeanne d'Arc.

Satisfied that we could be trusted, Jules informed us, "The engagement was announced a week ago last Saturday and the civil marriage was to be on the twenty-third of June, followed by a church wedding the next day."

"So soon?"

Bernhardt said, "Bertie, in France we don't go in for long engagements."

"The details of the marriage contract were settled in a most civilized way between the families," Jules went on to inform us. "I found Letissier senior a charming fellow to deal with. On Wednesday, the young couple dined with the Letissiers at the château, and on Friday we took them out to Magny's."

"Magny's. I frequently dine there myself," I told him. "Was it an agreeable meal?"

"The food, you mean? Absolutely. One couldn't fault it."

"And the conversation?"

"Oh, Juliette, as usual, had more to say than the rest of us put together. If possible, the engagement had made her more animated than ever. It was an ambition fulfilled. Not that the rest of us were silent, but you know how she can be. We talked until almost eleven and then went on to a dance hall."

"Saucy!"

"Oh, it was Rosine's idea. She'd planned all week that we would end the evening that way. According to our daughter, everyone is going to the Moulin Rouge in Montmartre these days. Respectable people."

"I've been there," put in Bernhardt, begging the question.

Jules went on: "Rosine insisted that it was terribly chic and there was supposed to be a marvelous cabaret. I've heard of such places before and I was none too enthusiastic, but Maurice said it was a stunning idea, so I felt obliged to fall in with the suggestion. You can't really stand in the way of a young couple when you're celebrating their engagement. Off we went."

"The four of you?"

"Five. We had Tristan with us—didn't I say?"

"Tristan?"

"My son. Rosine's young brother. He's eighteen now, in his first year at the Sorbonne. Naturally, the dance hall had his vote, too. We arrived about half past eleven, when the place was filling up with people coming from the restaurants. I was reassured to find that we weren't by any means the only party wearing silk hats, although it wasn't exactly the Alcazar. Some of the women we passed in the hall were blatantly *co-cottes*."

"And good luck to them," said I smoothly, at the same

time giving him a broad wink, for I happened to know that Bernhardt's mother had been one of the sisterhood.

"Oh, certainly," he succeeded in saying. "We were shown to a table at the edge of the dance floor and served with drinks. A band was playing for general dancing, so by turns we joined in, and I must admit that it was amusing to tour the floor with some of those exotic characters who patronize the place. Then at midnight, the floor was cleared and the cabaret announced. When I say 'cleared,' I'm referring to a space at the center not much larger than this room. In fact, it was the signal for people to crowd onto the floor in significant numbers and it rapidly became obvious that we would see nothing unless we abandoned our table and joined them, so we did. I remember feeling anxious about pickpockets." Jules sighed. "Pickpockets! If I'd known what was about to happen, I'd gladly have settled for having my pocket picked. We found ourselves in the thick of the crowd, with a partial view over the shoulders of people ahead. There were others behind us; everyone very excited, for this was one of the nights when La Goulue performed."

"That creature!" said Bernhardt.

Perhaps I should explain here that the lady who rejoiced in the soubriquet of La Goulue, "The Glutton," was at this time (1891) at the height of her fame, a performer of outrageous dances verging on indecency, yet unquestionably one of the chief attractions in Paris. Bernhardt's contempt may have been mixed with some envy.

"First we had the cancan, of which I saw very little from our position, although the music, so-called, was deafening, and then La Goulue was announced and made her entrance. She need not have bothered so far as I was concerned, because all I could see of her was the strange topknot of carroty hair that is her trademark, but her partner, a tall, thin man of grotesque features known as Valentin, was more visible in his top hat, leading her in a surprisingly subdued dance. All around us, people were calling out and straining for a better view. It was not unlike being close to the winning post at the races. I'm telling you all this because of what happened shortly after. The *chahut* was announced and the tempo of the music quickened."

"*Chahut?*" I said dubiously, for the word means "uproar" or something similar in the French argot.

Bernhardt rapidly informed me that it was a dance, an old-fashioned dance recently revived and made notorious by La Goulue and others and involving two athletic feats, *le grand écart* and *le port d'armes,* high kicks that required the dancers to perform the splits in the upright position while balanced on one leg.

"*Chahut*, it became in the literal sense," Jules resumed, "for just as the dance was reaching its climax, the dancers leaping like beings possessed, the music at crescendo, the crowd shrieking encouragement, there were two deafening explosions close at hand. I felt a terrific jolt the first time and another immediately after as people reacted, uncertain whether it was part of the performance. There were some screams and I caught the smell of cordite, though I still didn't fully understand what had happened. Maurice, you see, was still on his feet, though mortally wounded by two shots in the back."

"Dreadful!"

"Yes, it was. The pressure of the crowd kept him upright. There was some screaming from hysterical people, but I think no one appreciated that murder had been committed on the floor of the Moulin Rouge until the dancers stopped uncertainly and the crowd drew back. I gripped Maurice under the armpit and someone else was on his other side. Between us, we were holding him up. We let him down gently to the floorboards. He made no sound. I believe he was already dead. Of course a doctor came forward and after a few minutes we moved him to a dressing room. I could see myself that it was a matter for a detective, not a doctor."

"What an appalling crime," I said. "Is no one apprehended? There must have been a hundred witnesses."

Jules gave a Gallic shrug. "The Sûreté are investigating. They say paradoxically that too many witnesses are an impediment. It is difficult to find an assassin in a crowd."

"But who would want to shoot the young man? Did he have enemies?"

"None that my family has heard about."

"Could it have been a case of mistaken identity?" (You can see how actively my brain was working, reviewing each possibility.)

"They simply don't know, Bertie. Goron himself is at work on the case."

"Who's that?"

"Goron—*chef de la Sûreté.*"

"Is he any good?"

He stared at me as if I had insulted the Tricolor.

Bernhardt told me, "Marie-François Goron is a legend in Paris. He arrested Allmayer, the King of Rogues, and Pranzini, the triple murderer."

"But he has failed so far to find the killer of young Letissier," I remarked in a way that deflated them both. "Jules, I myself am not inexperienced as a criminal investigator. A mere amateur, yes. The resources of the Sûreté are not at my disposal. No gendarmerie, no whistles, no capes. However, I have Madame Sarah Bernhardt to assist me, and—without denigrating Monsieur Goron—I venture to suggest that she and I are as capable of solving this mystery as anyone else in Paris."

Bernhardt turned to me as if I'd tugged her bustle. Fortunately, poor old Jules didn't notice. He was far too occupied trying to think what to say to me.

I saved him the trouble. "Of course you are about to remark

that I shouldn't undertake so dangerous an assignment. It has been said before, Jules, and more than once. I appreciate the sentiment each time I hear it, I give my thanks, and then I ignore it completely. Good Lord, we're the oldest of friends. I can't turn my back on you in this hour of crisis."

His face creased with emotion. "Bertie, don't think me ungrateful—"

"Never," said I, placing a hand masterfully around his shoulder. "The decision is made. Tonight Sarah and I shall visit the Moulin Rouge to see where the poor young man was murdered."

Chapter 2

Feeling hungry, we stopped at the first wayside hostelry on the road back to Paris. The choice was a happy one, as it turned out, even though, amazingly, the *patron* failed to recognize either of his visitors. We had the dining room to ourselves, simply furnished, with a good log fire and an enormous dog asleep on the hearth rug—that is, until Bernhardt decided to embrace the "poor dumb creature." Nothing can be taken for granted where she is concerned. Having told me she was famished, she ordered onion soup and nothing else, while I lunched on chicken liver pâté (much of which Bernhardt fed to the dog), followed by roast quails in a mysterious and quite delicious sauce. On inquiry, I was advised that this small establishment employed its own *saucier*, who had no other duties. I expressed surprise, giving Sarah the opportunity to quote Voltaire's unkind remark that England is the country of one sauce. Unkind and untrue, as I pointed out, for what are applesauce, mint sauce, and bread sauce? She had no answer.

The shooting at the Moulin Rouge was hardly a suitable topic for luncheon, so I reminisced about the Jules d'Agincourt I'd known on happier occasions, at the races and down at Biarritz. "He is unfailingly kind. On one occasion, we took the children for a picnic in the country and the Agincourts came with us. This must have been about 1874, when Eddy, my eldest, the Duke of Clarence, was nine or ten. I say it myself—because I'm damned if I'll allow anyone else to say it—Eddy can be extremely tiresome when he's not watched. His sister Louise had brought with her a favorite doll, which at some point in the afternoon went missing. There was such a chorus of lamentation, with Victoria and Maud joining in, that for some peace and quiet we grown-ups were compelled to make a search of the area. I was convinced that Eddy was responsible and threatened to send him home directly if he didn't at once tell us where he'd hidden the wretched doll. The queen is always telling me that our children should have been whipped from infancy as we were, and I suppose they *are* inclined to rampage when excited, but Alix and I have never cared for corporal punishment. Well, to cut the story short, Jules informed the party in all seriousness that he'd spoken to a blue-bird, which had told him that Elizabeth, the doll, had met some pixies and been taken to fairyland. If there were no more tears, he solemnly informed us, Elizabeth would be returned to Louise before midnight with a gift from the fairies."

"What a charming notion!" said Bernhardt. "Had he found the doll?"

"Yes, but in no condition to return to a sensitive little girl. Someone had taken a knife to it. Most of the stuffing had spilled out."

"Eddy?"

"I fear so. I was so angry that I was ready to forget my principles and warm his backside there and then until Jules persuaded me to ignore the incident, pointing out that every boy has done something destructive at some stage in his youth. That night, the doll, invisibly repaired, with, I believe, an entirely new torso, was returned to the nursery. When Louise found it the next morning, there was a crystal-bead necklace around its throat and a larger one beside it, for the child to wear. Typical of Jules's kindness."

"He's such a lovable man," murmured Sarah.

"He's not alone in that," I was quick to remind her, "but he has a remarkable understanding of children. I'm sure that Rosine and the boy must have had a blissful upbringing. This horrible murder—you *have* finished your soup, have you?—has obviously affected poor Jules the more because of his closeness to Rosine."

"Do you think he is too close to see?" said she.

"I don't understand you."

"Sometimes a father who dotes on his daughter refuses to believe that she is human, a woman, with a woman's desires."

Bernhardt is so used to projecting her voice that she must have been audible in the kitchen. I cautioned her to speak more softly. "Are you suggesting that there may be a second young man in Rosine's life?"

She gave a nod.

"A *crime passionnel*, eh?"

"Look at the circumstances," she said. "The girl has just become engaged and pouff! The man is shot down in front of her. It shrieks of jealousy to me."

"So we look for the rejected lover?" To be truthful, I was more than a little skeptical of the theory. Bernhardt's passionate imaginings *would* run to melodrama of this sort.

"You don't sound impressed, Bertie," she commented. "Do you have a better proposal?"

"For the moment, yes," said I. "I shall try the crêpes suzette."

That evening I wrote a short letter:

Hotel Bristol
Paris

My dearest Alix,

Paris without you is indescribably dull. Weather barely tolerable—a wind from the North Pole, I am informed. Compelled to wear flannel underclothes, which always make me appear corpulent. But that's enough of me. This morning, I called on Jules d'Agincourt, our old friend of years past. The poor fellow was in low water, his prospective son-in-law having been dreadfully murdered in a Montmartre dance hall. Do you remember little Rosine, his daughter? Unbelievably she is grown up and the victim was her fiancé. The top man of the Sûreté is investigating and no doubt will make an arrest shortly. Scant consolation for the Agincourt family.

I shall endure a few more days of walking the dog here before taking the train to Cannes.

Kiss Toria and Maud for me. And my parents-in-law if I am in better odor this visit.

Ever your loving Bertie

The same evening, I escorted Sarah Bernhardt to the Moulin Rouge. Sometimes in the pursuit of the truth, one is obliged to venture into places one wouldn't normally patronize and make a show of enjoying oneself.

Montmartre is a revelation by night. No city in the world has as many restaurants and dance halls as Paris, and this is where most of them are concentrated. There's nothing special in that, you may say, but you should see their names written in flames in the gas festoons outside every one. You should see the magic-lantern projections making spectacular sights out of dull stone walls. Above all, you should see the Moulin Rouge.

This temple for worshipers of the cancan was built by Charles Zidler in the year of the Paris Exposition, the same year that they erected that monstrosity, the Eiffel Tower. The mock windmill outlined with red electric lightbulbs has been described as an excrescence on the boulevard de Clichy, but personally I find it less offensive to good taste than Monsieur Eiffel's so-called miracle of engineering on the Left Bank. We approached the Moulin by landau from the rue Blanche, and long before reaching the top of the rise we could see the night sky glowing crimson. The sense of anticipation was irresistible to a woman of Bernhardt's sensibilities. She squeezed my hand and said, "*Là là*, Bertie!" Swathed in sealskin trimmed with sable (nothing was said about the dumb creatures who had supplied their hides), she brandished an ostrich-feather fan that she seriously suggested she could use to conceal her identity. Of course we were recognized the moment we stepped from the carriage.

One enters through a lobby hung with posters and peopled with vendors of flowers, bonbons, and less innocent wares. I paused at a flower basket to buy a knot of spring flowers for my companion's bosom and we were importuned by a dozen other sellers. A few choice words from Bernhardt ensured a passage through the glass doors to the foyer, where the reek of cheap scent and face powder assailed us. The demimondaines were there in force.

"Your Royal Highness, Madame Bernhardt, we are deeply honored." Some functionary of the establishment had spotted that we were of two minds whether to continue with this adventure and had darted forward. "Would you care to visit the gardens first, or would you prefer to take a table in the ballroom? At this very moment, Zélaska, the queen of the belly dance, is performing inside the plaster elephant from the Exposition. There are merry-go-rounds, shooting galleries, and donkey rides—whichever you desire."

We told him that we desired a table in the ballroom.

"And I should like to speak to the manager, if that is possible," I added. "Would you kindly ask him to come to our table?"

"Your Royal Highness—"

" 'Sir' will suffice."

"Sir, I am the manager, Georges Martineau." Georges Martineau had the sort of physique that makes me feel slim. When he bowed, his face practically disappeared into his several chins.

"I am pleased to hear it. First, Monsieur Martineau, we should like to visit the cloakrooms."

He cleared his throat. "If I may be so bold as to offer advice, sir, you may prefer to retain your coats. It can be drafty in the ballroom."

I said frigidly, "Thank you for your advice, monsieur. Now, would you show us to the cloakrooms?"

(Answering a call of nature, I confide in passing, is no simple matter for members of my profession. The rest of the population appears to believe that the Lord provided royalty with a superior system of plumbing, but, alas, He did not.)

Comfortable again, we were shown to a fairy-lit table on a balcony overlooking the dance floor. The blare of what sounded like circus music was deafening at first; the orchestra—I use the term ironically—seemed to be engaged in mortal combat to see which instruments would prevail, the drums, cymbals, or trombones. Mind you, no one was interested. The players might have been silent, for all the attention they were getting. Every face was turned in our direction. And what did they see? Yours truly still in hat and opera cloak; Bernhardt rashly slipping off her sealskin to reveal one of Monsieur Worth's creations, white cashmere ornamented with silver braid, with an antique silver girdle. Sarah is not a beauty, not by conventional standards, but I have to say that she always contrives to look stunning.

While Martineau called for champagne, I surveyed the scene of the recent crime. The ballroom was as big as Victoria Station and quite dazzling to the eye, thanks to abundant chandeliers, globe lights, and mirrors. Drinks were being served at small tables around the edge, and behind the massive pillars supporting the gallery on either side of the long hall, people were promenading. At least, one hopes that is what was going on.

The lighting penetrated there only dimly and some of the promenaders in my view presented a rather Babylonian character. In the center, dancing couples wearing hats and coats cruised sedately around the wooden floor, observed by others chattering—and if they weren't chattering, I'm sure their teeth were, for there was a wicked draft coming from the gardens. I took out a cigar and our host stepped forward to light it.

"Now, Monsieur Martineau," I said, "shall we see the cabaret presently? I can't sit here shivering for long."

"Very soon, sir."

"And is the lady known as 'The Greedy One' performing tonight?"

"La Goulue—yes indeed."

"How did she come by such a name?"

"I think the explanation may be vulgar, sir. She is known for her amorous tendencies."

She was not alone in that; I avoided Bernhardt's gaze. "And is the man called Valentin also here tonight?"

"Le Désossé—yes."

"The what?"

Bernhardt said in English, " 'The Boneless One.' "

"He is there now, just below us," said Martineau, pointing to an exceptionally thin man—a veritable beanpole—partnering a woman wearing a faded yellow coat and a black feather boa. I'm no judge of dancing, but I could see with half an eye that they were moving more elegantly than any other couple on the floor. It was a bizarre spectacle because Valentin—this man guiding his partner with such sinuous grace—had one of the ugliest faces it has been my misfortune to see, his nose like the sharp end of a pickax, poised over a huge spadelike pointed jaw. He wore a battered stovepipe hat with a decided downward tilt, as if to hide as much as possible of the disaster. By the same token, his suit was cut to draw attention to those supple limbs, the trousers tailored like tights.

"Will he appear in the cabaret, as well?"

"Oh yes. He dances every dance, each night, sir. He can treat a waltz in a hundred different ways. The women queue up to partner him."

"No wonder," murmured Bernhardt. "The man is fascinating."

To restore some balance to the conversation, I observed, "I dare say dancing with such an ugly fellow tends to lend attraction to the lady."

"Oh, Bertie—he's a joy to behold!"

I turned to a more interesting topic. "Monsieur Martineau, I learned that there was a fatality here on the dance floor quite recently."

A quiver went through Martineau's more-than-ample flesh. "That is correct, sir, but I assure you we have taken steps—"

"I've every confidence, or we wouldn't have come," said I. "Where were you when the incident occurred?"

"On the step beside the orchestra. I announce the cabaret from there."

I glanced across to the wooden bandstand where the dozen or so instrumentalists were housed. "And where did the shooting take place?"

"Across the floor from there."

"How much did you see?"

"Very little, sir. Like everyone else, I heard the shots."

"This was during La Goulue's performance?"

"Yes, in the *chahut*. I suppose the assassin chose the time when everyone's attention was on the dancing. They crowd on to the floor for a better view and there's a tremendous crush. You'll see presently. There were two shots, followed by some screaming. The orchestra stopped playing and presently a man dropped to the floor."

"Someone must have seen the man with the gun."

"Apparently not. No one has come forward. The shots were

at close range, sir. I imagine that the murderer had the gun secreted inside an overcoat."

"Come now," I persisted, "the people around must have been aware of what happened. You can't tell me that if some idiot standing next to you fires a gun, you don't look to see who he is."

"Your Royal Highness, I couldn't agree more—in theory. With the utmost respect, you haven't experienced the crowding when La Goulue performs. People jostle for position, trying to get a view between the hats. You may turn your head, but you are unlikely to get a sight of what is happening below shoulder level. The shots were deafening even from my position across the room. It was impossible to tell with any accuracy from where they had been fired."

His explanation was beginning to sound plausible. "How many people were present that evening?"

"At least five hundred. Friday is a popular night."

I turned to Bernhardt. "A curious paradox. If you wish to commit murder and get away with it, choose the most crowded place you can find." Then I asked Martineau, "How soon did the police arrive?"

"Within a very short time, sir. I sent for them immediately. We moved the unfortunate young man to the dressing room and they came soon after."

"You stopped the entertainment?"

"Naturally."

"And I suppose some people left the dance hall?"

"Practically everyone. It would have been impossible for me to detain them. I was trying to comfort the Agincourt family. Such a tragedy!"

"But the show goes on," commented Bernhardt acidly. "You opened your doors again?"

"Not until this week, madame. Monsieur Zidler, the owner, discussed it with Detective Chief Goron. The police were in favor. They wanted to interview some of our regular clients. The only way was to reopen. I've had detectives here every night asking questions. It isn't very good for business."

"Have they learned anything useful?"

"Not to my knowledge, sir. Monsieur Goron describes the case as an infliction."

"I'm sympathetic if he has to spend his evenings getting chilled to the bone," said I. "No wonder some people are stamping their feet." In fact, in the last few minutes the drumming of leather on wood had become distracting.

"They are impatient for the cabaret, sir," answered Martineau sheepishly.

We detained him no longer.

A drumroll signaled his arrival beside the bandstand, and I saw precisely what he had meant. There was excited shouting. People were already gathering on the floor, coming in from the gardens and down from the galleries, more than I'd realized were in the building—and this was supposed to be a thin attendance. You could see their breath mingling with the cigarette smoke on the cold air. Bernhardt was all for our joining them, but I didn't relish being squeezed by Parisians reeking of garlic and tobacco.

Martineau shouted, *"Mesdames et messieurs, le cabaret."* A cheer drowned the rest, except for ". . . La Goulue!"

A gangway had to be forced in the circle before several dancers could run in, gripping their skirts. Behind them, alone, making the entrance of the star performer, strutted the woman known as La Goulue, in a red and white polka-dot blouse and black skirt, a black ribbon around her throat. She appeared preoccupied, eyes down, indifferent to the reception she was getting. I should have realized that it was done for effect, because suddenly she flung back her head, stared straight up at me, gave an evil grin, and shouted, "Ello, Wales!"

A great cheer from the audience greeted this overfamiliarity and I raised my hat in response—to their greeting, not hers. Hers was infernal cheek and I was not amused. If I hadn't been there for a very good reason, I'd have left at once. I'm told that the lady is known to present her rear view on occasions, flicking up her skirts to display the scarlet heart embroidered on the seat of her drawers. I'm no prude, but I have to be thankful that she spared me that spectacle.

I shall be generous. What followed went some way to expunging the incident. Rarely have I watched a performance as exotic, acrobatic, exceedingly naughty, and hugely entertaining, but I shall not dwell on it here except to say that La Goulue transformed vulgarity into art. Other dancers joined her in the so-called quadrille—unrecognizable as the sedate dance of that name performed in English ballrooms—but one's eyes were only on this virago with the Psyche topknot and the kiss-curls who flung herself into each movement with lunatic abandon, high-kicking, shrieking, whirling, and leaping.

The climax was the *chahut* with Valentin. Now, I've watched the cancan performed in other places, and, believe me, it is tame compared to the *chahut*. If the cancan is mainly skirt and petticoats, the *chahut* is—let us not duck the truth—all legs and drawers. As if goaded by the antics of her partner, La Goulue flung her black-stockinged, diamond-gartered legs ever higher and grabbed her foot with her hand, regardless of the expanse of white thigh she was revealing in the midst of that froth of lace. Now she released the foot and let it go higher, higher, as if to kick the chandelier above her: *le grand écart*. Scandalized shrieks from ladies in the audience only encouraged her more. Spinning on one foot, then the other, wriggling and bending, vulgar and athletic, witty and alluring, she went through her repertoire of movements. Some of the contortions appeared impossible as she repeatedly performed the splits while standing on one leg. And always Valentin le Désossé was there to complement the movements, his gargoyle of a face expressionless, even when, in a final dervishlike gyration, La Goulue spun with one foot high above her head and finished by kicking the hat from her partner's head. Valentin, being the artiste he was, retained his dignity by catching the hat and replacing it in one movement.

Did I say I wouldn't dwell on the performance? Obviously, it made more of an impression than I realized. I must add that the cabaret went on for some time after and nothing came up to La Goulue's *chahut*.

It was past midnight when we left. Bernhardt had overindulged in champagne and was beginning to become embarrassing in ways that I'd rather not go into, except to state that I have always insisted on decorum in public places, whether in Paris or anywhere else.

My investigation—if it could be so termed at this early stage—had not advanced so far as I would have liked, and I took the opportunity to put some more questions to Martineau while he escorted us toward the exit. "I take it that Letissier was dead before you got him to the dressing room?"

"You're speaking of the incident the other evening, sir?"

"Does it sound as if I'm discussing the racing form?" I said with sarcasm.

He reddened appreciably. "You must forgive me, sir. I was instructed not to discuss the tragedy."

"Who by?"

"The owner of the Moulin Rouge, Monsieur Zidler. It is not good for our reputation."

"Your *what?*" said I, wondering if I had heard correctly.

"To come back to your question, Monsieur Letissier was killed on the dance floor, sir."

"There were no last words?"

"I believe not."

Thus the frustrating difference between reality and fiction, I reflected. There are always dying words in a detective story, the half-finished sentence that only the investigator can interpret. "And—you must tell me if I have it wrong, monsieur—you removed the body to the dressing room and called the police?"

"Yes, sir."

"Who was present?"

"The family Agincourt, sir. The comte, the comtesse, and their daughter and son. Also a doctor and his wife who were in the audience and certain of the performers who used the dressing room."

"That La Goulue creature?"

He shook his head. "This was the gentlemen's dressing room, sir."

"I can't imagine that would trouble her. Was Monsieur Zidler present?"

"No, sir."

"And was anything said that threw any light on the mystery?"

"Not while I was there, sir."

Bernhardt gave an exaggerated yawn and leaned her head against my arm. My tolerance was severely strained. I asked Martineau to see if our carriage was waiting. Once he was out of earshot, I reminded Sarah why we were there. She said she was ready for bed and I said she'd made that transparently clear. She drew herself away from my person and promised to behave.

"You'll have gathered that I'm taking a personal interest in the case," I told Martineau when he returned. "Was any suspicious person seen here on the night of the murder?"

"That's impossible for me to answer, sir."

"Presumably you know the sort of clientele you get. They come to enjoy themselves. You'd notice anyone of a furtive demeanor?"

"That may be true, but my duties don't permit me to study everyone who enters and leaves the place."

"Is there anyone who does?"

We had reached the foyer. The answer to my question was all around us in the shape of members of the scarlet sisterhood.

Bernhardt cackled like a parrot and said in English, "I 'ope you're feeling strong, Bertie."

I disregarded her.

Martineau coughed nervously and said, "There is one of our habitués who may be willing to assist you, sir. He knows most of the working girls. They confide in him."

"A pimp, do you mean?" I said, shocked.

"No, sir, the artist, Toulouse-Lautrec. He is responsible for several of the posters that you see around us."

I had vaguely registered that there were some particularly grotesque drawings displayed on the walls. They were all over Paris, on posters in the boulevards. Valentin and La Goulue were pictured in a crude representation of the dance. To my eye, all the drawings looked unfinished, as if the artist had wisely decided to abandon them. "If that's the best he can do, I'd hesitate to call him an artist."

"He's here most evenings, sketching," Martineau said. "I haven't seen him tonight, however. His studio is not far from here, at twenty-one rue Caulaincourt."

"Was he here on the night of the shooting?"

"Yes, he was one of the last to leave."

"And you say that this Lautrec converses with the wretched creatures around us?"

"He paints them. Sometimes he visits the houses where they, er, conduct their business and paints them. They all know Toulouse-Lautrec."

"He sounds utterly depraved."

Bernhardt whispered in my ear, "Bertie, he is a nobleman. He is the Count of Toulouse-Lautrec Monfa."

Chapter 3

Hotel Bristol
Paris

Dearest Alix,

And how is Fredensborg this year? It cannot be more
tiresome than Paris, where the racing has been canceled
because the turf is frozen. That is not the whole story. The
theaters are half-empty because the plays are all written by
philosophers. The latest craze, would you believe, is an
importation from London or New York that seems des-
tined to supplant the traditional French café; it is the
"bar," complete in many cases with a British barman. I
don't come to Paris to sit up at a counter and stare at a
row of bottles. You can judge how desperate I am for
recreation when I inform you that I have decided to
dedicate this morning to art! As you well know, I can't
tell a Leonardo from a Landseer, but I propose to visit
the studio of a painter who is all the rage, I gather. I
saw some of his work yesterday, scenes of Parisian life
(interiors) done with a certain flair, though I can't imagine
that his style would pass the selection committee of the
Royal Academy. Not to prolong your curiosity, I shall
now reveal that he is a count, from one of the oldest

families of the provincial aristocracy, the Toulouse-Lautrecs, and the visit will be mainly social. Mind, I shall probably inform my new friend the count that my wife paints admirable watercolors. It's a pity you can't be here to give him some advice, because his colors seem to me to lack the restraint that is so characteristic of your little masterpieces.

No news of the police inquiry into the murder of that young man I mentioned in yesterday's letter. I decided to drive out to Montroger and visit the Agincourt family to express our sympathy and see if there was anything one could do—unlikely, but at such times the support of old friends can be a solace. Jules, poor fellow, is visibly depleted by the blow that this has dealt to his entire family. The others were too grief-stricken to meet me. I gather that they were all present in the dance hall when the wicked deed was perpetrated.

I am constantly looking out for a letter from Fredensborg, but I suppose tomorrow is the earliest I can hope for. My love as always to you, Toria, and Maud.

Your becalmed Bertie

Bernhardt really is the limit. She gave me no clue as to what I might expect on my visit to Toulouse-Lautrec; I think she wickedly relished seeing me in a state of confusion.

By day—by a sharp, clear day in March, at any rate—Montmartre is another place from the one I portrayed in the previous chapter. The *bon viveurs* had abandoned the quarter before dawn and the residents in respectable employment had left in droves for Paris soon after, so apart from the occasional nursemaid, we saw nobody. Rue Caulaincourt, where the count had his studio, was a few minutes only from the Moulin Rouge (which, like most of the pleasures of this world, is a disappointment in daylight). We stepped from the carriage into a street of respectable bourgeois dwellings that must have been built about twenty years before. Number 21, a three-storied apartment building with tall, shuttered windows, was at the corner of another street, the rue Tourlaque, giving it the novelty of a second address. The third-floor window, on the angle of the corner, had obviously been enlarged.

"That will be his studio."

"What time is it, Bertie?" Bernhardt asked me.

"A few minutes after noon. Even an artist should be on his feet by now."

We made ourselves known to the concierge, who was clearly a dyed-in-the-wool republican, for without batting an eyelid she asked whether *Monsieur* Toulouse-Lautrec was expecting us. Left to myself, I would have informed the lady at once how persons of rank are addressed. However, Bernhardt subscribes to the view that a Parisian concierge ranks as royalty in her domain, and perhaps she is right. After an ingratiating speech from Sarah, we were permitted to pass. The count, as we had surmised, lived on the third floor, the one with the studio window.

"You'd better tell me if you've met him," I said to Sarah while we were climbing the stairs, since she seemed to be on familiar terms with most of the French aristocracy, and I needed to know whether a formal introduction would be necessary.

"No—but I have seen a photograph."

"That's not the same thing at all."

"It 'elps," she said in English, with an impish glint in her eyes that I didn't understand. Each time I think back, I become more reproachful of her conduct that day. I am not without experience in the machinations of the fair sex, but, believe me, Bernhardt is irredeemable.

I knocked.

There was no sound of movement inside, so I knocked again, trusting that the concierge would not have sent us upstairs if the count had been away from home.

After a considerable delay, I heard someone coming.

"He was in bed," murmured Bernhardt.

The door opened a fraction. The shutters must have been across, because it was difficult to see inside. A whiff of cognac crept into my nostrils and that was all. I put my face closer and still saw nobody. Then the light from outside caught the shimmer of a pair of spectacles at about the level of the door handle. I assumed that a poor-sighted child had answered our knock. Bernhardt hadn't mentioned that the count had a family. I bent lower and started to say in an avuncular tone, "Good morning, would you kindly ask your . . ." when my words trailed off, because the crack in the door had widened sufficiently for me to see that the child had the head of a grown man sporting a mustache and beard. My sense of shock was the greater because, not to mince words, he was an ugly fellow, swarthy, with an overlarge nose and thick, moist lips. He was dressed in a flannel nightshirt that reached to the floor.

I am not sure how much of my astonishment showed. I know Bernhardt—the wicked hussy—would tell me if I inquired, but I have never given her that satisfaction.

I managed to say, "Sir, I must apologize. We have clearly called at an inconvenient time."

He adjusted his pince-nez and after an uncomfortable interval said, "Yes." There was another pause for reflection before he thought fit to add, "If you are who I think you are, I would have wished to receive you in better circumstances . . . Your Royal Highness? And . . . Madame Bernhardt?"

In the circumstances, it was as gracious a welcome as we could have expected. I nodded and took a step back. "No doubt you would prefer us to call again."

He opened the door fully. "On the contrary, sir. I can make myself more presentable, but I doubt whether I can make my studio more presentable, and since you have seen me already . . ."

One could only admire the little man's composure. When I say "little," I should qualify the word. I once met a truly little man, General Tom Thumb, who was just over three feet in height. Toulouse-Lautrec was almost five feet, but it is a trick of perception that anything a few inches below the norm appears freakish. To compound his difficulties, he walked woodenly and used a stick.

We were admitted to the studio while its owner hobbled back to his bedroom to change out of the nightshirt. Presently, we overheard subdued voices, and one was unmistakably female.

"Can you believe it?" I whispered to Bernhardt.

"He's popular with the ladies," she whispered back.

"A little fellow like that? He must have hidden charms."

She smiled. "They call him 'The Coffeepot.' "

I turned away. I can't in honesty say that I admired his paintings any more than the posters. There was a vast canvas lying against one wall that depicted a group of drinkers at— I think—the Moulin Rouge. It had been painted in reddish browns, ochers, and pale greens, with some black areas for the men's hats and overcoats. The people were drawn with some facility, but to my untutored eye, the brushwork was slapdash, the perspective faulty, and the whole scene at such an impossible angle that the drinks looked about to tip off the table.

"Do you recognize anyone, Your Royal Highness?" Toulouse-Lautrec had reappeared, decently attired in a morning coat and check trousers. Before giving me a chance to comment, he touched his stick against a figure in the background. "That, of course, is me, with my cousin, Tapié de Céleyran, the tall man."

"And the woman adjusting her hair must be La Goulue," I was pleased to be able to add.

"Ah, you know La Goulue, then?"

"We saw her perform last night."

"A phenomenal dancer. Let me show you some other examples of my work."

This, I realized too late, was fraught with embarrassment. He assumed that we wanted to buy one of his pictures. Why else would well-to-do strangers call? With the best will in the world, I didn't want a Toulouse-Lautrec adorning the walls of Sandringham.

He was tugging out canvases from a great stack behind an easel, and the strain on his small physique was all too apparent. "I am looking for one I did of an Englishman, an artist I know who studied at the Slade School."

Impulsively, I uttered a complete untruth. "It is your posters I admire the most, monsieur le comte."

He turned and the pince-nez flashed. "Oh, I don't use the title."

"But you are a count, are you not?"

"It doesn't make any difference to my painting, sir. People here in Montmartre call me Toulouse, or Lautrec, or Toulouse-Lautrec, or simply Henri. I was named after the Comte de Chambord, the pretender to the throne of France, but I am not interested in the royalist cause. I am a disappointment to my father."

"You don't see many people of your own class?"

He laughed. "Not in Paris. Sometimes in Albi, by force of circumstance."

"So you wouldn't know the Comte d'Agincourt?"

"We have not been introduced, if that is what you mean. I know the gentleman in the sense that I would recognize him. I sketched him at the Moulin Rouge last week."

Bernhardt clapped her hands in delight. "Marvelous! Was that the night the man was murdered?"

"Yes, madame."

"You were sketching the dancers?"

"The dancers, the onlookers, the orchestra, anything that caught my interest. I am often there."

Bernhardt's eyebrows soared like pheasants at a shoot. "Then it is possible that you sketched the man who fired the fatal shots."

"If I did, madame, there is no way of telling who he was. I saw no one pointing the gun at the victim."

"May we look at your sketches?" She was ahead of me, I have to admit. I was thinking of ways of getting out without having to buy a picture.

Toulouse-Lautrec said, "I thought you were interested in the posters."

I said quickly, "The sketchbook interests us more."

Bernhardt said, "May we see?"

"I am sorry, madame, but you may not."

"You refuse to show them to us? We are extremely interested."

"That is evident."

"And if I offered to buy them . . ." suggested Bernhardt after a pause.

"I would be unable to accept."

"But why? What is there to be secretive about?"

"That is not the point."

"But it is. What if His Royal Highness demands to see them?"

He was silent, but the expression on those fleshy lips didn't give me any confidence that a royal command would do the trick.

Bernhardt is used to getting her own way and was becoming shrill in her protests. "Don't you see? A murderer is at large and the pigheaded attitude you are taking may lead to a second killing."

He said, "I never heard anything so ridiculous."

The dispute was fast becoming detrimental to our investigation, Bernhardt was pursuing it so vehemently. The painter and she were liable to end up screaming at each other if I didn't intervene, so I said, "If you will allow me, Sarah, I think we should explain to monsieur le comte why we are here."

She gave a sigh of impatience and capitulated by sitting on a chaise longue and folding her arms.

With the absolute candor of one gentleman addressing another, I explained that I was investigating the murder of Letissier for two good reasons: the first, that I was a long-standing friend of the Agincourt family; and the second, that I was doubtful whether the Sûreté were capable of solving the crime.

"You can do better than the Sûreté?" asked Toulouse-Lautrec, sounding more skeptical than impressed.

I said, "I have had some modest successes as an amateur detective. Monsieur Goron of the Sûreté has admitted that this is a baffling case. I am not baffled. With the support of Madame Bernhardt, I am actively pursuing the murderer."

Bernhardt blinked and fortunately said nothing.

"A dangerous pastime, surely?" He picked up a sketchbook and I thought for a moment that my candid statement had won his cooperation, but then he opened the book at a blank page and reached for a piece of charcoal. "Kindly hold the pose, Madame Bernhardt." With no more preamble than that, he pulled a stool across the floor, climbed onto it and commenced a drawing of Sarah as she sat in her attitude of pique. "Have you considered the danger? The assassin has killed once, and that is enough to earn him a kiss from madame la guillotine. Why should he not kill a second time and a third? One kiss is all he will get. No, please keep your head quite still, madame. This will not take long."

I said deviously, "Perhaps if you cooperate, Sarah, my dear, monsieur le comte may be persuaded to show us the rest of his sketchbook."

Bernhardt said in a long-suffering voice, "He'll want me stretched out naked for that."

The artist smiled. "I am open to negotiation."

"I am not," said Bernhardt.

He worked fast. A passable likeness was already taking shape on the paper, although whether it would please the sitter was another question, for it picked out signs of middle age that Bernhardt probably never noticed when she looked in a mirror. I privately resolved not to submit to a sketch.

But I was not immune to his satire. "You must be familiar with Sue, Your Royal Highness," he remarked while continuing with the drawing.

"Sue?" I frowned, uncertain where this new avenue was leading and not caring for it. I'm not in the habit of discussing ladies of my acquaintance with comparative strangers.

He preserved me from making an ass of myself by saying, "Eugéne Sue, the author of *Mysteries of Paris*."

"A writer? I don't get much time for reading."

He said, "Forgive me, then. I thought perhaps he was your inspiration. Sue's chief protagonist is a prince, Prince Rodolphe, who visits the dens of iniquity and studies the habits and careers of thieves and murderers, exposing injustice and crime."

I said firmly, "Sir, I do not frequent dens of iniquity."

To which Toulouse-Lautrec replied cryptically, "I do. My best work is done in dens of iniquity." He held the sketch at arm's length and studied it. "You may move if you wish, madame. I have finished." He jumped off the stool.

"May I see?" Bernhardt reached for the sketchbook.

"Certainly. You may keep it." He tore out the sheet with her portrait and handed it to her. He was not parting so lightly with the rest of the book.

Poor Sarah—my sympathy went out to her as she frowned at the all-too-penetrating likeness. She said, "Is that how I look?"

The little man had the grace to say, "No. That is how I drew you, madame."

To forestall a second demonstration of his skill, I said, "We shall not detain you much longer, monsieur. There is much to do. It would oblige us greatly if you would give us your recollection of the fatal incident at the Moulin Rouge."

"Is that your reason for calling?"

"Yes."

With a shrug, he said, "My recollection will be no better than anyone else's. The cabaret was announced and a crowd formed on the dance floor as usual. Among them were the Agincourt party, new faces to me and quite helpfully positioned opposite me—I sit at a table on the dance floor—so I sketched them rapidly without knowing who they were, the distinguished older man and the youth so similar in feature that he must have been the son, and the mother built like a ship's figurehead and the rather pale, beautiful daughter."

"And the victim?"

"The man who was killed—yes. Like the father, he was in a silk hat and looked ill at ease so close to the dancers, who are rather risqué in their movements. These were thumbnail sketches, an artist's notes, of no practical value to anyone except me. Presently the *chahut* began with La Goulue and Valentin le Désossé as usual attracting all the attention. The next thing I recall were the two reports. People screamed. The dancing stopped and, as the audience drew back, the young man dropped to the floor. His hat fell off and I remember being surprised to discover that he was bald. Understandably, the people with him were very distressed by the attack. The victim was there some time before they removed him to the dressing room."

"Did you go over to see?" asked Bernhardt.

"No, madame, I am not very mobile. I continued to sketch the scene from where I was sitting."

Bernhardt's bluster hadn't succeeded in prizing the sketchbook from Toulouse-Lautrec, so I decided to appeal to his sense of duty as a citizen. I literally stood over him and said with authority, "I really must insist that you show us your sketches of that evening. However rudimentary they may be, they are evidence, and one shouldn't withhold evidence, you know."

Rubbing his hands vigorously to remove the charcoal dust, he said, "Sir, I would not dream of withholding anything from you or Madame Bernhardt. If I had the sketchbook here, you would be more than welcome to examine it. Unfortunately, I do not. It is in the hands of the Sûreté. Monsieur Goron was here last week and took it away. I can only refer you to him."

I was so taken aback, I could only repeat the statement. "Goron has the sketchbook?"

"He is a very astute policeman."

Bernhardt spoke a word that I cannot possibly translate here; the effect is strong in the French, but several times stronger in our own tongue.

Without disguising my disappointment, I said to the artist, "You could have told us this ten minutes ago."

"I am sorry. I was of two minds. Monsieur Goron particularly instructed me not to gossip to anyone about his visit."

"I'd hardly categorize a statement to the English heir apparent as gossip," I remarked. "However, it seems you acted from the very best motives, monsieur le comte."

"I assure you there is nothing to be learned from the sketchbook," he said to mollify us—and I thought I detected a nuance in the way he spoke, the promise of something he was tempted to mention.

Whereupon, Bernhardt atoned for previous lapses by shrewdly asking, "Were you able to assist the police in any other respect?"

Toulouse-Lautrec vibrated his lips and looked away from us. I was sure there was some other matter he was tempted to bring to our attention if only we could coax it from him.

I said tentatively, "Something overheard?"

He shook his head.

Bernhardt said, "Something you wish you had mentioned to the police but didn't?"

This drew no immediate response except that he shuffled across to the bedroom door and drew it shut. Turning, he said in a modulated tone clearly not for the ears of the person on the other side of the door, "There was the matter of the gun."

"The gun?" I said, my hopes revived. "You saw the gun?"

"Whether it was *the* gun, the murder weapon, I can't say with certainty," said he. "I saw a gun. It was after most people had gone. Because of my stature and my slowness in walking, I like to let the crowd leave before me. I was left alone in the ballroom, although there were still a number of police and other people in the dressing room where the dead man had been taken. I was at my table finishing a drink. The lights had been turned down, so I suppose I was inconspicuous, even more inconspicuous than usual. I heard the sound of someone coming from the dressing rooms. A man, a tall, thin man, crossed the floor of the ballroom, which is the most direct way to the foyer, and I noticed that he put a hand in an outer pocket of his overcoat and took out a pistol, silver in color."

"*Mon Dieu,*" whispered Bernhardt.

"He glanced briefly at it and then transferred it to an inner pocket and walked swiftly toward the exit."

I sent up a rapid prayer and asked, "Did you get a clear view of him?"

"No."

"Damnation."

"But he had a profile easily recognized. He was the dancer, Valentin le Désossé."

I felt my skin prickle. "La Goulue's partner?"

He nodded. "I didn't inform the police. You see, I know Valentin quite well. We have not been on the friendliest of terms of late, but he is still someone I would not wish to incriminate. I'm certain he could not have shot Letissier. He was dancing the *chahut* at the moment the fatal shots were fired. Letissier must have been facing him. Everyone was facing him, watching him. How could Valentin have drawn a gun and shot a man in the back?"

"It seems an impossibility," I conceded.

Our informant nervously fingered his necktie. "Now that I have told you, sir, I must entreat you to exercise discretion with this information. I would have spoken to Valentin myself if we had not fallen out over a poster he objected to. It requires more courage than I possess to visit him in the knowledge that he carries a gun."

"Is he dangerous?"

"How can one tell? Do you think you could speak to him without alarming him?"

"I shall have to, if I value my life," said I.

"And keep me out of it?"

"I make no promises, monsieur le comte, but we shall do our best. Where is he to be found?"

"His real name is Renaudin. He has a wine shop in the rue Coquillière, near Les Halles."

Chapter 4

Les Halles has a vile reputation. It is known as the belly of
Paris for the obvious reason that it is a food market in the
center of the city, but to anyone who has visited the area, a
more disagreeable symbolism is suggested. The market halls
are surrounded by narrow, malodorous streets and alleys of
intestinal complexity. Most of them date from the Middle
Ages. It is a pity Baron Haussmann didn't flatten the whole
of this squalid slum when he modernized so much of Paris
during the Second Empire. The driver of our landau could
hardly believe that people of our class intended to venture
there, and I had doubts myself when we came to it. Passing
down the rue Montmartre, you have no conception of what
lies ahead. At some point, we left the busy commercial street
and trundled through a cobbled lane lined with houses black
with years of grime, almost every window boarded over. Regardless of the bitter cold, groups of men in clothes I would
be ashamed to dress a scarecrow in, many of them barefoot
and all of them stained the color of coal heavers by exposure
to dust and mud, huddled in doorways, plotting the devil
knows what. These, surely, were descendants of the agitators
who had fomented the Revolution. The least decrepit and—
to my eye—the most threatening wore the black jerseys of

apaches, cut low at the neck and armpits, their arms covered only by a crust of grime. Some of these unfortunates no doubt resided in the slums of this street, but many were homeless, for there are no workhouses in France.

"We must be mad," I remarked to Bernhardt, "coming to this place to look for a man with a gun."

She said, "Bertie, I would cheerfully follow Valentin anywhere. He fascinates me." Which didn't address my concerns at all.

The rue Coquillière, when we reached it, proved to be slightly less odious than the lane we emerged from, yet not a street I would care to linger in. At the end closer to the actual market halls, a crowd of costermongers had surrounded a fellow in a countryman's blouse. He was doing nothing more provocative than carrying a huge empty basket on his arm. We were unable to hear what was being said, yet we could see plainly enough that they were prodding and goading him, and when the hapless wretch dropped his basket to defend himself, they kicked it into the middle of the street and pushed him into it, a spectacle that had them holding their sides with laughter.

With unfortunate timing, our cabman asked, "Where shall I put you down, sir?"

"As close to Renaudin's wine shop as possible. Do you know it?"

He did, and fortunately it was some distance from the thugs we'd just passed, a small establishment sensibly barricaded with iron bars in front of the window and casks of wine behind the glass. Bernhardt insisted on joining me, so after I'd helped her out and shooed away some ill-disposed dogs, I asked the driver to wait for us. He said he couldn't guarantee it; if he saw someone preparing to rob him, he'd be off and it would be up to us to find our own way home. I was indignant and told him so, threatening to have his license confiscated, but in his position I would have said the same.

The interior of the shop was built like a barricade. None

of the stock was in reach. A sturdy counter supported two large casks, allowing just a small space between in which an unsmiling fat woman was framed. The bottled wine, the little one could see of it, was on racks behind her. No customers were ahead of us, so I asked if Monsieur Renaudin was available.

"What do you want?" the woman rudely demanded.

I remained civil. "Just a few words with the owner, madame."

"I'm his wife. What's wrong with me?"

I was tempted to tell her, but Bernhardt got in first. "This is His Royal Highness the Prince of Wales and I am Sarah Bernhardt. Now will you kindly ask Monsieur Renaudin to step out from wherever he is?"

This impressed Madame Renaudin enough to make her turn her head and shout, "Visitors!"

It sounded as if we'd found Valentin at home. His wife remained staring at us as if we were from Timbuktu, and I suppose we might have been, for all the people of refinement she had seen from behind her counter. She was better scrubbed than the brutes in the street, yet she had the same Neanderthal cast of face, and one could well understand why Valentin spent most of his nights at the Moulin Rouge.

The scrutiny was becoming unnerving, so I occupied myself by looking around the shop—not that there was anything of interest, just more casks, some crates of empty bottles, a broken chair, and cigarette butts liberally scattered across the wooden floor. I glanced up at the crossbeams and saw last summer's flypapers still suspended there with their victims adhering to them. Then I happened to look beyond the flypapers to one of the darkest corners, copiously draped with cobwebs, and something moved—something too large for a spider.

My first thought was that I must have seen a bat, but I was wrong.

"What is it, Bertie?" Bernhardt asked me.

I was about to say that I was damned if I knew, when there
was another slight movement from the same corner. Two eyes
were watching me. Whatever it was up there had blinked.
Bernhardt had seen it, too. She's an extraordinary woman. I
don't think she has any fears at all. She crossed the floor to
get a closer look and immediately there was a sound, the
scraping of wood against wood.

I moved closer for a better view. A sliding hatch had just
been drawn shut: a spy hole. Someone had been watching us
from upstairs.

I said to Bernhardt, "We'll have to go up. I'm sure he's
there."

Rapid footsteps from upstairs punctuated my statement. I
looked for a way around the counter and found it barred by
casks. Our progress might have stopped altogether if Bernhardt
hadn't said, "Look, Bertie, one of them is on hinges. It must
be a door." And she was right. A cask had been sawn down
the middle and fitted with hinges and a hasp and staple. I
unfastened it and went through, only to meet a sturdier barrier
in the person of Madame Renaudin. Now that I saw the entire
lady and not merely the portion framed behind the counter,
I had a petrifying memory. In my youth, there were women
known as dippers employed at Brighton and other seaside
resorts to supervise the bathing machines and plunge the
wretched bathers into the waves. These grinning harpies would
stand for hours fully clothed up to their hips in water. Conse-
quently, the only women who could endure the cold were very
fat. The sight of Madame Renaudin reminded me all too
vividly of the mountainous creature employed by my parents
to force me screaming into the sea at Osborne at the age of
six.

"Don't stand there, Bertie!" Bernhardt urged me and gave
the woman—who would have made six of her—a volley of
abuse worthy of the roughest fishmonger in Les Halles. Our
way was cleared.

I mounted the first stair and prudently called out, "We are friends and admirers, monsieur."

If the man upstairs heard, he wasn't persuaded to remain. A strong draft from an open window hit our faces as we reached the landing and I caught sight of a trousered leg being lifted over the window ledge at the end of the passage. I dashed to the window and looked out.

Valentin—for it was he, beyond all doubt, in his battered top hat and brown suit—had shinned down a drainpipe into the yard at the rear of the shop and was in the act of climbing over a wall.

I shouted his name, and he ignored me. He jumped into the yard of the neighboring house and—so far as I could tell without falling from the window—ran inside the building.

"Aren't you going after him?" demanded Bernhardt, at my side. She seemed to think I was capable of matching Valentin's agility.

I looked at the drainpipe and knew it wouldn't support me. "Better to meet him the other way." Suiting action to the words before Bernhardt disputed them, I ran downstairs, dodged around the still-shocked Madame Renaudin, through the shop and into the street in time to see Valentin's thin form bolting like a startled gazelle toward Les Halles, with two dogs in pursuit. He must have come straight through the house next door to make his escape. He was a very frightened man.

Our carriage was still outside and there was a chance that with horsepower we might get closer to the fugitive. As soon as we had climbed aboard, I urged the driver to use the whip.

Like most cabbies in my experience, this one was a pessimist. "You want me to catch him? It's not possible, monsieur."

"Of course it's possible." I said tetchily. "A horse is faster than a man, and you have two."

He didn't argue the point any more, but he had to turn the carriage, and then I was forced to admit that his opinion had been sounder than mine. We had lost sight of Valentin. Refusing to be defeated, I ordered the driver to take us with all speed as far as the first of the market halls, the weird umbrellalike structures of cast iron and glass where it was obvious Valentin must have gone to avoid pursuit. We would take our chances among the market fraternity. Having heard Sarah's repertoire of abuse, I almost pitied the fishmongers.

By this time, the business of the vegetable market was over and only a handful of tradesmen remained, sweeping and tidying up. They didn't include Valentin, so we penetrated farther. There are ten halls altogether, two ranks of five, with narrow streets behind. *Halls* is a misnomer, really, because they are open on all sides but roofed over with glass, supported by iron girders. We hurried through what must have been the meat and fish markets by the odors that lingered, eventually to reach the last hall, a more salubrious area where flower stalls were still in place and people were buying and selling blooms that I suppose had come from the warm south. Oblivious of any who may have recognized us, we darted this way and that, looking up the gangways. Some of the stalls were tiered so high that even a man of Valentin's stature could easily dodge behind them and be missed.

This was an obvious place for a man to be hiding, and I told Bernhardt as much. Imagine my satisfaction, then, when we caught sight of Valentin again. He appeared briefly between two stalls only about twenty paces from us, the nose and chin unmistakable.

Bernhardt shrilled, "*Là! Là!* Bertie!"

Valentin didn't turn in our direction, but he must have overheard Bernhardt's cry, because he immediately started running toward the far end of the market.

Now, I'm fit for most things in this life, but running isn't my sport and never was. Never mind running—a quick walk leaves me gasping for breath. I'm perfectly sure that even Sarah Bernhardt could outpace me if she was suitably attired; skirts tend to hamper the fair sex in feats of athletics. So it was pointless for either of us to go haring after Valentin. Resourcefully, I did the best thing I could think of—climbed onto a flower stand to observe the direction he was taking.

A vase or two of daffodils were tipped over in the process, for it was actually a handcart about three feet high fairly packed with flowers, and it required quite some agility to step up there. Bernhardt did her best to pacify the lady owner while I ignored the rumpus and watched Valentin weaving between the stalls at a speed I could never have matched. I kept him in view until the moment he left the hall by the southeast side.

"Right—let's get after him," I said, climbing down and knocking over more pots in the process. This time the stall holder didn't shout at me. I think Bernhardt had convinced her that she would get a royal warrant—*HRH Albert Edward, Prince of Wales, kicked over some vases on this stall in March 1891*—and instead she insisted on attaching one of her broken daffodils to my lapel, just as if it was St. David's Day.

We made the best possible speed across the hall and found ourselves in a street heaped with rubbish from the markets, where children were scavenging for anything edible.

"We need some sous, Bertie," Bernhardt told me, and without waiting for a response, she turned to the children and asked which way the tall, thin man in the top hat had gone.

The urchins looked expectantly in my direction. I have never found room in my pocket for anything so humble as a sou, so I had to part with several francs before we got the information we wanted. The thin man, they told us, had gone in the direction of the rue des Innocents.

Paris street names bear no resemblance to their character. The prettily named rue de la Lingerie down which we passed was unspeakably shabby and the rue des Innocents, with which it connected, seemed consecrated to venery, for there were streetwalkers parading even at this hour of the afternoon. This actually proved helpful, because two of them knew Valentin from the Moulin Rouge and had just seen him enter a place known as the *caveau*.

The waiter behind the bar in this establishment, a man of saturnine looks, said nothing when we inquired, merely pointed downstairs—down a set of narrow stone stairs between plastered walls covered in penciled drawings and inscriptions that I hoped Bernhardt passed without noticing, because the ones I saw were unfit for even the most emancipated lady to inspect.

This was the *caveau* proper, a vault divided into three by arches that lent the place a quaintly ecclesiastical air; indeed, I learned later that this had formerly been a charnel house. It was now fitted with gas jets, by the light of which we could see six or seven derelicts at a wooden bench engaged in a game of dominoes. A blind man was playing a mournful tune on an upright piano. In one dim corner, a couple were locked in a passionate embrace. In another, trying to hide behind a newspaper, was Valentin le Désossé.

Up to this point, I have to state that the lady at my side had shown as much pluck as I, perhaps more. This was my opportunity for a show of derring-do. Without a thought for personal safety, I said, "Monsieur Renaudin, a word, if you please."

To my horror, he lowered the newspaper and revealed a silver gun in his right hand, pointing at my chest.

I turned rigid. I think one is supposed to speak calmly to a man holding a gun. I was dumbstruck.

There was a loud bang. I gasped and swayed back, certain that I was shot, but the sound I had heard was a domino being slammed on the table behind me. Rough men turn this innocent parlor game into a show of aggression. It surprised Valentin, too. His hand jerked up and he fired a shot into the ceiling. The report was deafening.

Pandemonium followed. I threw myself to the floor to avoid

being hit and so did Bernhardt. The domino players tipped the table over and sheltered behind it. The blind pianist grabbed his white stick and blundered into the wall, his free hand groping for a door that wasn't there. The young lovers fell off their chair and disappeared under a flurry of petticoats.

As for Valentin, he was so shocked that he dropped the gun.

At this juncture, I acted with commendable presence of mind by grabbing the stick from the blind man and using it to hook the gun out of Valentin's reach. Bernhardt snatched up the weapon, stood upright, and pointed it at him. Without a word, he raised his hands. I got up from the floor myself and murmured to Sarah, "Bravo!"

Behind us, everyone except the blind man was escaping up the stairs. If Valentin couldn't hold a gun without shooting into the ceiling, what would a woman do?

She would cope perfectly well, I was confident—for about two seconds.

Inconveniently, quite a cloud of dust had been raised by the commotion and poor Sarah suddenly erupted into a fit of sneezing. I grabbed the gun, which, through no fault of her own, she was waving about like a conductor's baton.

Pointing it steadily at Valentin, who had turned deathly pale, I told him, "You can put down your hands, but keep your distance."

He obeyed, his grotesque features rigid with terror.

I told him, "You have some explaining to do, monsieur."

It was some time before he succeeded in saying anything, and then it was only to ask, "May I sit down?"

We all sat down except the blind man, who was still pawing the wall. Bernhardt got up to reunite him with his stick and steer him to the stairs. Someone at the top shouted, "Are you all right down there?"

"Everything is under control," I called back, "and we should appreciate a few minutes' privacy."

Valentin said in a rush, "Monsieur, I appeal to you, while you continue to point that thing in my direction, I cannot speak a word. Not a word, not a word." A nice example of self-contradiction. He was talking nineteen to the dozen. The idol of the Moulin Rouge, the disdainful dancer who set female pulses racing, was reduced to a gibbering wreck.

Satisfied that he was no threat, I lowered the gun and examined it. A fine example of the gunsmith's art, I concluded. A silver revolver, elaborately chased on the side plate and along the barrel—a gentleman's gun, beyond question. I have one like it in the gun room at Balmoral, a useful weapon for putting a wounded animal out of its misery. I rested it on the table, out of Valentin's reach, but sufficient to signal that I was not proposing to shoot him. By now, his fit of hysteria had calmed somewhat. I would have introduced myself and Bernhardt, but it might have sent him into another paroxysm, so I contented myself with saying, "You had better tell us how you acquired the weapon."

He had gone silent now, his features rigid, producing a strong resemblance to those monstrous statues one sees in illustrations of Easter Island.

I prompted him: "This was at the Moulin Rouge, was it not?"

He managed to nod his head.

"On the night the man was shot there?"

"Yes."

"You've found your voice, then?"

He said, "Are you from the Sûreté? You sound like an Englishman."

"We are independent investigators. Please go on."

"Will you respect what I say as confidential?"

"Depend upon it."

"Then yes, I saw the man shot at the Moulin Rouge. That is to say, I heard the shot." His hand went to his throat. The scene was obviously vivid in his memory. "It happened right in

front of me when I was dancing with La Goulue. A tremendous
report, followed immediately by another. Everything stopped
and a young man dropped to the floor."

"Did you see who was behind him?"

"No. I was looking down at the victim. I was very shocked."
His brown eyes studied me intensely, making some kind of
appeal. "Paris is a terribly dangerous city. I live in constant
fear of being murdered. That's why I kept the gun."

"You're running ahead of your story, monsieur."

"I'm sorry. After the shooting, the poor fellow was carried
to the gentlemen's dressing room. I believe there was a doctor
in attendance, and the Agincourt family. The police arrived
and went in. Most of the audience had left the building by
that time and so had La Goulue and the other girls. I would
have gone with them except that my overcoat was still in the
dressing room and I didn't like to interrupt. I waited some
time. The ballroom was empty."

"Not entirely empty," said Bernhardt. "You overlooked
Toulouse-Lautrec."

"Don't we all?" I quipped, but my wit was lost on Valentin.
"Pray continue."

"When I went in, the corpse was lying on a table, covered
with a blanket. The family were talking agitatedly. I think
the young girl was crying and the father was trying to comfort
her."

"Who else was there?"

"The two policemen. The doctor had left. There was a
middle-aged lady talking to the police."

"The comtesse," I said.

"And a youth."

"Tristan, the son. No one else?"

"No one else."

"Did you speak to any of them?"

"It seemed inappropriate. I raised my hat, picked my over-

coat off the hook, and left. Only when I was outside did I put my hand in the pocket and find the gun there."

"You're telling us it was in the pocket of your coat?"

"I don't know how it got there, monsieur and madame. I swear I don't know."

"Why didn't you show it to the police immediately?"

"I was afraid."

"It was your public duty, surely?"

His mouth tightened. "You don't know our police. They would think I was the prime suspect. Anyone from Les Halles is labeled as a criminal."

"But you were dancing when the shots were fired," Bernhardt pointed out. "Hundreds of witnesses must have seen you."

"If the police find a man in possession of a gun at the scene of a murder, they are not interested in witnesses, madame. They expect a confession, and they usually get it."

All this was said with an intensity that I found persuasive. However, the story begged two important questions: Why did the murderer deposit the gun in Valentin's overcoat, and when? Unless plausible answers could be found, Valentin's part in the affair could not be dismissed as innocent.

"If you are so fearful of the police, monsieur," said I, "why did you not dispose of the gun? They might have called on you at any time and found it in your possession."

Deep creases appeared under Valentin's eyes and for a moment I thought he would burst into tears. "You don't believe a word I've said."

"On the contrary," I told him with a trace of impatience, "I am doing my damnedest to find the rational explanation for your behavior."

"But I have told you. Les Halles is a jungle. Savages roam the streets in gangs. Through no fault of my own, I have a conspicuous appearance. To some of these brutes, my face is an incitement to violence. Returning late at night from dance halls, I have been set upon and assaulted three times. I go in constant fear of my life. Is it so surprising that when a gun is put into my pocket I should think twice about keeping it for protection?"

My thoughts returned to the bullying we had witnessed in the rue Coquillière in broad daylight and it wasn't difficult to put myself into Valentin's shoes walking home some time in the small hours, fearful of what might be lurking in every doorway. I wouldn't care to attempt it without arming myself. Yes, the opportunity to carry a gun might outweigh the dangers of being found in possession of a murder weapon.

I picked up the revolver again and examined it closely to confirm something I had noted before without fully absorbing its importance. The implications, I now realized, were devastating.

"What is it?" Bernhardt asked.

I didn't respond. Instead, I asked Valentin, "Have the police questioned you about the murder?"

He rolled his eyes upward. "They keep coming back to the Moulin Rouge. I was questioned last Monday by the *chef de la Sûreté* himself. He simply asked me what I saw when the shots were fired. Nothing was said about what happened to the gun. I didn't lie to him, monsieur. It wasn't mentioned."

"Then with luck, you won't hear from him again," said I, a statement so morally irresponsible that I drew a gasp from Bernhardt, who had the grace to stay silent after that. "I suggest, monsieur, that you take some lessons in pugilism, because I can't allow you to keep the revolver."

"May I go?" he asked, relief flooding across the furrowed face.

"Let us all go," I said. "The air in this cellar can't be improving our health."

In the rue des Innocents, the lamplighter was busy. We watched Valentin's spindly figure scuttle into the dusk and then we made our way in the opposite direction as far as the rue Saint-Denis, where with some relief I succeeded in hailing a cab.

"Bertie, what are you going to do with the gun?" Bernhardt asked anxiously when we were aboard.

"It's safe with me," I assured her.

"It ought to be taken to the police. I think we should have escorted Valentin to the police, whatever he said. You can't allow sympathy for the man to outweigh civic duty. The revolver is vital evidence."

Her pious tone needled me somewhat. "I'm aware of that, Sarah, and I, of all people, don't need lectures on civic duty. I think you may form another opinion if you examine the weapon." I took it from my pocket and handed it to her.

She turned it over in her hands. "Is there some doubt that this is the gun used in the murder?"

"No doubt, so far as I'm aware," I said. "But if you will look closely at the chasing on the side plate above the trigger, you may understand why we are not at this minute speaking to the *chef de la Sûreté*."

She held it close to her eyes and waited for the carriage to pass a streetlamp. "Well, I see some kind of emblem engraved in the silver. Is that what you mean? A shield with something written under it in Latin. I don't read Latin, Bertie."

"Look above the shield, at the crest."

"The letter *A* surrounded by these curly bits, do you mean?"

"That is precisely what I mean, Sarah. You are looking at the coat of arms of the Agincourt family. Unless I am very mistaken, the weapon that killed Maurice Letissier was from their private armory."

Chapter 5

That evening, I dined with Sarah Bernhardt at Magny's, where the cuisine has never failed to please. You will recall that the Agincourt family dined at this highly regarded restaurant on the night of the murder, so our visit was mainly investigative in character. Smile at the "mainly" if you wish, but who would deny that Sarah and I had earned a decent dinner after risking life and limb in Les Halles? Besides, there was much to discuss and my brain works best over a toothsome meal.

My companion was ravishingly dressed in another of Monsieur Worth's creations, sky blue damask lavishly trimmed with embroidered lace and pearls. As usual, she wore white gloves to her armpits, for she is terribly conscious how thin her arms are. At her breast was a magnificent brooch with the letters *LN* worked in diamonds. Without too blatantly staring at this area of the lady's anatomy, I spent an interesting time trying to decipher the significance.

"Who is he?" I asked eventually. "A lover?"

Smiling, she gave an evasive answer. "This brooch? I've had it more than twenty years."

"Yes, but whose initials are they?"

"The emperor's."

I blinked. "You and Louis Napoleon . . ."

"My reward for a command performance, Bertie." Now her eyes mocked me wickedly, inviting me to decide whether the gift had been earned on the boards or in bed. I knew she'd had scores of lovers, but until that moment I had confidently assumed none of them outranked me.

Slightly piqued, I said, "Personally, I think messages in jewelry should be more discreet. My engagement present to Alix was a ring with six stones—a beryl, an emerald, a ruby, a topaz, a jacinth, and a second emerald."

I let her puzzle over this for a while before explaining that the initial letters of the gems spelled my name. "But of course," I was quick to add, "I could not duplicate the gift for another lady, however intimate a companion she might become."

"That would be unforgivable," she agreed, then added coquettishly, "but you would think of some other keepsake for such a lady, if one existed. You have a fertile imagination, Bertie."

"A fertile imagination, but poor credit with Monsieur Cartier, I'm afraid," said I, not entirely untruthfully. "These days, a monogrammed handkerchief is the very best keepsake I can run to."

She laughed, not believing a word of it. After all, we were dining at one of the finest restaurants in Paris. Who would believe that the Prince of Wales was so underfunded by his own nation that he was obliged to borrow from his foreign friends? Who would believe that he was prey to moneylenders touting for trade who virtually laid siege to the Hotel Bristol?

Over some delicious Ostend oysters garnished with anchovies and radishes, I returned to the vexing question of the murder of Letissier. "We can't duck it, Sarah. That revolver belonged to the Agincourt family."

"Can we be certain?"

"There is no question, my dear. In my youth, I was given an excellent grounding in heraldry and it is quite a passion of mine. I can recognize a coat of arms, be it English or French."

She said she didn't doubt me, but she felt it right to point out that it was Valentin le Désossé, and not one of the Agincourts, who had been caught with the gun in his possession.

I said, "That is immaterial, in my opinion. Valentin's coat happened to be hanging in the dressing room and the murderer slipped the revolver into the pocket."

"For what reason?"

"In case the police decided to conduct a search."

She set down her knife and fork and sat back in her chair to meditate on the matter. She had scarcely touched her oysters, but then her appetite is birdlike.

"If you're not going to finish those . . ." said I.

"Please do." She pushed her plate toward me. "Bertie, let us be clear about this. You are suggesting, are you not, that one of the Agincourt family must have fired the fatal shot?"

"That is the obvious conclusion," I concurred.

"Meaning Jules or his wife, Juliette."

"Or the daughter, Rosine."

"Or the son . . . what was his name?"

"Tristan, a mere lad of eighteen."

"Young males on the threshold of manhood can be very antisocial, Bertie."

"Insufferable. I've had two of my own," I reminded her while I helped myself to oysters from her plate.

"Then you don't need telling how disorderly the male of the species can be at that age."

I gave her a sharp look to satisfy myself that the remark was innocent. No one is more stern a critic of my two sons than I, but I won't hear them maligned by anyone else. I took a sip of Chablis. "I must have met Tristan when he was a small child, but I've no idea how he turned out."

"Nor I," said Sarah.

"It's a queer fellow who shoots his sister's fiancé in the back."

She said, "It's just as queer when the girl's parents do the deed."

"Or the girl herself."

A twitch of the mouth, the tiniest movement, told me that Bernhardt, too, had her suspicions about Rosine. "She faced a lifetime tied to this man."

"She'd agreed to marry him."

"Do we know that, Bertie?"

I gazed at her in mystification.

She explained, "The father's choice of a son-in-law doesn't always coincide with his daughter's."

"Sarah, do you know something? Is there a lover?"

"Intuition, pure intuition."

I told her candidly, "We should be dealing in facts, not fancies."

"All right. Do you know for a fact that Rosine loved Maurice Letissier?"

"Come, come, Sarah," I chided her. "People of rank don't marry for love. They do it to produce sons." As I spoke, I was all too aware how difficult this would be to convey to Bernhardt, the love child of a courtesan. Poor Sarah had loved many men and married only one, a Greek, on a whim of passion, and he had been utterly unsuitable, addicted to morphine, which had killed him at forty-two. How could a woman of her romantic nature and experience understand the fine discrimination that goes into the uniting of two young people of family? "In society, you marry the girl your parents invite to sit next to you at dinner. Love is what happens with someone else, preferably after you have produced an heir."

She said, "You can't legislate for love, Bertie. It can happen at any time."

"I know that only too well, my dear."

"Didn't you have lovers before you married?"

"I was not without experience," I said guardedly, "but I am a male. Young ladies of Rosine's class are entirely ignorant of such matters, and rightly so."

"In England, possibly," said Bernhardt with disdain. "You are in France now."

The task was hopeless. She didn't understand a word I was saying, and anyway, we were interrupted by the first violin from the quintet. He was at liberty among the tables, playing at people with a view to francs, so I finished the oysters to a rendering of some mournful chanson. I paid him and pushed the plate aside. "The only certainty is that we are faced with a domestic murder. Another visit to Montroger is essential."

The fish course I had chosen was salmon trout with whitebait. Before I could intervene, she sent hers back and asked for a smaller portion.

I told her, "I could have helped you with that."

She said, "Bertie, shouldn't we take that gun to the police?"

"Keep your voice down," said I.

"It may be important to their investigation."

I told her confidentially, "This may be a case the Sûreté should not be encouraged to pursue. Jules d'Agincourt is an old friend."

She frowned. "Are you seriously suggesting that we should obstruct the police in their inquiries?"

"I wouldn't *obstruct* them," I said in a shocked tone. "I'm merely proposing to pursue an independent investigation, subject, of course, to Jules's permission, and if you and I succeed in unmasking the murderer, the outcome must be more satisfactory from every point of view."

"But the murderer is almost certainly one of the family."

"Exactly. And the family is one of the oldest in France. They can deal with it in their own way. They won't want their name besmirched in the courts."

"Bertie, I don't think the police will approve of this at all."

"I'm not seeking their approval, my dear."

For this, she treated me to a lecture on the French system of justice that I won't bore you with, the gist of which was that an examining magistrate wouldn't take any more kindly to interference than the police. I listened with restraint, finished my fish course, called for the next wine, a Saint-Estèphe, and repeated that we would definitely make a second visit to Montroger in the morning.

She said, "You haven't listened to a word I said."

"Every word, my dear," said I. "Call me old-fashioned if you wish, but I put loyalty to an old chum above kowtowing to magistrates and policemen."

"Loyalty to an old chum! It's not a matter of sentiment. It's dangerous," she said.

"Why?"

"Well, if one of them is a murderer . . ."

"Oh, that won't arise," I reassured her. "No, no, the great advantage we have over the police is that we can go into the house as friends of the family. I've done this before, Sarah. I'm an expert at lulling the guilty into a sense of security. Now, I think the waiter is approaching with your pheasant and truffles. Let us enjoy the meal. Do you know, I'm beginning to get an appetite?"

And, my word, Magny's excelled themselves. The bird was roasted to perfection, those truffles looking like ebony apples. There's much to be said for the skills of a French chef, as I conceded to my companion, deftly moving the conversation into a different area of controversy. "But of all the cooks I have known, I award the palm to Rosa Ovenden, an Englishwoman of Cockney descent. Delightful creature. She is cook to Lady Randolph Churchill."

"And before that, she was kitchen maid to the Duc d'Aumale at Chantilly," Bernhardt said in a way calculated to undermine my claim. "Then she joined the staff of the Comte de Paris. She learned everything she knows from French chefs."

Warily I said, "You know the lovely Rosa, then?"

"I have sampled her cooking."

"Weren't you enslaved?"

"I wouldn't put it in quite those terms. She is an adequate cook of simple meals."

I would not be downed. Bernhardt is no more generous to her own sex than she is to foreigners, so I relished telling the story I had been leading up to. "The first time I met Rosa, I had no idea of her occupation. I was attending a shooting party at Chieveley Park and happened to slip into the dining room sometime before dinner in search of something to keep me going. I was not the first. At the sideboard was a stunning creature dressed in a white gown and sipping champagne. We chatted agreeably and I found her so charming that I couldn't resist planting a kiss on her cheek before leaving. But later when we all sat down to dinner, this vision in white wasn't at the table. Somewhat disappointed, I made inquiries of my hostess and it was revealed to one and all that I must have kissed the cook. After a moment's embarrassment, I laughed and then everyone else laughed, too, though a little uneasily. Then my hostess charmingly declared that I must have guaranteed them an excellent dinner."

Bernhardt forced herself to smile. The French sense of humor leaves much to be desired.

However, Monsieur Magny judged it a suitable moment to approach the table and ask if we were enjoying our meal. I assured him that the fare was delicious and Bernhardt added waspishly, "Incomparable."

I told Magny that we would appreciate a few words with his headwaiter and his sommelier over coffee.

Before that, I enjoyed a savory dish of quails garnished with peeled grapes, accompanied by Chambertin 1884, followed by some splendid rum babas and chocolate patisseries. Bernhardt had long since placed her napkin on the table, but she joined me in coffee and a small *chasse café* in the form of a cognac.

Having verified that the headwaiter remembered meeting

the Agincourt party on the evening of the murder, I asked him whether he had been able to observe their demeanor toward one another.

He said, "Your Royal Highness, I noticed nothing untoward."

I said, "You don't have to be discreet just because you're talking to me, my good man. Be candid. Were any harsh words spoken between them?"

The fellow was a typical stuffed shirt. You could tell straight away that he was going to say nothing of substance whatsoever. "I was not in a position to hear very much of what was said, even if I had been disposed to listen, sir."

"Of course, but you must have sensed the atmosphere at the table. Were they convivial?"

"Cordial would be closer to it, sir."

"Cordial? They were celebrating a betrothal. 'Cordial' sounds like a funeral. No high spirits? Toasts to the happy couple?"

"None that I noticed, sir."

"Do you recollect who was in the party?"

He described the four Agincourts and Letissier.

"At least we're talking about the same people," said I in some frustration. "No one joined them, I suppose?"

"I believe not, sir."

"Did you sense any unease at the table?"

"Unease, sir?"

He was a washout. A headwaiter should be as vigilant as a bride's father. This one's daughter could have married the sweep and he wouldn't have noticed.

"Be so good as to ask the sommelier to step over, will you?"

I suppose it is in the nature of their work, but sommeliers in general are more forthcoming than headwaiters. This one was not much taller than Toulouse-Lautrec, Oriental in feature and indeterminate in age, but with a disarming grin that displayed some wide gaps in his teeth. Yes, he had attended the Agincourts' table and brought them champagne. To his eye, they were going through the motions of an engagement party without the expressions of joy normal on such occasions. "Madame la comtesse had much to say, very much, and it seemed to discourage the others."

"What was she talking about?"

"Whenever I approached the table, the subject of her discourse was the impossibility of finding reliable servants."

"They were discussing the servant problem at an engagement party?" said Bernhardt in disbelief.

"The comtesse was expounding her views, madame. It was not a discussion. She held forth from the hors d'oeuvres to the savories and no one seemed willing to change the subject."

"Perhaps she was giving advice to the young couple," said Bernhardt.

"No doubt you are right, madame."

"There must have been some breaks in this monologue," said I.

"Once started, the comtesse is like—" He stopped himself.

"A steam engine? We know the lady," said I. "However, one of the party was murdered later in the evening, as I'm sure you know. Are you able to tell us anything at all about the others at the table? The daughter, for instance?"

He put a hand to the silver corkscrew that he wore on a chain suspended from his neck and stroked it thoughtfully. "May I be frank, sir? She is a stunningly beautiful young girl, but that evening she was not so radiant as others I have seen on similar occasions. Her eyes should have flashed like the chandeliers. They were almost opaque."

"How extraordinary! And her manner?"

"Demure and dignified."

Sarah exchanged a glance with me that said I had better take seriously her theory about a lover.

"Tell us about the others," I urged the man. "About Letissier. How was his behavior?"

"My impression was that he was not displeased. Slightly ill at ease, perhaps, but no more than one would expect when his new fiancée was looking so wan. Yes, I would say that he was acting normally under the circumstances. And the comte, too, was doing his best to raise the spirits of the party by ordering some excellent wines. He knows the great years and he is generous enough to order them."

"But he wasn't interrupting his wife?"

"You mentioned that you know the comtesse, sir?"

"Point taken. That leaves the son, young Tristan. How was he holding up under *Maman*'s dissertation?"

"When he wasn't actually eating, his eyes were on his sister, sir."

"Interesting. He was sensitive to her mood, I take it?"

"That is difficult for me to say, sir."

I nodded. The sommelier had more than compensated for the headwaiter's blandness and I thanked him warmly and put something into his hand.

I gestured to Magny and called him to the table. "We have had an excellent evening, *patron,* so I shall let you into a secret about one of your confrères. It was some years ago in another restaurant and the Swiss waiter was making pancakes for me beside the table on one of those contraptions."

"Flambé?"

"Exactly. Unfortunately, the poor fellow betrayed some nerves and it was quite obvious that he was burning the first one. It was thin as lace. I told him not to be dismayed but to baste it immediately with curaçao and brandy, which he did. The result was delicious. That evening, we had discovered a new delicacy. He asked me if I would permit him to name it after his sweetheart. I suppose I could have insisted that he named it after me, but I am magnanimous about such matters. Instead of crêpes bertie, we gave the world crêpes suzette."

"*Magnifique*, Your Royal Highness!"

"Is this true?" said Bernhardt.

"You can ask the waiter concerned. He has an establishment not far from here. His name is César Ritz."

Magny held up his hands, bereft of speech.

"All of which leads me to add," I continued, "that a few crêpes suzette and a little more champagne would not come amiss at the conclusion of this excellent meal. What do you say, Sarah?"

Chapter 6

Knollys, my private secretary, was fussing as usual when I called at the Bristol next morning to walk my dog.

"We had no idea where to look for you, sir."

"Splendid," I said.

"But your bed wasn't slept in."

"Francis, this is Paris, not Balmoral," I told him good-naturedly. "The city wakes up at night. You should get out and see for yourself. Meet a charming mademoiselle and take her to a show and dinner afterward. It'll do you no end of good and you'll very soon understand why my bed wasn't slept in."

He said, "I'm fifty-three years old, sir."

I said, "Well, I hope if I'm spared to live so long I won't consider it an impediment to pleasure. Oh, I appreciate your concern, Francis, really I do, but it isn't necessary."

As it happens, I was a little tetchy from having spent another innocent night with Bernhardt. After Magny's, the lady had insisted on visiting an extraordinary entertainment in the boulevard de Rochechouart, with a notice outside that proclaimed: *Le Mirliton, for Audiences that Enjoy Being Insulted.* A vulgar man called Bruant, dressed in velvet and a wide-brimmed hat, had fulfilled the promise with a series of unrepeatable songs and repartee that Sarah found enchanting but that I didn't particularly care for. I put up with it manfully until dawn was breaking, seeing that she was so enraptured, and then took her for an early breakfast, but afterward I fell asleep in the cab on the way back to her apartment. It was the driver who wakened me in front of the Bristol, acting, he said, on Madame Bernhardt's instruction, she having left the cab and paid our fare.

"What do you have for me this morning?" I asked Knollys. "Any post?"

There was a letter from Fredensborg—at last.

> Fredensborg Castle
>
> Beloved Bertie,
>
> I am writing this at once in response to your letter, which has just arrived. What dreadful tidings for the Agincourts! Such a kind, devoted family. I remember Rosine as a pretty child in ringlets and I can scarcely believe that she is old enough to have become engaged— but then our own darling boys grew up too fast. Life moves on so rapidly and so much that one has to face is cruel. God knows, we have had our share of heartbreak, but nothing so violent as this tragedy that the Agincourts must endure. When you send our condolences to Jules and Juliette (and Rosine, of course), be sure to mention that they are in my prayers.
>
> And now, my dearest, I venture to say something that you may find difficult to accept. I have never sought actively to curtail your freedom, nor would I, but these are difficult times—you said to me yourself that we are walking on eggs until that disagreeable business about the game of baccarat at Tranby Croft is resolved in the courts—and I have a strange presentiment that out of your generous nature you run the risk of becoming in-volved in the unhappy event that has befallen the Agin-

courts. You declare confidently that the Sûreté will make an arrest shortly, but what if they do not?

Bertie dearest, we both know that from time to time you have interested yourself in an active way in cases of murder, and yes, I admit, the guilty parties were eventually apprehended. This time, if the opportunity arose, you would be in no position to usurp the role of the detective police, and even if you were, the risks of being misunderstood are too appalling to contemplate. Paris may seem like a second home, but you are still in a foreign country. Their methods are not ours. With Tranby Croft hanging over us, we cannot afford more misunderstanding and the scandal that always comes in its wake. So I implore you most earnestly not to involve yourself in the Agincourts' tragedy, however much your chivalrous feelings may prompt you.

Now to other matters. If Paris is so cold—and I can believe it, for we have twelve degrees of frost in Copenhagen today—why don't you travel immediately to the Riviera? I am sure Francis Knollys would make the arrangements speedily. He never seems entirely relaxed in Paris. And I do not like to think of you in a state of boredom.

For me, here in the castle, life is tolerable, though I *do* wish they would serve something besides currant jelly for dessert. It is a great consolation to have Toria and Maud with me and we play loo every evening, but I think constantly of Louise, praying that she will not deliver prematurely. I am determined to be home in good time.

Write again soon, my dearest. Remember I shall look first at the postmark to see where you are.

Ever your devoted Alix

Poor Alix! She is utterly loyal to her aged parents, but in truth, every hour she spends in Fredensborg is like a prison sentence. Part of the problem, I think (though she never admits it), is the difficulty of communication, for the old couple are both very deaf and so is Alix. A family conversation sounds like the Trooping of the Color.

The rest of the letter was predictable, and of course matters had moved on so rapidly since it was written that Alix couldn't possibly expect me to follow her advice in every particular. What a good thing her thoughts were so taken up with Louise's pregnancy and the forthcoming arrival of our first grandchild.

I stuffed the letter into my pocket, called for my terrier, Jack, and went for a stroll in the Champs-Elysées. The sun was out at last.

For the rest of the morning, I was forced to take a nap.

Jules d'Agincourt was surprised to see Bernhardt and me on his doorstep a second time, but he took it in good part. Having invited us inside and poured us cognacs, he said, "I need not ask why you are here. The police are getting nowhere."

"Have they been back?" I asked.

"The *chef de la Sûreté* himself had long interviews yesterday with Juliette and Rosine. But he should be making his inquiries in Montmartre, not here."

I gently disabused him of this opinion. "Jules, the police may not be so far astray as you believe. They do not know it yet, but this was found hidden at the Moulin Rouge on the evening of the murder." I handed him the revolver with the Agincourt coat of arms.

He let it rest on his hands and stared at it in silence for a long time.

Finally he said in a voice tremulous with emotion, "Found at the Moulin Rouge?"

"And recovered later by Sarah and me."

I watched him keenly. After all, no investigator worthy of the name can permit friendship to get in the way of the truth. Those patrician features and the pale blue eyes and the lines

around them that formed into an expression of absolute genial-
ity when he smiled (and you always expected him to) had to
be treated as suspicious. I had always taken his intelligence
to be a force for good and never known any cause to doubt
that assumption, but I understand enough about human nature
to know that in extremis a clever mind may be artful in deceit.

His lips formed a word and then closed as if his voice was
unable to function. He made another try. "You said the police
are not informed yet?"

"That is so."

"It means . . ." He was unable to go on.

I said, "We believe the truth is to be found in this house,
Jules."

He lowered his head. I can't begin to tell you how distressing
it was to see my old friend in such a state of shock, but I had
to be firm with him.

I lifted the revolver from his open palms. "We have a choice.
We can hand this to the police. Or we can conduct our own
investigation here, in the family and among friends."

He managed to say, "The latter."

I told him that in that case we would require his cooperation
in persuading the rest of his family to submit to questioning.

The voice tried to be steady. "I shall see to it."

"Not yet," I said. "Before we go any further, Sarah and I
would like to know where this gun was kept."

"It's from the gun room. All the firearms are kept there."

"May we see?"

The way to the gun room was through the dining room and
the smoking room and across a cobbled courtyard. He led us
there and pushed open the door.

I said, "You don't keep it locked, I notice."

"There is a key," he pointed out.

"Yes, but it's not much use if you don't remove it when
the door is shut."

"Bertie, I've never had reason to lock it—or never thought

I had," Jules said, sounding sheepish. He pushed open the door.

Reader, I have seen the gun rooms of every great house in England and Scotland and, believe me, this would have ranked among the finest. Oak-paneled and as high as a coach house (which I dare say had been its original purpose), it was furnished with twenty or more rosewood gun cabinets, each holding a dozen shotguns. The walls just below the open beams were hung with the mounted heads of animals bagged by Agincourts over half a century, including wild boar and some big game. At a lower level were a series of exquisite oil paintings of hunting scenes. They were interspersed with photographs of shooting parties. The floor was carpeted and dominated by two magnificent tiger-skin rugs. The morning newspapers lay undisturbed on a table. The pleasant smell of cigars lingered. A black retriever was asleep on the hearth, at least until Bernhardt gave a cry of delight and woke the poor beast.

I am not by temperament a sybarite, but I could easily picture myself resorting to this companionable room on a foggy morning when shooting was impossible, fanning my hands in front of the huge log fire before settling into one of the leather lounging chairs with a glass of sherry and a volume of Surtees (or his French equivalent) from the bookshelves behind the door. In fact, the atmosphere was more to my liking than the smoking room. In no way could one think of the room simply as an armory.

"I spend many a cosy hour in here," Jules said, reading my thoughts. "I've never cared to keep it locked."

"So anyone may come in?"

"Yes."

"Including the ladies?" Bernhardt inquired, looking up from where the dog was lying in a most undignified position having its chest massaged.

"Certainly, when they wish."

"And do they?"

"Not as a rule, but occasionally they'll come for a newspaper or a book."

"Or a gun, if they had a use for it," said I, quick to catch the drift of Bernhardt's questions.

Jules missed the point entirely. "The ladies in this house don't go in for field sports."

"Where do you keep the pistols? I don't see any on display."

"They're in the top drawer of the gun cabinet at the end, or should be," Jules informed us. "We possess four revolvers, all engraved with our coat of arms." He went to the cabinet he had pointed out and opened the drawer. It was not kept locked, I noticed. Clearly, no one had seen any reason to enforce security.

"How many are left?" I asked with a strong hint of irony. To tell the truth, I was not a little shocked by the easy access to the weaponry. Given that Jules liked using the room to lounge in, you would think that he'd still see the wisdom of keeping the cabinets locked.

"Three."

I looked inside. The silver guns lay in no particular arrangement on the black velvet lining among a scattering of loose cartridges. "Would you by any chance have checked this drawer in the past few days?"

He shook his head. "I had no reason to."

"So you had no idea that one of these revolvers was missing?"

"No idea at all." He looked apologetic, but what use was that?

"Tell me, Jules, in the week of the murder—that is, the days before the murder took place—do you recall any visitors, anyone who might conceivably have come in here?"

He fingered his cravat as he made an effort to remember. "No, we've had no visitors recently, other than Maurice, rest his soul. Lord, I shouldn't say this, but I wish there *were* someone else."

"Is there any one of the servants you might suspect of taking the gun?"

"The servants." He sighed and frowned. "Most of my staff have been with me for years. I can't believe they would steal from me."

"It's not so unusual," said Bernhardt, trying to be helpful. "I once caught my maid wearing my underclothes. I found out only when my pet monkey got under her skirt and made her jump onto a chair. A lady's maid wearing a Breton-laced petticoat from Beer's! My God, she was out of my house in thirty seconds."

"Sans petticoat?" said I.

"Sans everything except the mark of my boot on her derriere."

Jules listened blankly. Not even an image like that would lift his spirits.

At my suggestion, we prodded the fire into more activity, threw on a couple of logs, and sat in front of it in the huge leather armchairs. Sarah had already draped herself on one of the tiger skins, where she could fondle the by now utterly shameless gundog. I wanted Jules to relax sufficiently to tell us how young Letissier had met Rosine and how each member of the family had reacted to the prospect of this outsider becoming one of them. He began with much sighing and hesitation, as if the exercise was too painful to undertake, but with no end of coaxing from Bernhardt and me, he gradually became more fluent.

"How were they introduced?" He echoed my question. "I think it must have been at a dinner party."

"A dinner party?"

"It could have been somewhere else," he hedged. "A salon. No, it was supper in Cubat's."

"I know Cubat's," I said, for he was speaking of one of the better restaurants in Paris. Cubat was the former chef to the

Tsar, and the Romanov family know how to eat well. "So they met over supper?"

"It was during the Grande Semaine the year before last. 1889, the year of the Exposition."

"The Grande Semaine. No wonder your memory was hazy," said I.

The Grande Semaine, reader, is the climax of the Paris season, a week of racing in August followed every night by balls, parties, and suppers that last until dawn, a social program so exhausting that it can only be undertaken in the knowledge that immediately the week is over, everyone departs for the summer resorts.

Jules explained, "The whole thing was got up at Longchamp by some Yankee millionaire in a straw hat who was looking in at all the boxes, announcing, 'Cubat's at midnight. See you there.' It became quite a joke along the racecourse. As soon as one of us spotted a friend, we all chanted in chorus, 'Cubat's at midnight. See you there.' And so we had to be there."

"All the family?"

"Yes, Tristan had finished at the lycée."

"Cubat's must have been crowded that night," Bernhardt prompted him after a longish pause.

"Crowded, oh, yes. But it was a gloriously warm evening and the tables were laid in long rows in the garden. A candlelit supper. No prearranged seating. Americans like informality, don't they? And that was how we found ourselves at a table with Maurice Letissier. He was seated at the end, as if he was presiding, and in a way he did, because the waiter couldn't get to everyone along the table, it was such a crush. Maurice called us all to attention at the appropriate moment and announced the soup of the day and so on. He did it all with great charm and wit."

"You were impressed by him?"

"One couldn't fail to have been."

"Was he handsome?" Sarah asked.

"Not by conventional standards, but he was very animated, very articulate, and I'm sure the ladies found him attractive. He sported a particularly fine mustache. He was seated beside Juliette and for once my dear wife didn't monopolize the conversation. She was intrigued by the young man."

"And where was Rosine seated?"

"Along the table, on my left, close enough to observe Maurice without exchanging too many words."

"Was it love at first sight?" Bernhardt asked.

"I think he fell for Rosine straight away, yes. His eyes hardly left her."

"And Rosine?"

Jules hesitated. "She was only eighteen at the time."

"An impressionable age."

"That's a fact!"

My remark had hit the bull.

"Well, you may as well know that Rosine was already in love with someone else," he added. "Someone utterly unsuitable."

At this, Bernhardt sank her hand so powerfully into the retriever's furry chest that the creature gave a yelp and scampered under the table for refuge. "So there *is* a lover."

Jules covered his mouth as if he'd said too much.

"Unsuitable in which way?" I pressed him. When he declined to answer, I said, "I realize how delicate this matter must be, Jules, but clearly it has some bearing upon our investigation. I must insist that you tell us."

He shifted in the chair. "Sarah, you will understand what I am saying, but bear with me while I explain our French customs to Bertie. We are old-fashioned enough to believe that marriage is a contract between families. A bride must accept that she takes not only her groom for better, for worse, for richer, for poorer, but his entire kith and kin. It is more than a personal matter; it is a joint-stock affair. There is a matrimonial settlement. A French mother doesn't cry on the wedding day because she has lost a daughter; she rejoices at gaining a son."

The speech seemed like flannel to me. "This is not so different from marriage among English people of rank, as I was trying to explain to Sarah only yesterday," I commented, leaving him in no doubt that I was irritated at being lectured on French customs.

"Ah, but it must be handled with delicacy in France," he said with want of tact. "We have to abide by the Code civil. If a daughter of twenty-one or older should choose to defy her parents and promise herself to some young man of her own choice, and if the parents will not give their consent, she may make what is called a *sommation respectueuse*, a kind of extrajudicial protest. After three such *sommations*, if her parents continue to resist the match, the Code allows her to marry the man whatever his character and habits."

"Good Lord!"

"Be he a vagrant, a philanderer, an anarchist, anything," Jules added. "It is diabolical."

"But it is the law," said Bernhardt firmly, and for a moment I feared that she was about to give us a lecture on the rights of women. To my great relief, she spared us that.

"So do you see the difficulty parents labor under?" Jules went on. "We are not insensitive to our children's wishes. Matchmaking is a delicate process that continues for some time until a desirable partner is found. Parents—and I suppose I should say mothers, for they are usually the more instrumental in the process—will make discreet inquiries about the circumstances of prospective families. If suitable, they will approach the other parents and suggest opportunities of acquaintance, such as garden parties, or croquet, or dinner parties."

A little wearily, I said, "Jules, old friend, this is all very familiar. Remember, I have three daughters and two sons, and only one is married."

"Yes, but your daughters aren't threatening you with a *sommation respectueuse*," he blurted out.

We were coming to the crux of it.

"Has Rosine resorted to that?"

"She can't. She is not twenty-one yet, but she will next October."

"And who is the young man she so admires?"

"He is not young at all, Bertie. He is older than I am."

"Come, come," I said in disbelief.

"He is a worthless painter called Morgan and he is fifty-one."

"Well, I'll be jiggered!"

Bernhardt for once was lost for words.

Jules informed us, "She met him in church, of all places."

"That's some consolation, surely?" I commented. "The fellow can't be entirely bad."

Jules quickly put me right on that point. "He is a pagan. He followed her in there to talk to her when she was arranging the flowers. The ladies of the district take turns to decorate the village church. You'd think your daughter was safe to perform a pious duty like that unchaperoned. I gather Morgan happened to be in the churchyard in front of his easel when he saw my little Rosine coming up the path with her basket of flowers. He went in and started a conversation with her, just like that. No one introduced them. In a house of God, Bertie!"

"It does seem sacrilegious," I agreed. "When did this disgraceful episode take place?"

"Some time early in the summer of '89."

"Before she met Letissier?"

"Yes. She is totally infatuated with Morgan. I can't understand it."

Bernhardt said to console him, "The ways of the heart cannot be analyzed, Jules."

"Yes," he said, "but this is an old man. He's over fifty."

"That's not so old," said I, with my own half century looming in November. "The difference in ages is cause for comment, I grant you."

"Well, he looks a damn sight older than he is," Jules said. "It's the long beard streaked with gray that does it, I suppose, and the scruffy clothes."

"You've met him, then?"

Our host spread his hands in a gesture of helplessness. "Last summer, Rosine invited him to paint a landscape of the park. We've had him wandering about the estate ever since. The gardeners kept asking if he was a tramp. I had to tell them he was there by invitation. I don't know what the girl sees in him."

Bernhardt made the obvious point that some young girls were attracted to older men. "It's their experience, their urbanity—"

"Not forgetting their money," said I.

"Not in this case," Jules put in. "Morgan is practically without a sou. His paintings don't sell. He says he doesn't care about material needs. Mind you, he makes short work of lunch when it's brought to him on a tray."

"You made him welcome, then?"

"We tolerated the fellow, Bertie. I didn't want him sitting at my table, so I had the meals sent out to him."

"But you met him yourself?"

"I went to look at his painting out of curiosity. I didn't have the slightest suspicion that Rosine was in love with him. I thought we were helping a poor painter as a charitable gesture. She had mentioned that she'd met him at the church, which was true, and I assumed they had been properly introduced. She'd said after painting the church he was looking for other local scenes to render in oils and I gullibly agreed to give him the freedom of our estate. We French have a high regard for the arts, as you know."

"Is he a talented artist?" Sarah asked, like me looking for crumbs of comfort.

"Did I call him an artist?" said Jules, by now quite pink in the face just talking about the man. "If I did, it was a mistake. He's one of these Impressionists—all dabs of paint in garish colors straight from the tube. He does the whole thing in two hours. You have to stand ten meters away before you can pick out anything at all in the picture, and then it's very crude in outline. He'll never sell anything, as I keep telling Rosine."

"Was he civil when you met him?" I asked.

"Depends what you mean by civil. He didn't have much to say. Didn't even have the decency to put his brush down. And he didn't once look me in the eye. I didn't object at the time. I put it down to eccentricity. After all, I didn't know I was speaking to a prospective son-in-law."

"Is that what he has become?" said I.

"Heavens, no, Bertie. I'm speaking from the point of view of my deluded child."

"You said they met two years ago. When did you meet him yourself?"

"Last summer, when he started painting here. The fellow hasn't gone away yet. Sometimes he sleeps in empty buildings on the estate. And he appears to think that he has carte blanche to roam across my land with his easel at any time. He was painting a snow scene within a hundred meters of the house when I last saw him."

"Haven't you warned him off?"

Jules sighed and shook his head. "I've always tried to be civilized in my dealings with local people, and they respect me for it. I gave permission for Morgan to paint on my land without specifying that it was only for a limited time. He's done no damage. He closes gates after him. If I ban him from the estate, I've got to justify my action."

"But if he was pursuing Rosine—"

"He wasn't, not in any obvious way. He was clever, you see. If there was any pursuing, it was Rosine who did it. She goes riding around the estate every day—has done for years, and I can't stop her. I'm sure she knows where Morgan sets up his easel. I'm not suggesting that there was any misbehavior. She's a virtuous girl and I trust her. But if I put a ban on Morgan, it won't be his reputation that suffers in the village; it will be Rosine's."

"So he does have carte blanche."

"Well, now that you point it out, I suppose he does," Jules admitted. "But only to paint, not to fraternize with my daughter."

"Rosine was promised to another."

"Exactly."

"You and Juliette thought him suitable, I take it?"

"Maurice? Well, I wouldn't have promoted the engagement otherwise," said Jules, still tetchy about the whole unfortunate business. "He was from an excellent family, decently educated, completed his military service with some distinction. And he had a very confident, charming manner. Juliette and I discussed him and decided after making some inquiries, as responsible parents do, that we should meet the Letissiers. It was easy, because they are racing folk, as you know, and I'm a member of the Jockey Club, so I got a mutual friend to introduce me to Letissier senior. It was arranged that our families should meet at a costume ball given by the von Winslows."

Bernhardt boldly asked, "Did you consult Rosine?"

"Of course. She said at first that she wasn't ready yet to meet young men, but she was twenty, for heaven's sake, as I had to remind her. In the end, she said she was willing to accompany us to the von Winslows'. Maurice paid particular attention that evening to Rosine, who later agreed that she could find nothing to object to in his character. Juliette, as mothers do, pressed his case as a prospective husband. Perhaps she pressed too hard."

"Why do you say that?"

"Because Rosine resisted. Juliette, being the kind of woman she is, pressed all the harder. By degrees, we began to learn the reason—our child's infatuation with the painter. One day, she told us that nothing on earth would induce her to marry anyone else, in spite of the fact that Morgan was in no position to support her. We were appalled. We had some tearful scenes, I can tell you, and it went on for months. Eventually, Rosine saw sense, or Juliette's iron will prevailed, and the engagement was agreed. Believe me, Bertie, I wouldn't have let Juliette make such an issue of it if I hadn't believed myself that Maurice would be a good husband."

"So the engagement went ahead."

"Yes, it was announced—what is it?—just over two weeks ago and the wedding was arranged for June, as I mentioned."

"And I commented that it seemed a short engagement," said I.

"We don't require long betrothals in France, as you do across the water. No young man in this country will seek a wife before he is in a position to marry her." Jules was proud of his nation, and I don't blame him for that. I didn't take him up on the point, but I don't necessarily agree that short engagements are something to wave the flag over. Couples who rush to the altar may have something on their consciences.

Bernhardt asked another penetrating question. "Did Rosine stop seeing the painter?"

Jules looked shocked. "I assume so."

"Did you and Juliette insist on it?"

"I don't think we gave her an ultimatum. She agreed to marry Letissier and that was enough."

"She still goes riding each day?"

"Yes."

"And Morgan is still about?"

"I haven't heard that he has left. But I really can't see that this is a matter you should pursue." He was becoming twitchy, tugging at his hair and crossing his legs. As if unable to contain himself, he sprang up from the chair and put another log on the fire and then stood staring at it.

I said quickly, "Depend upon it, Jules—Sarah and I will employ the utmost tact in questioning young Rosine. Is she now in a calmer state of mind than the other day?"

"I believe so."

"She'll see us, then?"

He took this as his chance of escape, offering to go and look for her at once. The dog, too, made a dash for freedom.

The minute Jules was out of the room, Sarah said, "He's hiding something from us, Bertie. He's a dear man, but he hasn't told us everything."

I thought it proper to exert my authority as the senior detective in this team. "Let's not make unfounded assumptions, Sarah. You have to understand that his family are now under suspicion of murder, of the murder of a young man they were supposed to be embracing as one of their own. That must be a terrible blow to any father—and the Agincourts are one of the most respected families in France. No wonder he is guarded in his replies."

She said, "One thing is very clear. He feels extremely guilty about forcing this engagement on his daughter. And another thing, Bertie—there is a lover. One of my assumptions, at least, proved to be true." She followed this with a triumphant long look that reminded me of my mother when Mr. Gladstone lost the election.

I said, "Personally, my dear Sarah, I look at these matters with an air of detachment. That is the mark of a good detective."

She said, "Yes, but what have you detected?"

Quick as a nun's kiss, I answered, "A new suspect."

"Morgan?"

"Yes . . . a *crime passionnel*."

She said, "That was my suggestion."

I said, "But we didn't know about Morgan then. He had the motive and the opportunity. He was permitted to roam freely around the estate. It wouldn't have been difficult to pick his moment to come in here and steal the gun. He'd only have to find his way into the courtyard and open the door. As one of those Impressionist people, he must know Montmartre and the Moulin Rouge. And as Rosine's confidant, he must have known that the family were going there that evening with Letissier."

Bernhardt said after a stunned pause, "Bertie, you're doing so brilliantly on your own, do you really require an assistant?"

Chapter 7

I was in the act of kissing Sarah Bernhardt when we were interrupted.

Let me explain the kiss. My clever deduction about Morgan, the painter, had the curious effect of demoralizing poor Sarah. You see, she hadn't thought of it first. She was practically inconsolable. As she expressed it in a faltering voice, she felt that her contributions to the investigation were so puny that she would be better employed packing her trunks for the Bernhardt World Tour. Do you know, I'd almost forgotten by then that she was the world's greatest actress.

She sank into one corner of a large leather sofa and managed to look pitiably small and the very picture of dejection. Quick to reassure her, I sat beside her and said that her questions to Jules had been uncommonly helpful. She was my support.

She said, "I'm just a crutch, am I?" And a gleaming tear escaped from the corner of her eye and rolled down her cheek.

Now it has often been written that Bernhardt is so skilled an actress that she can weep at will, but I prefer to believe that this tear was involuntary.

What could I do but draw the poor waif to me and embrace her?

Next thing, we were up from that sofa like rocketing pheasants when a voice said, "Who are you?"

The speaker was a youth in a brown suit. He was a more paunchy version of Jules and I took him, correctly, to be the son, Tristan. Dark and disapproving, he stood just inside the door with a shotgun in the open position over his shoulder. When I say that he resembled Jules, I should qualify the description. The boy lacked his father's slightly languid manner. But the eyes of that disturbing light blue color so unusual in a dark-haired man were unmistakably those of Jules's son.

Allowing that we had arrived at Montroger unannounced, it was not unreasonable that Tristan inquired who we were, and I introduced Bernhardt and myself. The lad pricked up his eyebrows, blushed, and gave a courtly bow.

Bernhardt said, "You must be Tristan."

"Yes, madame."

"We are waiting to meet your sister," I informed him without any reference to the scene he had chanced upon. Never go into explanations when you're caught spooning. "Your father went to fetch her."

Tristan said, "How typical of Father."

"What do you mean by that?"

"I don't mean to be disloyal, sir, but he won't find her. She's out riding. She goes riding every afternoon at this time. Father is terribly absentminded." He rested the shotgun on a table.

"What were you shooting?" I asked with an effort to be at my most amiable.

"Rabbits, sir. Do you mind if I attend to my gun?"

"Please do. Any success?"

"Five, actually." He went to a drawer and took out a cleaning kit.

"So you're a good shot?"

"Better than average, sir." He attached the swab to the cleaning rod in a practiced way and pushed it into the bore.

"Have you ever used a revolver?"

He looked up. Those blue eyes were as still as the frost on a window. "It's an unreliable weapon, sir."

"You have fired one, then?"

"Only for amusement." The young man was beginning to impress me. He was mature in manner, polite without obsequiousness. I've noticed that most French children are quicker to mature and more socially adept than our own. This, I am sure, is because they join their parents in the dining room at an age when ours are confined to nursery meals.

"I'm sure you know that your sister's fiancé was shot with a revolver," I said, watching for his reaction.

He nodded. "So I was informed, sir."

"But you were there."

"I heard the shot, sir. I didn't see the type of gun that was fired. If I had, I would have told the police."

He would make an impressive witness in a court of law, I thought, if it should ever come to that. "The detectives questioned you, then?"

"They questioned us all, sir. Not one of us saw the gun. How could we? It was fired from behind."

"Whom were you standing next to?"

"My father, I suppose."

"You must know, Tristan."

"With respect, it isn't so simple, sir. There was jostling. Everybody wanted a good view of the dancers. I had a tall woman with a wide hat in front of me, so I moved to the right to see better. When the shot was fired, I wasn't literally next to Father, but I was close by. I turned to see what had happened and Father was beside Maurice. My sister, Rosine, was on Maurice's other side."

"And your mother?"

"She stood next to Rosine, I think, sir." He put down the gun and it was obvious that there was something else he wanted to say. "If I may be so bold, why are you asking these questions about my family?"

I said evenly, "Because your parents are valued friends of mine and I want to find out the truth about this tragedy. Did you like Maurice Letissier?"

He frowned. "He wasn't family." As if to soften the response, he added, "My sister didn't really want to marry him."

"Is that your observation, or did she tell you?"

"We all knew it, sir."

"You felt some sympathy for her, I dare say?"

He gave me another ice blue stare. "That's no reason to kill a man, is it, sir?"

This had developed into a duel and I wasn't sure who was winning. I said, "Your parents clearly approved of Letissier."

He parried with, "Sir, I think my parents would prefer to speak for themselves."

Bernhardt cautioned him, "Have a care how you speak to His Royal Highness."

He immediately apologized, but I didn't press the question. To be frank, I had some sympathy for the boy's point of view. I still feel pain remembering my elder sister Vicky, at seventeen, being married to Prince Frederick of Prussia, even though the marriage turned out to be a happy one and Fritz one of the finest and noblest of men. The tie between brother and sister is stronger than most people realize. I was fifteen and I wept for Vicky, I don't mind admitting. For the whole of her adult life, she has written to me regularly and I have always scribbled something back at once, notwithstanding my dislike of writing letters.

Tristan had picked up the gun again and was working methodically on the bore with a bristle brush. He wasn't skimping.

I said, "You shoot regularly, do you?"

"As often as I can, sir."

"Every day?"

"That would be impossible, sir."

"You attend the Sorbonne?"

"Yes, sir." He smiled faintly. "We get a few hours for private study."

"You don't have lodgings nearby, as some students do?"

"No, sir, I live here."

"And bag a few rabbits when you can fit in the time, eh?" I winked and he grinned more readily.

"And have you ever seen anyone except your own family in here?"

"The servants attend to the fire and sweep up, sir, but it's very unusual for anyone else to come in. That's why I was surprised to discover you and Madame Bernhardt."

"I'm sure." Passing smoothly on, I said, "Tell me about the servants. How many live in?"

The question was never answered because before the words were out, we all heard a shot fired, followed immediately by the screeching of rooks alarmed by the sound.

Tristan dropped the shotgun he was cleaning. "What on earth. . ."

A rash of gooseflesh afflicted me. I'm accustomed to gunfire, but not sudden, unexpected gunfire. I said, "Should anyone be out there shooting this afternoon?"

"Absolutely not."

"The gamekeeper?"

"He's laid up with sciatica."

"Does anyone in the family use a gun?"

"Father. But he's in the house, isn't he? The shot came from outside."

I said, "I think we should investigate."

We all stepped outside, across the yard, around the stables to an open area with a view of the estate. Nobody was in sight, and the colony of rooks was settling in the trees again.

The vista before us reminded me rather of Sandringham, the flat meadowland made interesting by clumps of trees and small woods. We could probably have seen a great distance if the mist had not been so reluctant to lift.

I said, "It's anyone's guess where it came from. Do you get poachers?"

"If we do, they don't come in broad daylight, sir."

"Then who do you suppose it was?"

He didn't answer.

Some scuffling and panting at our feet signaled the arrival of Bernhardt's friend, the black retriever. It nuzzled her skirt companionably. From behind us, Jules appeared, striding from the house. He called sharply, "Ezra!" and the dog came obediently to heel.

"What are you doing here, Tristan?" he asked. "I thought that shot just now was yours."

"No, Father. I was in the gun room."

"Then who the devil is shooting on our land?" Jules said. "I'm sorry about the language, Sarah, but this is very irregular. Would you mind fetching my field glasses, Tristan?"

While his son went on this errand, Jules explained that he hadn't yet been able to find Rosine.

I said, "We were told she is out riding."

"Of course she is," said Jules. "Should have thought of that." As another thought struck him, he put his hand to his mouth. "If Rosine is out riding and some idiot is loosing off a gun, she could be at risk. I don't care for this at all, Bertie."

None of us cared for it particularly, but there wasn't a lot we could do to remedy the situation. The glasses, when they were brought, didn't assist us.

Then came two more shots.

They echoed across the entire countryside, but there was no mistaking the direction they had come from.

"Just beyond the wood," said Jules, pointing to a copse a

good half mile away practically enshrouded in mist. "Infernal cheek! I'm going to saddle a horse and ride over there. Would you excuse me, Bertie?"

"Excuse you? If you have a nag strong enough, I'll join you,"I offered.

Whereupon, Bernhardt gamely said, "I'll come, too."

"We ought to be armed," said Tristan, making it clear that he meant to be one of the posse.

Within a few minutes, all four of us set off across the turf at a canter, Bernhardt riding sidesaddle as if she'd done it all her life. My days of riding to hounds were over and I was grateful to find myself on a mount more used to trotting than galloping, a strong, broad, underbred mare. Out of courtesy, Jules and his son went ahead to take whatever risks might be involved in engaging the enemy first, and fine horsemen they were, both of them, each with a shotgun slung across his back. They were soon out of sight.

By the time Bernhardt and I reached the copse, I was glad of slower progress as our beasts picked their way through dead bracken. Bernhardt remarked that I looked red in the face and asked if I was winded. This was her way of asking me to pause awhile, for I'm sure it can be no comfortable experience trotting sidesaddle across a field, so out of consideration, I halted.

"We'll go to the rescue when they need us," I told her with a confident air. "Actually, I would hazard a guess that young Tristan can see off most of the perils lurking in these parts. He knows how to handle a gun."

"He knows more than that," said Bernhardt. "I thought him remarkably self-assured for eighteen."

"Without the deplorable manners so typical of adolescence," I concurred. "At his age, I was the despair of my parents. I overate and was bone idle. They had diet sheets prepared for me and they stopped me wearing carpet slippers."

"Carpet slippers—how decadent, Bertie!" said Bernhardt, smiling. "When I was seventeen, I made my debut with the Comédie-Française."

"That was precocious."

"It was disastrous."

She didn't expand on the statement, and I didn't press her. "The question is," said I, "how seriously should we consider Tristan as a suspect?"

"I rather like the boy," Bernhardt remarked.

"That's beside the point."

She said, "I thought Morgan was our suspect. He sounds contemptible."

"We can't eliminate all the others just because they're nicer people," I told her as gently as possible, because I didn't want her piping her eye again. "Personally, I'd be more than satisfied to find that Morgan is the murderer, but until he confesses to the crime, we must keep an open mind about the Agincourt family."

"Very well."

"I was about to say that when investigating a murder, you have to take stock of each suspect's opportunity and motive. Tristan had the opportunity to fire the fatal shot. He uses the gun room regularly, so he knew where to find a revolver. He was at the Moulin Rouge on the night in question."

"But what would have been his motive?"

"Sympathy for Rosine, being dragooned into marriage with a man she didn't love. Boys can be very protective of their sisters. Tristan is on the verge of manhood, at the mercy of his glands."

She frowned, uncertain of my drift.

I explained, "Lads of that awkward age often feel compelled to prove themselves in some way."

"By murdering somebody?"

"That would be an extreme case," I admitted. "However, one should never underestimate the glands." I took out a cigar and put it to my lips, deciding that I'd probably said enough on the matter.

"Are you speaking of aggressive tendencies?"

"Er, yes, that sums it up nicely." I struck a match.

Then Bernhardt said in the most innocent of tones, "I thought you meant that he was in love with his sister."

The match went out.

"Then the motive would be simple jealousy," she explained.

I was deeply shocked. "A brother and sister? I don't care for that."

"Neither do I," said she, "but it can't be discounted. Never underestimate the glands."

We might have continued this unedifying discussion for some time had it not been for a sudden sound behind us, a definite rustling in the bracken. My steed whinnied in fright and reared, and I only stayed up with the greatest difficulty.

"What is it?" Bernhardt asked.

It was black and breathless. It was Ezra, the retriever.

We resumed our progress through the copse until the view opened up. We must have been climbing without being aware of it, for a considerable tract of parkland lay below us. At the foot of the declivity was a stream where some rather scrawny sheep had come to drink. There was a derelict cottage with some of the eaves exposed. In front of it, we could see Jules and Tristan. They had dismounted and were about to enter the ruin, their guns held at the ready.

"What are they doing?" Bernhardt asked.

"They appear to believe someone is holed up in there," said I. "There aren't many other places he could be. Let's watch for a moment."

It was fascinating as a spectacle, better than watching the Volunteers on maneuver in Windsor Park. Jules appeared to be guarding the front, while Tristan, bent low like a Red Indian, prowled around the walls to the rear. We couldn't hear what was said, if anything. I imagined they would invite the occupant (if one there was) to step out, for it was a safer procedure than walking into a possible ambush.

"Bertie."

Peeved at having the sport interrupted, I said, "Yes?"

Bernhardt said, "Look at Ezra."

"What?"

"Look at the dog. He's behaving strangely."

I turned and saw exactly what she meant. Ezra was obviously stalking something in the bracken behind us, his belly low to the ground as he emitted a peculiar growling sound. "A rabbit hole, I dare say," said I.

"I think not," said my companion. "There's something there, something quite big."

Just as I turned, Ezra gave a full-throated bark and leapt into the patch of brown and sodden bracken.

There was a scream, but not from Bernhardt and certainly not from me.

"Someone's there!" cried Bernhardt.

A man leapt up, wild-eyed, stocky, with the waxed mustache that many Frenchmen have. His tawny-colored hair was cropped and he looked very like a rat. Ezra had him by the sleeve of his brown overcoat, but the man swung the dog away with remarkable strength and bolted toward the thickest part of the wood. Ezra gamely stood upright again, gave a vigorous shake and set off in pursuit—with me in pursuit as well, still in the saddle.

The rat-man didn't get far. Ezra somehow contrived to get between his legs and he tripped heavily, hit the ground hard and groaned. My mare almost trampled him.

I didn't dismount. The fellow was craven, as I'm sure I would have been with a black retriever on my chest, with its teeth sunk into my collar, growling ferociously.

"Ezra, that will do!" I commanded, but the dog ignored me. "Ezra, you can stop now. Ezra!"

It was Bernhardt who succeeded in calling off the dog.

When she said, "Heel, Ezra," the beast immediately desisted and ran to her, wagging its tail. The fuss she had made of it in the gun room had paid a dividend.

Unarmed as I was, I had no fear of the man.

"On your feet and sharp about it!"

He rose unsteadily from the bracken, now a pathetic little figure in a brown overcoat, his shirt collar ripped from its moorings, his face smeared extensively with mud and one end of his mustache dangling where the wax had snapped. He had angry brown eyes under bushy eyebrows. The epitome of a trespasser caught in the act.

"Hands away from your pockets," I ordered him, remembering the shots that had started us on this manhunt. He might well be carrying a pistol. "Now, remove the overcoat and let it drop to the ground."

With a scowl, he obeyed. The coat fell in a heap on the bracken. Rather to my surprise, he was wearing a passably decent gray pinstripe under it.

"And the jacket, if you please."

He protested, "Monsieur, it's cold and I suffer from asthma. Can't you hear my breathing?"

I said, "Do it!"

The jacket joined the overcoat.

"Step away from the coat. Any tricks from you, my man, and you'll answer to the police—that is, after the dog has finished with you. Waistcoat."

He looked up at me with malevolent eyes before removing the waistcoat.

To be quite certain he was unarmed, I could have insisted that he remove his trousers, as well. Out of respect for Bernhardt, I spared the fellow that indignity. He looked pretty unthreatening in his suspenders and shirtsleeves.

"Now, you had better identify yourself."

He shivered, gave me a murderous glare, drew in a breath, and wheezed. "I am Marie-François Goron, *chef de la Sûreté.*"

Chapter 8

My Dearest Alix,

Yes, I am penning this from wicked old Paris, but do not despair, for I shall be leaving directly for the Riviera. Nothing can detain me here any longer.

I remember complaining the last time I wrote that Paris was becoming tiresome, or dull, or both. I am happy to report a distinct improvement. In fact, today has been a bracing experience. I thought I had better drive out to Montroger, the Agincourt residence, to convey the kind thoughts and condolences you expressed in your latest. (Before you throw up your hands in alarm and declare that I ignored your appeals, I went merely out of a sense of obligation to you and our old friends the Agincourts. Detective investigation was furthest from my thoughts.)

Jules was deeply comforted by your concern. I didn't see Juliette, but I met their son, Tristan, now grown up to be a fine young man of good intelligence and cultivated interests, too. He is a keen sportsman and we had an intelligent exchange about shooting. But I mustn't digress. I gave your message to Jules, and he particularly asked me to let you know how much your support means to him. With the best will in the world, I couldn't prevent our old friend from asking me for an opinion about the murder. He insisted once again on giving me all the grisly details and it was soon transparently obvious to me that this was a crime of passion and that the culprit was young Rosine's lover, a man of mature years, a painter by the name of Morgan. He is one of the Impressionist school and seems to lurk around Montroger ostensibly to paint scenes, but in reality to effect assignations with Rosine, who is quite besotted with him, notwithstanding her betrothal to Letissier. Impressionism in Morgan's case is the pursuit of an impressionable young girl.

We were discussing these matters when the sound of gunfire came suddenly from outside. No one had permission to shoot on the estate, so Jules and his son saddled horses and rode off to investigate. I observed them from a safe distance while exercising their dog. As you know, there are few activities I enjoy better. I assure you, Alix, my dearest, I was well out of range of any gun. But you may imagine my astonishment when Ezra, the retriever, discovered a man skulking in the undergrowth. Ezra and I between us treated the ruffian with the severity he deserved for giving us such a fright.

Now this is the bombshell. The wretched man turned out to be Monsieur Goron, the most senior policeman in Paris. A fine pickle! Fortunately, Goron's powers of detection were sharp enough to tell him who I was, or I might have found myself in a French clink. He and I were soon on better terms, but he kept his distance from Ezra.

Goron, it emerged, had been keeping watch on the same derelict building that Jules and Tristan were about to search. Several of his officers, also in plainclothes, were hidden at vantage points nearby. After carrying out the most intensive investigation lasting almost two weeks, the Sûreté had reached the conclusion that I had come to in five minutes: namely, that Morgan the painter was Letissier's murderer. Morgan was known to be in the ruined house, supposedly for some kind of assignation with young Rosine, who goes riding at this time each afternoon. I was relieved to learn that she had not yet been seen. Morgan was certainly armed, for he had bagged a rabbit before entering the house; these were the shots we had heard.

This was alarming, because Jules and Tristan had posted themselves at either end of the building and might any minute go in! We were not close enough to warn them of the danger. But it all ended benignly, with Morgan stepping outside, unarmed, and being apprehended at the point of Tristan's shotgun. The police closed in and made the arrest. The painter is now being questioned at the Sûreté.

You may imagine the sense of relief at Montroger that the Agincourt name has emerged from this affair unsullied. No opprobrium can be attached to young Rosine, for the lawyers will make it clear that she had no foreknowledge of the murder. Morgan plotted his dastardly crime independently, motivated, no doubt, as much by pecuniary gain as passion. Few will have any regrets when he goes to the guillotine. He is no great loss to the world of art if his painting is anything like the other Impressionist works I have seen. If I had my way . . . No, better not say it to one who takes so much pleasure in fine art.

Now, to far more important matters. I have it on excellent authority from Fife that Louise is in the pink of health and the doctors are entirely satisfied with her progress. There are no indications of premature labor, so you may continue to enjoy the games of loo and—dare I say?—the currant jelly for a few weeks yet.

Give my love, as ever, to your pretty antagonists at the loo table. I think of them constantly, as I do of my own darling wife.

Showers of kisses,

Bertie

"Francis."

"Sir?"

"I shall be going to the Théâtre des Variétés tonight with Madame Bernhardt. I see from the paper that they have revived one of my favourite operettas, *La Belle Hélène*, and I must on no account miss it. Have the hotel reserve my two boxes on the pit tier and send two decent armchairs. The furniture in French theaters is impossible to sit upon for more than ten minutes."

"I shall attend to it, sir."

"Tomorrow we leave for Cannes."

"Very good, sir." An expression of the most ineffable relief spread over Francis Knollys's face. He regards himself as my unofficial moral guardian (by appointment to HRH the Princess of Wales), and while Cannes is not without its temptations, it possesses fewer than Paris. The worst that has happened there (in the view of Francis) was the year I attended the Battle of Flowers dressed as Old Nick, in a scarlet costume and with horns attached to my head. Everyone but Francis thought it a marvelous lark.

Memories. While sitting beside Bernhardt in the gilded splendor of the Théâtre des Variétés that evening listening to Offenbach's matchless music, my thoughts drifted back more than twenty years to another Belle Hélène, dear little Hortense Schneider, who for one glorious season instructed me personally in *La Gaieté Parisienne*—until word got back to Windsor and I was given a jobation by Mama for neglecting Alix.

"Bertie!"

I sat forward with a start. The crystal gasolier had been turned up for the interval.

Bernhardt—dressed fetchingly in lemon-colored taffeta that rustled when she moved—turned to me with eyes narrowed and declared, "A tear has just rolled down your cheek."

I said, "The story is very moving, don't you agree?"

She said, "You were remembering an old flame."

I shook my head.

"We Frenchwomen aren't so dense as you think, you know," she said. "Your conquests here are well known."

"Name one, then."

"One!" She laughed. "The Princesse de Sagan."

"Jeanne is an old friend," I said.

"An old friend with an absent husband," said she, as if that settled the matter, and then she started counting on her fingers. "The Duchesse de Mouchy, the Duchesse de Luynes, Giulia Beneni, known as La Barucci, the Comtesse de Pourtalès, the Baronne de Pilar, the Baronne de Rothschild, Emilienne d'Alençon, Madame Kauchine, Liane de Pougy, Cora Pearl—"

"She's Irish," I pointed out.

"French by inclination. Where was I?"

"You've used up all your fingers," said I.

"Then I can start again. The widow Signoret, the Comtesse de Boutourline, Miss Chamberlayne, Hortense Schneider, Yvette Guilbert, Jeanne Granier—"

"This is the silliest nonsense," I broke in, for it was obvious that she intended to continue for some time. "And you haven't mentioned the only one I'd be willing to admit to."

"Who's that?" she demanded fiercely.

"Sarah Bernhardt."

She thought a moment, frowned, and blushed. "But you and I have never—"

I placed my hand over hers. "You didn't listen properly. I said I'd be willing. It was an offer, not a boast."

She clicked her tongue and said, "You've had too much champagne."

With more than a hint of invitation, I told her, "We are partners, successful partners, my dear. We solved the murder together. Tonight is for celebration."

She said, "The police solved it without our help."

"But we were absolutely right in our deductions. Morgan was the murderer and it was a crime of passion, just as you said at the beginning. More champagne, partner?"

Charming as the music was, when the show resumed, my concentration had gone. I spent the whole of the second act making mental lists, counting furtively on my fingers. Sarah had been wrong over several names, but I hadn't challenged them. It would only have strengthened her suspicions about those that I didn't challenge. There's no winning a game like that. Besides, there were others she might have mentioned, and hadn't.

At the end of the performance, she turned to me and said without prompting, "That was naughty of me. I got carried away. In my case, it *was* an excess of champagne."

I said, "In mine, an excess of lady friends, apparently."

She laughed and leaned toward me for a kiss, which she received. Then she said, "Let's eat at Maxim's."

I had to be careful here. I pondered the matter with a judicial expression before saying, "Do you like caviar?"

"I adore it," said Bernhardt with a little quiver of anticipation.

"The caviar at my hotel is quite the best I've tasted," said I.

"Oh, I couldn't possibly eat at the Bristol," she said at once. "I'm sure the food is divine, but we'd be seen."

I said, "That, surely, would be a cause for congratulation. Most ladies of my acquaintance—" I stopped myself just in time. "If you wish to be discreet about it, my dear, I have a key to a back door. We shall eat in my rooms and no one will hear of it."

Of two minds, she said, "I do think Maxim's would be simpler."

Not for what I was planning. I said as if the world was coming to an end, "This is my last night in Paris. Tomorrow we leave for Cannes."

This did the trick. She said, "Then let us both be quite clear, Bertie. I would be coming only to try the caviar."

I said, "I don't think it will disappoint you, my dear."

And we took a carriage almost to the Bristol. I say "almost" because I instructed the driver to put us down at the Place Beauvau and we walked the short distance to the hotel. I shepherded Bernhardt to the back door and not a soul spotted us. There were two flights of back stairs to negotiate, but it was exceedingly quiet and poorly lit. At the first landing, my companion stopped unexpectedly, faced me, tipped my hat upward, put her arms around my neck, and kissed me passionately.

Then she said out of the blue, "Did I tell you that to reach the stage door at the Théâtre des Variétés you go up the Passage des Princes?"

Bemused, I said, "Really?"

She said, "In the profession, that is what we call Hortense Schneider—the Passage des Princes."

It was a wicked slander on a dear old friend, but I couldn't stop myself from smiling.

Humor is the best aphrodisiac. On the next landing, I returned the kiss with interest and told my own Schneider story. "One royal admirer of Hortense was Ismail, the former khedive of Egypt. Once when he was at the spa at Vichy, he got bored with the cure and told his equerry to write to Hortense. But through a mistake, the letter was delivered to an American salesman called Harold Schneider. This gentleman could not believe his good fortune when he read, 'By order of the khedive, a suite is reserved for you at the Grand Hotel at Vichy and your presence will be to Ismail as an oasis in the desert.' "

Bernhardt clapped her hands in delight. "And what happened?"

"Believing a large order was in prospect, Harold Schneider took the first train to Vichy and, my word, he was impressed by the welcome he got at the Grand. He was taken up to the suite, which was full of flowers. There were chocolates and champagne. Feeling tired from the journey, he got straight into a relaxing bath. Shortly afterward, the door opened slowly and Ismail peered around it to look at his oasis."

"Wonderful!" said Bernhardt with relish.

"Whether the coconuts stayed on the palm tree is not recorded."

At this, she burst into such a belly laugh that I had to warn her to keep her voice down. After the trouble we'd gone to, I didn't want one of my staff discovering us. However, we negotiated the corridor leading to my suite—Bernhardt so paralytic with my story that I was holding her upright (no hardship)—and I let us in.

"What an elegant room!" She let the cloak slip off her shoulders and attempted a pirouette, compelling me to catch her again.

We held each other in a close embrace.

I murmured, "Let's postpone the caviar."

Sarah gave me a lopsided smile. "Coconuts instead?"

It was at this more-than-promising moment in my romantic career that I happened to glance over Sarah's shoulder and was subjected to a surprise no less than if I had been knocked down by a London omnibus while strolling up the Champs-Elysées. Against the wall opposite, inconspicuous between a satinwood secretary and a tall fern in a brass pot, was an upright chair. Upon the chair, motionless, sat a young woman in black.

Neither of us had noticed her upon entering, we had been so occupied with each other.

What could I do next? I said gently to Sarah, "Don't be alarmed, but we are not alone."

She said muzzily in my embrace, "Mm?"

My paramount concern was not to create a panic. In a voice as even as a billiard table, I told her, "Sarah, there is a third person in the room." Then I relaxed the embrace, allowing Sarah to turn around and see for herself.

Before I could get any further in unraveling this mystery, Sarah reached her own conclusion, and it was not to her liking. "*Mon Dieu*! I have never been so humiliated. What sort of perverted creature do you take me for?"

"Sarah, for pity's sake," I protested, "I don't even know this young lady."

"Then it's even more vile than I thought. Don't ever speak to me again, you . . . you Bluebeard!" She snatched up her cloak and dashed from the room.

Naturally, I went after her, but she refused to stop. I called down the stairs, "Sarah, will you listen? I don't know who she is or how she got in there." I ran down the first flight of stairs after her, but she was far too quick for me. All that I saw was the end of her cloak trailing around the corner.

Whatever may be said about me—and plenty is—I am not a bad sportsman. In a fair contest, I can take defeat as well as the next man. This was palpably unfair. I trudged upstairs simmering with resentment and frustration. Worse was to follow, for the commotion had brought most of my retinue out of their rooms to find out what was happening. Just about every door in the corridor stood open and they goggled at me as if I was the Wild Man of Borneo: my valet, footmen, brusher, equerries, lord-in-waiting, groom-in-waiting, pages, even my dog, Jack, was there barking.

Knollys, in a purple dressing gown, stood at the head of

the stairs and said in his unctuous voice, "Can I be of assistance, sir?"

I said loudly enough to be heard by everyone, "You can tell the gallery that the poppy show is over for tonight." When all the doors were closed, I said to Knollys, "Now perhaps you will account for the young woman who is sitting in my room."

"Is she still there?" he said. "Oh, my word, I forgot all about her."

"You invited her in, I take it?" I demanded acidly.

He fiddled with the tassels of his dressing gown as if milking a cow. "Sir, I had no idea she would still be here at this hour. She arrived much earlier this evening. I thought you had gone for a short walk before dressing for the theater. I meant to explain when you came back."

I said, "You must have taken leave of your senses to allow a person we don't know from Adam to install herself in my suite. It has resulted in extreme embarrassment for me. Aside from that, she could be out to assassinate me. An anarchist."

Knollys cleared his throat in a way that suggested I was mistaken. "I beg your pardon, sir, but the young lady in there is not unknown to us."

I said with certainty, "She's a stranger to me."

"She is Mademoiselle Rosine d'Agincourt, sir."

"Rosine?"

"I thought you knew her, sir."

"Years ago. What does she want?"

"She won't say, except that she insists on seeing you, sir, about a matter of surpassing importance."

"Something to do with the murder?"

"I would imagine so."

"And she is still here at this hour? It's past midnight. She must be desperate."

My evening was already a lost cause. Bernhardt was convinced I was debauched. My staff had seen me in undignified pursuit. I hadn't eaten yet. And now there was this young girl waiting to drown me in tears because her lover was going to the guillotine.

I should never have stayed in Paris. Alix was right. She is always right.

Chapter 9

She was still seated, half-hidden by the fern. And she still looked petrified.

"Why don't you come out from there?" I suggested with admirable restraint, considering the embarrassment I had suffered. "I won't eat you."

After some hesitation, she rose and curtsied, keeping her eyes modestly averted from mine. I had been led to expect beauty in this young lady and the description could not be faulted. She possessed a type of French face that I have seen nowhere else in Europe and it is difficult to convey in words, but I shall try. Superficially, the hair is dark, the face oval, eyes deep-set and olive or brown, nose straight or with the slightest curve, jaw well defined. You'll have noticed that I left the mouth till last. This is deliberate. Of the features in this singularly French face, the mouth is the most characteristic. The lips are precisely defined, yet fuller and more prominent than you might think perfection requires. The flesh above and below the mouth contrives to curve outward at the edge of the lips, giving the merest indication of a pout, as if confident of a kiss. The effect is charming. The lady may be a paragon of virtue, yet incapable of changing the promise in her expression. I have even been amused to spot these kissable mouths among certain sisters of the church.

"Well, Rosine, I have been told who you are," I informed her, doing my level best to be dignified again. "Frankly, I didn't recognize you just now, as you must have gathered."

She said in a low voice, "Yes, Your Royal Highness."

"I was not expecting you to be here."

"No."

"You have been waiting some hours, I was told. May I send for some coffee or tea, or would you care for a drink?"

"No thank you, sir."

"Then you had better sit on the sofa and tell me why you are here. Would you like to remove your cape?"

Under the cape, she was dressed in a mourning gown buttoned to the neck and with no ornamentation whatsoever. She positioned herself opposite my armchair, demurely at one end of the sofa, her gloved hands nervously fingering the strap of her handbag. Her tragic demeanor and appearance could not fail to arouse sympathy.

"My dear, after waiting so long you had better not waste your opportunity," I prompted her compassionately. "You have my undivided attention."

"They have taken poor Glyn and he is innocent!" she blurted out.

"The painter?"

"Yes, sir. He is falsely arrested and I don't know what to do!"

"This *is* the man called Morgan you are speaking of?" said I, knowing full well that it must be; I was being pedantic merely to let her know that I would not be sunk by a tide of emotion.

"Yes, sir. Glyn Morgan." She gave me a penetrating look. "He is a countryman of yours."

I was wary and probably sounded so. "The name sounds

Welsh to me." Between ourselves, reader, it is good advice
to be wary of the Welsh. A nation with so many chapels must
have sinners in abundance to give the preachers employment.

"Forgive me, sir," said Rosine. "But you are the Prince of
Wales."

This, I thought, despite that "forgive me," shows want of
tact. I may be obtuse at times, but it isn't necessary to remind
me who I am. Worse still, she takes me for a Welshman.
"And you believe he is falsely arrested?"

"I know it. Glyn didn't murder Maurice. He is the most
gentle of men. An artist. Artists don't kill people."

"You'll have to think of something more significant than
that to save him," said I. "I was with Monsieur Goron of the
Sûreté this morning and he is in no doubt. Morgan had a
powerful motive and an opportunity second to none. They
expect to get a confession very soon."

She was saucer-eyed. "Sir, that is monstrous! They are treating him as if he is guilty. The truth is that Glyn was as
shocked as any of us when the shot was fired."

"Oh, really!" said I at once, for not much escapes me when
I'm hot on the scent. "So he was definitely present at the
Moulin Rouge that night?"

She put her hand to her mouth like a child who has spoken
out of turn. "Didn't you know that?"

"I had my suspicions."

"You won't mention it to the police?"

I said, "I'm sure they will have heard it from Morgan himself
by now. If he is innocent, what possessed him to go there?"

"He knew that my parents intended to take us after we had
dined. He said . . ." She lowered her eyes modestly. "He said
he wouldn't be denied an opportunity to see me."

"Even in the company of your fiancé?"

"Glyn's love for me is unshakable, sir."

Incredible as it may sound to the reader, this made sense

to me. You would think the sight of his heart's desire on the arm of his rival would have rubbed salt in the wound, but the Welsh are second to none in the art of suffering.

"Did he speak to you or any of the party?"

"No, sir. He merely observed us."

"And you, in turn, observed him?"

She blushed. "Well, yes. He took care to stand at some distance from us, or my father would have recognized him."

"I can imagine," I said with conviction. I could picture all too vividly the infatuated painter pacing the outer reaches of the ballroom. "And did he continue to keep his distance for the whole of the evening?"

A shrewd question, which caused her to hesitate. "Until Maurice was shot, Glyn did not venture anywhere near us."

"But after the shots?"

"Naturally, he was anxious to know whether I had been hurt. In the confusion, he appeared at my side and asked if I was all right. My parents didn't notice. They were too occupied with what had happened to Maurice, but my brother saw Glyn in conversation with me." She pressed both hands to her cheeks. "Tristan may have told the police. Oh, how a noble action can be misconstrued!"

I said to calm her, "It is best to know the worst of it. Tell me, where was Mr. Morgan standing at the moment the shots were fired?"

"Sir, I do not know. I lost sight of him when the dancers appeared."

Morgan sounded as guilty as Cain to me. "And after he spoke to you, did you see him again that night?"

"No, sir. He left with everyone else."

"Have you seen him since?"

She colored a little. "Yes, sir."

"Does he profess to be innocent?"

She said with a catch in her voice, "Sir, he is innocent. I know it."

I said reasonably, "That wasn't what I asked, my dear. The question is whether Morgan himself has told you he is innocent."

She answered with fervor, "But there's no need! Glyn is incapable of committing such a wicked crime. The possibility has never been mentioned between us."

I said, "The police won't flinch from asking him."

"That is what terrifies me."

Trying not to distress her more, I commented, "If he is innocent, as you say, he need have no fears, nor should you."

"You do not know Marie-François Goron, sir."

"Do you?"

She shivered. "He has an evil reputation. He will get the answer he wants, regardless of whether it is true. Glyn is doomed."

"Then why have you come to me?"

"Because you are the Prince of Wales and all of Paris respects you. The police would be compelled to listen to you."

This I could not deny and I rather liked the way she expressed it. Flattery would not have impressed me in the least, but she was speaking the truth. No one was better placed than I to intervene. I was seriously tempted to play the gallant prince coming to the aid of the maiden in distress. Young Rosine sensed it and shed a tear. Because I cannot abide women who weep, I gave her grounds for hope. "If I am to be of any use at all in this matter, I must know exactly what has happened between you and the painter."

She uttered a shrill cry as if unable to believe her ears and then answered in a rush of words that ended in another fit of weeping, "Sir, I don't know whether I understand you correctly, but nothing has happened. Nothing! Nothing!"

I got up and poured two cognacs, the smaller for her.

She said, "Sir, if that is intended for me—"

I said sternly, "You will drink it. You are becoming hysterical."

"I am not allowed."

"You are commanded. Every drop, before we speak any more of this."

It was only a small measure. She obeyed, screwing up her face as the spirit warmed her throat, then taking the rest like medicine. Not the way to treat fine cognac, but it had the desired effect. She said, "It makes my head feel strange, as if I am floating."

"It will pass. Now, I was told by your papa that you first met Morgan in the village church."

"That is correct." She gave me the story almost exactly as I had heard it from Jules.

"You make him sound like a young man, but I am told he is over fifty," I said.

"I don't think about his age when I'm with him. Glyn is so much more charming than boys of twenty. He is wise and he sees beauty in everything. He may lack material possessions, but he is infinitely rich in talent and vision."

"You mean his painting?"

"Sir, I mean his mind. What is painting but marks on a canvas? His mind directs the brush."

"Forgive me, I haven't seen his work," said I, striving to keep the conversation from becoming too ethereal. "He is one of the group who call themselves Impressionists, is he not?"

"Glyn would not be fettered to any movement. He is happy to spend many a long hour discussing theories of art with people like Monet and Renoir, but he is a free spirit."

He sounded to me like a windbag. "And you have been meeting him regularly? You had better be frank with me."

At this, the color might have risen to her cheeks, but she was already flushed with the cognac. "I can't deny it, sir. Glyn has lately been painting landscapes in the park around Montroger—with my papa's permission, I must add. I go riding each afternoon, and that is when we have tended to see each other."

I was amused by the innocent-sounding "tended to see each other," as if she cantered past him with no more than a wave of the whip. "Where do you meet—in that ruined house?" When she hesitated, I said, "For heaven's sake, child, I'm not going to stand in judgment."

"We meet there sometimes, yes," she answered, adding quickly, "but in no way could our meetings be construed as shameful, or furtive. We have conversations, marvelous, inspiring discussions about art and poetry and the meaning of life. Everything Glyn says is so . . . so liberating."

Perhaps fatigue was setting in, or perhaps I am becoming jaded as I approach middle age, but all this talk of poetry and philosophy struck me as depressingly juvenile. Don't misunderstand. I can respond to a young girl's beauty as well as ever I did, but some of the drivel they talk is depressing. Give me a lady of maturity every time, only let her be passably handsome, as well. "And did you discuss the murder?"

"Only to agree that killing can never be justified."

"He said that?"

"No, sir, I did. But Glyn did not demur."

I fetched the decanter and poured more cognac into both glasses. She gave me the look of a trapped deer as she put hers to her lips and took a gulp. I selected a cigar from my case and trimmed it thoughtfully. "There is something I ought to point out to you, Rosine. If, as you maintain, your friend Morgan is innocent of this murder, some other person must be guilty. Now we know that the revolver used by the murderer came from the gun room at Montroger. The inescapable conclusion must be that one of your own family shot Maurice Letissier. Have you considered this possibility?"

"I cannot bear to think about it."

"Four people," I pressed her, "including yourself."

She said passionately, "I didn't kill Maurice."

"I'm relieved to hear it. That leaves your parents and Tristan."

She put down the brandy glass and covered her eyes.

After a pause, I said, "If you know of anything suspicious . . ."

She was silent.

I took some time over lighting the cigar. "Let us talk about the victim. You and Letissier were first introduced during the Grande Semaine two years ago, I gather from your papa."

"Yes, sir." She proceeded to give me her version of the candlelit supper at Cubat's, which didn't differ markedly from her father's, except that she told it in a tone of icy disenchantment.

"You said that your mama was seated beside Letissier and got on well with him."

"She declared him to be the most eligible young man she had met since my father," Rosine admitted.

"But you did not? I sympathize, my dear. If anything is calculated to turn one against a prospective suitor, it is the enthusiasm of one's parents."

"I didn't dislike Maurice," she told me. "He was a good conversationalist. Anyone who can keep my mother from talking for minutes at a time must be a social asset. He was handsome, too, with a big mustache that he got rid of recently. He should have kept it, because his hair was rapidly getting thinner on top—he was practically bald, in fact." She hesitated, conscious that she might have given offense. "I know it happens to some gentlemen, most gentlemen, but not when they are young."

"It was probably inherited," said I.

She said generously, "I think all gentlemen look better with mustaches. And beards, ideally."

"How right you are!"

"But even if he'd been the most handsome man in the world, I couldn't have brought myself to love him," she declared. "By then, I had already met Glyn, and beside Glyn, Maurice was shallow. Papa arranged a dinner party with the Letissiers—

a real ordeal—when I was supposed to succumb to Maurice's endearing personality. I did not. He was amusing, attentive to me, and paid me compliments, but he couldn't compare with Glyn."

"Did you say this to your parents?"

"Of course—from at least the time it was made clear to me that they wanted him as a son-in-law. When I told Mama about Glyn and she learned that he was a poor painter more than twice my age who despised the sort of life we led, there were terrible, painful arguments. Mainly, the onslaught came from Mama, because she has always had most to say in our family, but Papa made it clear that he supported her. It went on for many months. Cruel things were said on both sides. They even suggested I must have allowed Glyn to seduce me, which was a vile slander and showed how little they understood Glyn or trusted me. And I threatened them with a *sommation respectueuse*. Do you know what that is?"

"Yes," I said, "your papa explained. You can enlist the Civil Code to marry against your parents' wishes. After three declarations, you are at liberty to wed the man of your choice."

She nodded. "But I didn't tell them that Glyn and I would never marry."

"Oh." This pronouncement took me so completely by surprise that I bit on my cigar and ruined it.

"Glyn doesn't believe in marriage," she explained. "He says it was invented because most people are too weak-willed to trust each other. He believes we should be free to make whatever arrangement we like with the partner of our choice. It can be just as binding as a formal marriage if we choose, but it should be no concern of the church or the state."

"He *is* a freethinker. So he had no intention of marrying you?"

"Absolutely none. That is why, in the end, I agreed to marry Maurice."

I frowned, unable to follow her reasoning. "But you say you loved Morgan."

"I still do," she said with conviction. "I have never wavered."

And who could doubt her, even if the brandy glass was wavering perilously? I was hearing things I would never have heard without the aid of the cognac.

"So why marry a man you do not love?"

"Because after a married lady has provided her husband with a son, she may take a lover," she confided, her eyes shining at the prospect. "Have I shocked you, sir?"

"No," I said after a moment's thought. "You have just persuaded me to speak to the *chef de la Sûreté*. If Morgan had no intention of marrying you, then the obvious motive for murdering Letissier is removed. This was not clear to me until a moment ago. It is imperative that this information is communicated to Monsieur Goron. I shall visit him in the morning."

She sprang up from the sofa and reached for my hand. "Sir, you are a hero! *Un preux chevalier*! Let us drink to your success!"

"I think not," said I, reaching for her glass. "I shall arrange a carriage to take you home and a maid to escort you, and I think it would not be wise to have another drop of brandy before you meet your parents and explain why you were out so late."

After she had gone, I ordered the supper I had denied myself for so many hours. Feeling famished, I chose for my main course *côtelettes de bécassines à la Souvaroff*, a snipe dish guaranteed to quell the pangs, for the bird is well stuffed with forcemeat and foie gras and the whole is grilled in a sow's caul and served as cutlets with truffles and Madeira sauce. On reflection, I was mistaken to choose a fish dish quite so substantial as sea bass, coming after pea soup, because by the time everything was served, the night was well advanced, and my stomach didn't take kindly to the horizontal position that the rest of my constitution demanded. In consequence, I sat up in bed for some hours regretting the French version of plum duff that completed the meal.

Between interruptions I need not go into, I reflected on what I had learned from Rosine. Far from confirmed by the arrest of Morgan, the identity of the murderer was once again a mystery. Of course I could not ignore the possibility that Rosine had lied to me to enlist my support. She had the intelligence to deceive, I was sure, and she would do anything to secure Morgan's release. Yet her statement that he rejected marriage as an institution fitted the impression I had gained of the man. If he had not killed Letissier to thwart the match with Rosine, what could have been the motive? It was certainly time I met him and formed my own judgment.

Chapter 10

Carrying an armful of daffodils, I called early next morning at Bernhardt's lair, 56 boulevard Pereire, resolved that the misunderstanding of the previous evening would be put right. Our friendship was too precious to sacrifice for want of a few words of explanation. Besides, I wanted Sarah in support when I tangled with Monsieur Goron of the Sûreté.

Her factotum, Pitou, received me. Pitou is a failed violinist who at some time in the past insinuated himself into the Bernhardt establishment and will never leave. I had forgotten he existed until he opened the door and stared at me with his spaniel eyes.

"Pitou, my dear fellow!"

"Your Royal—"

"Is she up and about?" I asked.

"Madame Bernhardt?"

"Who else? I must see her at once."

"Sir, begging your pardon, that is impossible."

"Why—is she in the bath?"

"She gave me instructions."

"She is laboring under a whopping misapprehension. Are the animals at liberty in the house?"

"Not the larger animals, sir."

"Stand aside, then. I'd like to come in."

Poor Pitou. He was in a fearful dilemma. Clearly, Bernhardt had banned me from the house, but it was not in the man's character to stand in anyone's way, let alone mine. He is one of nature's doormats.

I strode into the entrance hall. The house is furnished like a rajah's palace, with exotic rugs and cushions everywhere, and hardly a square inch of wallpaper to be seen for oil paintings of Bernhardt in various dramatic roles.

Her voice came from upstairs. "Who was it, Pitou?"

I gestured to Pitou to remain silent. In a servile tone, I called up, "A gentleman delivering flowers. Flowers from Wales, madame."

Bernhardt said, "That's not Pitou. My God, if it's that philandering old goat from England, I'll castrate him with my bare hands." She rushed to the top of the stairs, where she could see me. "It is, you monster!" She grabbed a vase and hurled it at me. It smashed a yard from my feet.

Somewhere deep in the house, a parrot cackled at the prospect of a fight.

Forty-five minutes later, forty-five minutes I shall not dwell upon except to state that I needed at least thirty of them to secure a hearing, a carriage left the boulevard Pereire to convey Bernhardt and me to the Ile de la Cité, that island in the Seine that houses not only Notre Dame but the Palais de Justice and the Préfecture de Police.

"I don't know why I agreed to this," Bernhardt complained to me halfway down the avenue Marceau. "This place has an evil reputation."

"You agreed because an innocent man is incarcerated there," I said tersely, not wanting more of her tantrums. "And because, like me, you want to know the truth about the murder at the Moulin Rouge."

"What use will I be? You are perfectly capable of talking to Goron."

"Yes, but who will talk to the prisoner? From what I know of Morgan, he is a rampant anarchist. The very notion of royalty is anathema to him. He'll regard me as the enemy. But we know he is susceptible to feminine charm. You'll coax the truth from him."

She clicked her tongue and stared out of the window.

"And more importantly," I added, "I can't bear to be apart from you."

Millions of women would have given their eye teeth to hear words like that from me. Not Sarah Bernhardt. She made a vulgar sound with her lips.

I must admit that when we crossed the Pont Neuf, I shuddered, for, like Bernhardt, I knew the vile history of the Ile, the unspeakable sufferings that people of refinement had endured there. I have heard that the island is a warren of underground tunnels, more than twenty miles of them linking countless cells and dungeons with the Préfecture; the sinister Conciergerie, where, during the Terror, thousands of the aristocracy spent their last days; and the Palais de Justice, where those bloodthirsty hags, the *tricoteuses*, would look up from their knitting and cry, "To the guillotine!"

I wouldn't say it to a Frenchman, but in these supposedly more enlightened times, the concentration of police, prison, and law courts on one small island is itself sinister, to my mind, laying them open to the suspicion of summary justice.

We were put down outside the Préfecture at 36 quai des Orfèvres, our driver having assured us that the Sûreté also had its headquarters there. We made ourselves known to the guard and were permitted to enter.

It was an intimidating place with a high ceiling, where voices echoed, and the stone floor reeked of disinfectant. After a short hiatus while the usual panic ensued at an unexpected royal visit, we were escorted upstairs to where the *chef de la Sûreté* presided, in a barn of a room overlooking the river. Marie-François Goron was behind a large ebony desk. He had the grace to stand and receive us properly and I noted an improvement in the state of his mustache since our last encounter in the bracken at Montroger. The ends were beautifully waxed. But he still looked an unlikely policeman, stunted in height and wheezing with the effort of getting up. This time, he was wearing pince-nez; a shipping clerk, conceivably, or a teacher of Latin. Never the top detective in France.

Not wanting to declare my hand too soon, I inquired how the investigation of Morgan was progressing.

"Satisfactorily," he said, equally guarded. "Forgive me, I was not expecting such distinguished guests." He snapped his fingers and some minion working at the opposite end of the room brought chairs for us. "May I presume that you have fresh information touching on the case?"

"Presume whatever you wish, my dear fellow. We would like to speak to Mr. Morgan," said I, refusing to be drawn into some kind of interrogation.

Goron regarded me speculatively over the pince-nez. "With what purpose, Your Majesty?"

I could not be certain whether the way he addressed me was calculated sarcasm or a foreigner's gaffe, so I ignored it. "He is, I believe, a British subject."

"That is true, sir."

"It is the practice in civilized countries to enable foreigners in custody to be visited by their consuls."

"Certainly."

"The British consul is the representative of the queen. If you wish to go to the trouble of verifying with the consul that I have my mother's authority to make this visit . . . "

"Good Lord, that won't be necessary, sir," said Goron, faced by the specter of a diplomatic incident. "He is being held downstairs, but I can have him brought up. He has already been questioned intensively."

"With what result?"

Goron gave that peculiarly French shrug that involves every

muscle in the upper half of the body and conveys absolutely nothing.

"Then has he admitted anything at all?"

"It is too soon, I think, sir." The implication was clear. Goron expected to extract a confession regardless of how long it took. "I will have him sent up."

"No," I said astutely. "We would prefer to see him in the place where he is being held."

The pince-nez flashed. "Whatever you wish, Your Royal Highness, but it is not very agreeable down there." He gave a patronizing smile. "Madame Bernhardt may care to remain here."

Which showed how little he knew of Sarah. She wasn't the frail female. She gave him a murderous look and said, "Monsieur, I didn't come here to twiddle my thumbs in an empty office."

Goron shrugged again, took a key from his desk drawer, got up, and unlocked a door to our left. He led us along a paneled corridor and down an iron spiral staircase to a level that felt markedly colder, a dimly lit brick-lined passage that appeared to stretch to infinity. A uniformed warder stepped in behind us without a word, the keys at his belt clinking. "Be careful of your clothes, madame," Goron cautioned Bernhardt. "There is mold on the walls."

A row of cell doors presently came in view and we stopped outside one. The turnkey took down a lantern from a ledge opposite and lighted it. Then he made a selection from his key ring. Goron turned to us and said, "I would advise you to remain outside for a moment."

Presently, an evil-smelling bucket was conveyed from the cell. Even without it, the place was not the most fragrant I have ventured into.

The lantern's flickering light showed us a standing figure wrapped in a blanket. The face was broad, the eyes focused above our heads, the mouth down-turned in defiance. With the blanket and his fine growth of beard, Morgan looked not unlike some Old Testament prophet.

"You have just been told who we are, I take it?" I said in English, to put him at his ease. "Would you care for a cigarette?"

He gave a nod.

In fact, we all lit up, including Bernhardt, for cigarette smoke was much to be preferred to the odors latent in the cell. Morgan's hand shook when I held the flame to his cigarette, due more, I am certain, to the cold than his state of nerves. He had the deep-sunken dark eyes of the Celt and they glittered with offended pride. He betrayed no sign of being unmanned either by his predicament or my presence.

I explained that Bernhardt and I were taking a personal interest in the case, adding that we had spoken yesterday to Rosine d'Agincourt.

"Rosine?" His eyes narrowed. "Have these bastards arrested her as well?"

"No, no. She came to see me. She asked me to take up your case with the Sûreté."

"She's plucky."

At this point, Goron interrupted to ask if we would conduct the conversation in French, and I answered that I had no objection, provided that we could be frank. He gave me a stare that I took to be his consent.

"You heard that," I addressed Morgan in French. "How are they treating you?"

"Abysmally," he replied, and went on to say in fluent French, "I have not been given a bite to eat since I was brought here yesterday. They keep me in this stinking cell in darkness and bring me out every two hours for interrogation. I have had no sleep. I am chilled to the bone. They don't believe a word I say. What do they expect—that out of hunger and despair I'll confess to something I didn't do?"

I turned to Goron. "Did you know about this?"

Before the *chef de la Sûreté* could respond, Morgan cried out, "Of course he knows, the bugger. He is my interrogator."

Goron flicked ash from his cigarette and remarked, "Prisoners who persistently insult their questioners can hardly expect us to provide privileges."

This incensed me. "Basic meals are not privileges, Monsieur Goron. The man has not been convicted of any crime. He is cold and hungry. I insist that he is fed at once. And he requires another blanket. Kindly arrange this with the warder."

Goron was apparently unmoved—until Bernhardt turned her cannon on him. "What are you waiting for? Can't you understand, you cretin? You make me ashamed to be French. Have some breakfast brought in for Monsieur Morgan, and a good one, or we shall go straight from here to the Minister of the Interior. This place may stink to hell, but we can make a bigger stink, believe me."

It was a mite excessive and I had my doubts what result it would bring, but the mention of the minister was decisive.

Goron capitulated, while muttering, "This is flagrant interference." He gave a nod to the turnkey and the man left the cell.

In a complete change of tone, Bernhardt said almost seductively to Morgan, "Monsieur, are you innocent?"

"Innocent of what, madame?"

Slightly nonplussed, she said, "Of the crime of murder."

"Of course I am not a murderer."

"It may not be so obvious to others as it is to yourself. Speak up. This is your chance."

He said, "I'm a simple painter. All my life I have only wanted to paint. I should be out there now."

I said, "Tell us about your friendship with Rosine d'Agincourt."

He drew his blanket more closely around him. "I refuse to implicate her in this."

Bernhardt addressed him with the air of the grande dame

she sometimes became when it suited her. "You had better listen to me, M. Morgan. The only reason we are here is because that young lady went to extraordinary trouble to persuade us to come. She loves you. She believes in your innocence. You won't get her into trouble by speaking the truth. You owe it to her to speak out."

Just how prickly a character Morgan was became apparent when he responded to this uplifting statement by saying, "Look, I've been battered by questions most of the night. They threaten me with the guillotine one minute and promise me my freedom the next. Why should I believe anything you buggers say? How do I know you're not hand in glove with the Sûreté?"

I was about to admonish the fellow for using unparliamentary language in front of a lady, but just in time I realized that he was doing it to provoke me. Given half a chance, he would have lectured me on the iniquities of the monarchy. I said in a tone that admitted no nonsense, "Mr. Morgan, if you don't need our help, we'll cancel the breakfast and leave you as you were. There are other places I would rather be this morning, I can assure you."

Almost certainly it was the threat to his breakfast that did the trick. Morgan inhaled on his cigarette, blew out a cloud of smoke, and said as if we were his oldest chums, "All I ever gave Rosine was a few kisses. Poor little scrap, she was put through the mangle by those pigheaded parents of hers, trying to shackle her to Letissier. She came to me for the sympathy they should have given her. They're her own flesh and blood, for Christ's sake. Rosine is just a pathetic young girl with romantic ideas about people like me who ignore the chance of a comfortable life for the sake of art. I could have taken her to my bed anytime I wanted, and she would have let me, but I didn't, not once. When I want a woman, I know where to get one. Is that what you wanted to know?"

His blunt speaking didn't derail me. I responded firmly,

"The way you conduct your private life is of no consequence, Mr. Morgan. The point is, would Rosine have married you?"

He gave a bleak smile. "She had childish ideas of eloping with me. Can you imagine? I'm over fifty, for God's sake. I told her I don't believe in marriage. I'm a painter, first and last. I'm in no position to keep a wife. I can't even keep myself."

"I thought you Impressionists made a decent living," I remarked.

"I'm not any kind of '-ist,' " he said sharply. "Anyway, you have to be an Academy painter to make a decent living, and I'm not one of those fossils, thank God. But don't go thinking that there's money in Impressionism. Most of that bunch are from the bourgeoisie. They had money in the bank already, or they wouldn't have survived—Manet, Degas, Bazille, Sisley. Old Pissarro dresses like a pauper, but he's bloody rich. Renoir and Monet were not so flush, but they feathered their nests as Salon painters first, both of them. Made themselves secure and then turned their coats. I'm the bloody fool who tries to do it on a shoestring. I've known one or two others who tried and starved, or went mad. As I told young Rosine time and again, it wouldn't be fair to take a wife."

"You didn't actively discourage her?"

"I didn't send her away, if that's what you mean. I pitied her."

"How did you feel when she finally agreed to the betrothal?"

He glanced upward as if the answer were written on the cell roof. "Not surprised, to be frank. She had no choice, really. Her parents were always going to get their way in the end. We talked about it. She had this idea that if she presented Letissier with a son, she would be free to take a lover. She made me laugh. Not bad to be thinking so far ahead when you're still a virgin. She was serious, though."

"You would have us believe that she did all the chasing, yet you went to the Moulin Rouge on the night of her engagement dinner."

"Ah, we've come to it now," said Morgan bitterly. "This is what they kept asking me all night."

"You don't deny you were there?"

"Certainly I was there, but I didn't put two bullets into Letissier."

"Why did you go at all?"

"It was a chance to get a squint at this young buck she was being mated with."

This wasn't the version I had been given by Rosine, and I didn't care for the vulgar way he expressed it, but it struck a note of truth. We had been given opinions of Morgan by Jules d'Agincourt and his daughter and neither altogether matched what was presently being revealed to us. "Did you speak to him?"

He stared back as if unable to believe I'd asked such a preposterous question. "I may be a fool, but I'm not that daft. I wasn't there to make a scene. I kept my distance."

"Kept your distance all night?"

"Until after the shooting, anyway."

"How much did you see of it?"

"Practically nothing. I was across the room with a full glass of beer. I didn't want it spilt in the rush, did I? I heard the shots and thought some maniac was loose. I bolted into the garden with some others. Lost most of my beer in the process."

"Did you return to the ballroom?"

"Pretty soon, yes. Someone said a young toff in a silk hat and dinner jacket was the victim. I thought of Letissier and went to see. A lot of people had run out, like me, but there was a cluster around Letissier. He was in the middle of the floor. The comte was kneeling beside him and the comtesse was talking to people, asking what they saw. I think a doctor was there. I saw Rosine with her brother, a little back from the group. She was holding her arms across her chest. Thinking she might have been hurt, I went over to ask. She hadn't been hit. She was in a state of shock."

Bernhardt unexpectedly asked, "What was she wearing?"

Morgan stopped, his flow of thought interrupted. "A blue dress, I think, Prussian blue, if that means anything to you, and a velvet cape over it, dark gray or black, with gold fastenings. People keep their coats on at the Moulin Rouge this time of year."

What this had to do with the fatal incident we were discussing was far from clear, and I was nettled by the interruption. Some of the fair sex think of little else but fashion. Until this moment, I had had a higher opinion of Sarah Bernhardt.

"You were saying that she was in a state of shock," I reminded Morgan.

"Yes. Oh, and she had one of those small black bonnets that are high tone now, with an ostrich-feather trimming."

I turned to Bernhardt and said cuttingly, "Do you have the picture now, or would you like to know about the shoes?"

She glared at me and I am sure she was about to say something sulfurous when the door opened and the breakfast was brought in on a tin tray. The turnkey placed it on the stone shelf that also functioned as the bed. And he handed Morgan an extra blanket that he'd slung over his shoulder.

I told Morgan he had better make a start on the food. He needed no second bidding and started wolfing bread rolls as if he hadn't eaten for weeks. I suppose he'd had little else to look forward to. To my eye, it wasn't much of a breakfast, but then if he'd been sitting at the best table in the Ritz, he would have been served nothing more appetizing than coffee and rolls. The French have no conception of what the first meal of the day should consist of. They don't even give it the status of a proper word in their language, calling it the "little luncheon." (They don't go in for afternoon tea, either, indulging instead in what is called a "five o'clock" at a public tea-room, where you nibble at pastries that could be consumed in a mouthful. Not a poached egg in sight.)

Goron was becoming restless. He asked if we had finished the interview and I told him frigidly that I would advise him when we were ready to depart.

He said morosely, "The prisoner has all morning to eat."

Unmoved, I said, "I would prefer to see for myself that he is allowed to finish what is in front of him."

One thing was certain: I had not made a friend for life of the *chef de la Sûreté*.

Only when every crumb was consumed did I prompt Morgan to resume his narrative.

"I told you practically all of it," he said. "I can't tell you who fired the shots, but it wasn't me. Rosine urged me to leave at once. I think she was alarmed that her father or someone would think I was the killer. Well, it could have looked suspicious, me being there. I took her advice and left on the double."

"You left the building immediately?"

"Isn't that what I just said?"

The man's uncivil tone wasn't helping his cause, but the conditions he'd been kept in were enough to test anyone's temper. I strove to remain tolerant. "You didn't go into the dressing room?"

He shook his head. "Why would I do that? I don't even know where the dressing room is. Are they going to release me now?"

Goron gave a sarcastic laugh. "You think you have talked your way out of here, do you? You think all these lies have fooled me? You are as guilty as hell, and you will confess; you will confess."

I said witheringly, "If he is kept in these appalling conditions and deprived of the most basic necessities, I am sure he will confess, Monsieur Goron. There can't be a person alive who would not. I demand to be told your reasons for detaining Mr. Morgan."

"Sir, I'll do better than that," said Goron with the confident air of a man who knows more than he has revealed. "Kindly step upstairs and I'll show you the evidence."

"Evidence?" said Morgan. "You've got no bloody evidence. You've got nothing on me."

I said, "We should like to see it at once."

"And so would I," said Morgan with disbelief.

Goron said tersely, "Not you."

Bernhardt made a heartwarming speech, pure Joan of Arc, promising Morgan that he would not be forgotten, and then we left the wretched fellow to endure more hours in the darkness and the cold.

The barnlike office upstairs now seemed homely and agreeable. "You will appreciate why I was reluctant to invite you to the cell," Goron said as we drank coffee together. "The conditions are harsh, but there is a method to the treatment. I am an educated man, not a torturer. I have studied law enforcement intensively and achieved considerable success in interrogation. These days one does not resort to the thumbscrew and the rack to get the truth from a man unwilling at first to supply it. Morgan is a typical case. Intensive questioning is the first step. We keep the suspect literally in the dark and question him at regular intervals. Food and water are sparingly given and sleep is discouraged. But he will not be quartered in the dark cell for many more hours. We shall move him to a pleasantly lit one. He will be offered an adequate meal and wine in return for a statement. I am confident he will supply it—or we shall begin the whole process again." He extended his hands elegantly, as if he had just informed us how simple it is to lace one's shoes.

I couldn't stomach much more of this. I said, "This statement you expect to extract is the one that will incriminate him."

"Certainly."

"But what if he is innocent of the crime?"

"That is not my opinion," said Goron.

"Now look here. I came to this place pretty sure in my own mind that he was guilty. Having heard what he has to say, I am far from convinced."

"Nor I," chimed in Bernhardt.

"We thought this was a simple *crime passionnel*," I continued. "It seemed obvious that he was a jilted lover driven to murder by young Rosine's decision to wed Letissier. But having listened to the man—"

Goron interrupted. "Not a *crime passionnel*. Oh no. Morgan is too old for that. Young Rosine d'Agincourt—who knows he is guilty, by the way, but won't admit it—would like to believe it is a *crime passionnel,* but she is deluded. The passion is all on her side. On his side, there is calculation." He took off the pince-nez and polished it. "Consider. Morgan is an unsuccessful painter. He lives a hand-to-mouth life, occupying empty houses when he can. He meets the young girl, Rosine, rich beyond his imagination. Sees an opportunity, not of romance, but of money and patronage. She is flattered by his foreign charm, by the romantic idea of the artist as her lover, and he sets out to insinuate himself into the Agincourt ménage. He gets permission to paint on their estate and takes up residence in a derelict cottage, where he bestows secret kisses on the girl."

I said, "All this may be true. He may be on the make, but a murderer? I have grave doubts."

"I'm coming to the murder," said Goron. "Does anything I have said conflict with what you have heard?"

"It's one possible interpretation," I conceded. "Please go on."

"Then Letissier appears on the scene. After being put through the mangle by her parents, as Morgan colorfully expresses it, Rosine is persuaded to become engaged. For Morgan, this is a disaster. He is about to lose the milch cow he has reared so diligently. If Rosine goes, he will surely be turned off the estate. He will lose his place of abode. He will no longer be able to tap Rosine for gifts of food and money, as I'm sure he did. So he decides to do away with Letissier. He acquires a revolver—from where, I do not know yet, but I have strong suspicions, and I will confirm them. In the Moulin, he picks his moment to perfection and shoots when everyone's eyes are on La Goulue. In case Rosine should suspect him, he appears at her side briefly to inquire whether she was hit. Then he leaves. A cold-blooded murder, carried out with cunning. He will confess. If not by tonight, then sometime tomorrow."

I didn't care for Goron's methods in the least, but I was compelled to admit that he had laid his case before us persuasively. I was swaying back to the conclusion that Morgan was guilty.

Bernhardt was less impressed than I and wasn't afraid to say so. She told Goron, "You promised to show us some evidence. All you have given us are theories."

"No," said Goron with a thin smile. "I have given you coffee. I thought you would enjoy that first. If you would like to see the evidence, be so good as to step into the next room with me."

We got up and followed him into a smaller room. And one couldn't deny that it was stuffed with evidence. Two trestle tables practically groaned under the weight of items connected with the case. A uniformed policeman was at work there, inscribing labels. With a wave of his hand, Goron dismissed the man from our presence.

Most of the objects already had labels attached to them. I noted a dinner jacket laid facedown to display two holes with scorched edges below the left shoulder. Beside it was an over-coat similarly holed. In case we missed the significance, there were postmortem sketches of the victim's back and chest. The spent bullets had been recovered and were laid on a sheet of white paper. There was a floor plan of the ballroom at the Moulin Rouge. And there was a large sketchbook.

I picked up the latter and started turning the pages. Bern-hardt, eager not to miss a thing, came to my side. Toulouse-Lautrec's excesses with the pencil were unmistakable. If that was art, give me a photograph every time. Without question, this was the sketchbook he had been using on the night of the murder.

"You will find what you're looking for if you start at the back," said Goron with a supercilious air.

I continued to examine the pages in the proper sequence, refusing to hurry. In my own good time, I came to a series of sketches recognizably made at the Moulin Rouge. They included people seated at tables and standing for the cabaret. As the little artist had insisted when we interviewed him, most of the drawings were rudimentary, barely recognizable as likenesses. I picked out one standing group that might have been the Agincourts. Then I turned the page and saw the final sketch, a more carefully executed study of a group of eight or nine figures clustered around a prostrate form that could only have been the corpse of Maurice Letissier. Mercifully, it was drawn from a foreshortened viewpoint, the hairless top of the head the most notable feature. Somewhere to one side lay a silk hat. Beside the victim, two figures were kneeling, one—presumably the doctor—supporting the head; the other, lean-ing over him in an attitude of concern, undoubtedly Jules. It was a simple matter to pick out the pigeon-chested Juliette, standing beside a man of vast girth I recognized as Martineau, the manager of the Moulin Rouge. Juliette had her mouth open, holding forth as usual. Slightly to the rear but just recognizable was Tristan, in the floppy black tam-o'-shanter that you see everywhere in the Latin Quarter, standing with his sister Rosine and the bearded figure of Morgan.

Goron stepped closer and jabbed a finger at the likeness of Morgan. "Proof positive that the suspect was there that night. I confirmed it with Lautrec. He knows Morgan as a fellow artist, of course."

Making no comment, I closed the sketchbook and returned it to where I had found it.

The other table was heaped with paraphernalia that I assumed had been brought here from the cottage at Montroger where Morgan had been arrested. There were cups, plates, and cutlery; some clothes; a stack of canvases; an easel; a box of paints and brushes; and a double-barreled shotgun and some cartridges.

"Your Majesty, have you heard of Cesare Lombroso?"

I looked across to Goron, who was now holding a large leather-bound book open at a page with a bookmark inside.

"An Italian?"

"The professor of criminal anthropology at Turin University, a man of genius who has made exhaustive studies of the criminal class. This is his book, *L'Uomo Delinquente*. Do you know Italian, sir?"

"*Criminal Man?*" I hazarded.

"Precisely. Professor Lombroso examined the physical characteristics of over seven thousand convicts and reached the interesting conclusion that criminals may be recognized by their physical appearance. This is the fruit of his research, a standard work of reference for investigators. The indispensable guide to the malefactors it is my job to find. Look at this page of murderers, for example. Note the receding foreheads, the heavy jaws, and the characteristic ears."

I took the book from him. The illustrations showed an unlovely set of profiles, but no more intimidating, I would have thought, than a picture I could recall of the bishops of England and Wales.

Beside me, Bernhardt thought otherwise. She said in a tone of high alarm, "Oh, Bertie! Look!"

"I think you have anticipated me, Madame Bernhardt," Goron said smugly.

"This one in the bottom row," said Bernhardt in a shocked whisper.

"I am glad you agree," murmured Goron.

I studied the portrait to which Sarah was pointing. Undeniably, there was a distinct resemblance to Morgan. "I suppose if the beard was slightly fuller . . . " said I.

"The beard is of no significance, sir," said Goron. "Criminal anthropology is based on the physical features that cannot be altered. The criminal type can be recognized as the modern embodiment of primitive humanity. The typical criminal exhibits the ferocious instincts of uncivilized man. The shape of the head, the structure of the features and their relative sizes—these are the significant indications. The man downstairs conforms in every significant particular to the archetype of a murderer."

"I'm sure you're right," said I. "But this fellow in the row above looks uncannily like my brother Affie, the Duke of Edinburgh, and he's no murderer."

"Pure coincidence," said Goron. 'Does your brother have long arms?"

"Not that I have noticed."

"The criminal type always has arms longer than the average. We have measured Morgan's and found them to be two centimeters longer than the norm."

"He's a large fellow."

"He also has acute eyesight, another criminal tendency."

"Really?"

"The evidence is overwhelming."

"I shall suspend judgment," said I, closing the book and returning it to him. The science of criminal anthropology didn't impress me at all. "And speaking of evidence, I cannot see the point in labeling some of these objects. What's this shotgun, for example?"

"It was recovered from Morgan when we arrested him. You will recall that he was shooting rabbits that morning. We found these cartridges in his pocket."

"But the victim was killed with a revolver. What is the significance of the shotgun?"

Goron picked it up and handed it to me. "Examine the metal plate inlaid into the stock. That is the Agincourt coat of arms. The gun was removed from the gun room at Montroger—clear evidence not only that Morgan stole this weapon but that he had access to a variety of weapons, including revolvers."

I may have reddened slightly. Certainly I cleared my throat in an embarrassed way. It happened that in my pocket was the murder weapon. I had fully intended to hand it over, having foreseen that this meeting would be the opportunity to unburden myself of something for which I had no further use. To retain it any longer could lead to embarrassment, even incrimination. By producing it now, I seemed to be sealing Morgan's guilt, but one should not manipulate justice.

"What is this?" asked Goron when I placed it on the desk.

"Well, if you of all people don't know, I fear for Paris," said I, recovering my poise. "It's a six-chambered silver revolver and it was found in the pocket of an overcoat left in the men's dressing room at the Moulin Rouge on the night of the murder. You will note that the arms on the side plate are those of the Agincourts."

He stared at the gun without moving a hand toward it. "How did you acquire this?"

"By vigorously pursuing inquiries."

His eyes locked with mine and I discerned some respect in them, but antagonism also, and the antagonism was driving out the respect.

I said loftily, "I am not at liberty to say more, except that the owner of the overcoat is unquestionably innocent. The murderer placed the gun in the pocket at some time after the shooting but before everyone left the dressing room. The coat's owner found it when he put on the coat to leave the ballroom."

"Is it loaded?"

"I removed the remaining bullets." Taking three from my other pocket, I placed them beside the revolver. "One shot was fired at the time the weapon came into my possession."

Goron's eyes widened. "I shall need to know more than you have seen fit to tell me, Your Majesty."

"Royal Highness," I said with formal coolness. "You must accept my word that what I have told you is true."

Bernhardt spoke up. "Monsieur, I can vouch for every word that His Royal Highness has spoken. I was present when he acquired the gun from the person concerned."

Goron picked up the revolver and examined it. "This is certainly the Agincourt coat of arms."

"It reduces the number of suspects by several hundred," I remarked to pacify him. "It will save you no end of time."

"When did you acquire the revolver?" Goron demanded.

"Quite recently."

"The details are confidential," reiterated Bernhardt.

Goron said, "Like the shotgun, apparently, it was stolen from the Agincourts."

"That, we cannot say for certain. It comes from the gun room at Montroger, without any question. I have seen the cabinet where it was kept. Neither the gun room nor the cabinet is kept locked."

"You have already checked these matters?"

"Yes."

"So you acquired the gun before today?"

"A fair deduction. But I shall give nothing else away."

"It seals Morgan's guilt," stated Goron with certainty. "This is fascinating. He must have meant the gun to be found, or why would he have gone into the dressing room and dropped it into someone's overcoat pocket? He could have walked off with it and thrown it in the Seine. What made him change his mind?"

We were silent.

"I'll tell you," said Goron. "He wanted the Agincourts to come under suspicion."

"But why?" said Bernhardt. "They were his providers, if all that you have said is true."

Goron brooded on this for a moment. "It begins to look as if something very provocative happened on the day of the murder. Suppose the comte chose this day to banish Morgan from Montroger. After all, Rosine was now engaged to Letissier. It was most undesirable that she should continue to rendezvous with the painter. The comte must have spoken to the fellow and told him to go. Morgan was so incensed that he used one of their own revolvers to kill the wretched Letissier and then left it to be found. Naturally suspicion would fall on the family."

"In that case, why did he continue after the murder to trespass on the estate?" said Bernhardt—cleverly, I thought. "Wouldn't it have been more sensible to leave the district?"

"No." The *chef de la Sûreté* was adamant. "That would have looked suspicious. He kept his nerve and stayed, confident that the revolver would be found and point inexorably to the guilt of one of the family. If it had been handed to me on the night of the murder, as Morgan intended, he would not be in custody now. I might well have suspected someone else." He smiled. "A few minutes ago, I was ready to accuse you of obstructing the work of the Sûreté, Your Highness. I was mistaken. Quite inadvertently, you have foiled Morgan's cunning deception."

Chapter 11

"After that, I need fortifying," I told Bernhardt. "Shall we find ourselves some lunch?"

This being a fine morning, the first promise of spring, we strolled in the sunshine as far as the Pont Michel and crossed to the Left Bank, to the boulevard Saint-Michel, or Boul'Miche, as it is known to all Parisians. At the top end, it is lined with cafés and restaurants catering to every nationality. We walked past several where we would have looked conspicuous. The Vachette was filled with elegantly dressed Africans from, I would guess, Madagascar and Martinique, who would, I am sure, have welcomed us. A band of cadets of the Ecole Polytechnique in their cocked hats had occupied the Soufflet; and the Café Steinbach was emphatically given over to Germans drinking beer at fifty centimes a glass. We wanted a table on the sunny side of the boulevard, and we finally settled for a discreet place in the third row outside the Café d'Harcourt, where the English tend to congregate, and ordered aperitifs. I suppose the weather had put people in a larky mood, because we could hear much laughter from the other tables. A pretty grisette unselfconsciously lifted her skirt to place a handkerchief in her stocking top, whereupon a young man at another table created much amusement by slyly imitating her, slipping his matchbox into his sock. It was difficult to credit amid this gaiety that people were languishing in dark cells just across the bridge.

I made an effort to dismiss the thought. "Cannes is calling to me," I told Sarah. "Do you think if I left this afternoon I could be there before midnight?"

She turned to me and placed her hand over mine. "Bertie, you can't leave Paris."

Ever the optimist, I took this to mean that she wanted to rekindle the flame so unkindly extinguished the previous evening, but she added immediately, "We must do something about that odious little man."

"Goron?"

"Unless we stop him, he'll force a confession and an innocent man will go to the guillotine."

"Oh, I don't think that's likely," I told her. "No one but Morgan could be the murderer."

She said nothing, making her disagreement clear by staring across the street as if I was no longer at the same table.

Tolerantly—for I knew she was genuinely troubled—I reminded her that her own country's law has its safeguards. "It isn't only up to Goron. The *juge d'instruction* will see that the police are conducting the investigation properly."

She was unconvinced. "Can you imagine a magistrate who would disbelieve the famous Goron?" Turning to face me, she said in a tone that was almost accusing, it was so forceful, "Bertie, you conscripted me as your assistant and now you must listen to me. Morgan is innocent. I understand him, because I, too, am an artist. I value my talent above all things. Morgan cares too much about painting to put it at risk by killing a man. His supposed motive for the crime isn't at all convincing. Look, the man has been living on the edge of poverty all his life. If he's ejected from the cottage at Mont-roger, so what? It's no different from all the other hovels he's had to leave for want of payment. This has been his way of life; he expects to be asked to move on. Why should he suddenly become so angry about it that he commits murder— and not even the murder of the man who evicts him? Why kill Letissier? Why not Jules?"

I had no answer.

She said, "This is a simple man, not Cesare Borgia."

I nodded. She'd argued with her usual clarity and there was a certain amount of good sense in what she said. Goron's version of events had sounded plausible enough in the Sûreté. Here in the sunshine, I was being swayed again. "The case against Morgan looked cut-and-dried before we met him, when we thought it was a *crime passionnel*," I conceded. "But we're asked to believe something else. Whatever one may say about Morgan, he isn't a frustrated lover."

"He's too old for that nonsense," Bernhardt said sweepingly. It was meant to support what I had said, so I let it pass.

I said, "I just can't conceive of one of the Agincourts murdering Letissier."

She looked at me with intensity. "You must face it, Bertie— one of them is guilty."

"They're respectable people. I've known them for years."

"The daughter and the son?" said Bernhardt sharply. "You told me you hadn't seen Rosine since she was a child and you couldn't remember Tristan at all."

"My dear Sarah, their parents are people of refinement."

"No one—not even you—can make statements like that with absolute certainty," she told me. "All my life people I took to be respectable have given me shocks."

"I dare say you gave some in return," said I.

I meant the remark lightheartedly, wanting to relax her. Instead of smiling, she put her hand to her mouth and looked away. What was in her mind, I cannot say for certain, but I'd once heard the story from another source that at eighteen she had met a Belgian nobleman, the Prince de Ligne, at a masked ball. At the end of the evening, this young man in the costume of Hamlet had presented her with a rose. Enchanted by his charm and blond good looks, Sarah had given herself to him. Some weeks later, her prince was having a housewarming and unkindly neglected to invite her. Being Sarah, she arrived dramatically on his doorstep and informed him that she was expecting his child. He told her with appalling cruelty that she should realize that if she sat on a pile of thorns she would never know which one had pricked her, and he sent her away. To her eternal credit, she had raised their illegitimate child with no help from de Ligne. Her son Maurice was now himself married.

The waiter asked for the order. Bernhardt, as usual, had no appetite and settled for a brioche and black coffee. I ordered plovers' eggs, followed by salmon, lamb cutlets, and stewed fruit. "I have always taken the view that a man in my position should eat lunch," I explained to lighten her mood. "My brother-in-law George, the king of Greece, eats frugally at lunchtime, thus causing his guests to swallow their food in gulps for fear of being caught conversing with their mouths full, because George will keep asking them questions. With me, there is no risk of anyone choking to death."

She said without the glimmer of a smile, "Bertie, I keep thinking back to something that poor man Morgan told us. He said that after the shots were fired, he went across to Rosine, supposing that she might have been hurt."

"That's right."

"He said she was standing quite still, a little apart from the group surrounding Letissier. She appeared to be in a state of shock and—the phrase I particularly noted—her arms were across her chest."

"Well?"

"That was when I inquired what she was wearing. Remember?"

"All too vividly," said I. "I wasn't expecting the interrogation to stop for an excursion into fashion."

"Yes, but do you recall what Mr. Morgan told us?"

"My dear, I was too peeved to listen."

"He said she was wearing a velvet cape, dark gray or black."

"Ah," said I, trying to keep up.

"A cape, Bertie." Her eyes widened encouragingly, but I wasn't able to supply the comment she expected. Too impatient to wait, she said, "She had her arms across her chest, but nobody could see them because she was wearing the cape."

"Oh, I don't think that's important," said I. "He probably guessed she had her arms folded from the shape of the cape. The elbows would project a bit, like so."

A small sigh escaped her lips. "I wasn't questioning that. I was speculating that if she was holding a revolver, nobody would be able to tell."

"Rosine—with the revolver? You're not suggesting that *she* fired the shots?"

"Certainly I am," she said, and she would have thumped the table as well if it had not been so rickety. "She's the obvious suspect now. She was infatuated with the artist. Everyone agrees on that, including herself."

Smiling, I said, "It's our old friend the *crime passionnel* after all, is it?"

She frowned. It was no joking matter to Sarah. "Yes, and why not?"

"My dear, if Rosine is the guilty party, why did she come to see me last night? A murderer doesn't assist the investigation."

"She was driven to it. The man she loves—the man she killed for—is being unfairly accused of the crime. When she shot Letissier, she didn't expect her lover to be arrested. She came to you hoping you could use your influence to free him."

"Which I have failed to do."

"Only because Rosine didn't tell you the whole truth. Bertie, if only for the sake of Mr. Morgan, we have to go back to Montroger and get her to confess."

Hotel Bristol

Paris

My dearest Alix,

The quickest of notes to let you know that in spite of my best intentions I am delayed in Paris another day. One more wearisome engagement that Francis Knollys couldn't put off. Rest assured that my next letter will be sent from Cannes.

Ever your loving,

Bertie

Imagine my dismay when we were received not by Rosine, but her garrulous mother. The French have a phrase—*"une femme formidable"*—that is so apt for Juliette d'Agincourt that it must stand. It would lose something in translation. If you have no French at all, let me put it another way. Occasionally before a dinner, I have secretly slipped into the dining room and switched the place card of one of the fair sex. I once did it for Juliette—to locate her as far from me as possible.

This dowager was in what I believe was known as a Directoire costume, an attempt to disguise a bulging middle with stays that creaked each time she moved. The top layer was dark green plush—the material footmen's breeches are made from—and looked most unappealing. I had to remind myself firmly that Juliette was a crucial witness and we needed to speak to her.

Not much chance of that. She was going like a barrel organ. "Your Royal Highness, Madame Bernhardt, you shouldn't do this! Jules has gone to Paris for the day. He won't forgive himself for missing you, and I'm in no state to welcome you properly. You'll have to excuse me. You'd like to speak to Rosine, I was told, but she is indisposed today. It's to be expected after all she's been through. I say 'indisposed' and it sounds like a mild dose of indigestion, but she's suffering terribly, poor child. This tragedy has affected us all in different ways. Such an enormous shock. I detest shocks, don't you? I swear that dear Jules has grown a crop of silver hairs he never had a month ago. We hardly ever see Tristan except at meals, and then he is silent as the grave. Would his age have something to do with it, do you think? He goes out shooting by the hour. As for me, I'm quite unable to do any tapestry for the shaking of my hands."

She paused for a breath and I seized my chance. "Would you be good enough to let Rosine know that we are here? She may rally a little at the news, I fancy."

"What news?" she said, her eyes the size of donkey droppings.

"The news that we are here."

The droppings shrank to rabbit size. "Oh, I thought you were going to say that Morgan had confessed. The sooner he does, the better for us all, including Rosine. How can I persuade her that this parasite she calls her friend is utterly without morals, capable of absolutely anything? He would have seduced her. That was the only thing he had in mind, you know. That was why he was lurking about the estate for months on end like some horrible tomcat. I'm sorry to sound indelicate, Madame Bernhardt, but this is the reality we had to face. The guillotine is too quick for a man like that. He deserves a lingering death, like being eaten alive by crabs."

"So far as we know, Madame la Comtesse, the worst he is guilty of is a few stolen kisses," said Bernhardt with such scathing hostility that my own skin prickled.

"He's under arrest, isn't he?" said Juliette. "You don't get arrested for kissing. He's a murderer. No one else had any reason to shoot poor Maurice. Well, did they? Did they?"

"Juliette, kindly be so good as to let Rosine know that we are here," I repeated before Bernhardt got another word in.

"She won't come down," our hostess stated as if it was carved in stone.

"I am not insisting that she comes down."

"Very well." She rang for a servant and started up again before either of us opened our mouths to speak. "What exactly is your interest in this dreadful business? This is the third time to my certain knowledge that you have visited Montroger in as many days. Jules said something about your wanting to solve the mystery, but the Sûreté have solved it."

"Not to our satisfaction," said Bernhardt.

With nice timing, a manservant answered the summons and prevented Juliette from launching into another tirade. She instructed him to convey our message to Rosine.

Precisely as he closed the door, I said, "To answer your question, Juliette, I like to think of myself as a friend of the Agincourt family, and I would be a poor friend if I failed to apply my deductive talents, such as they are, to unraveling the mystery. Sarah has generously agreed to join me in the quest. Up to the present, we are far from satisfied that the truth of this matter has been revealed. In fact, it would oblige us greatly if you would answer some questions."

She made her most unlikely statement so far. "I'm sure I can add nothing to what you have been told already." And immediately she contradicted herself with another outpouring of words. "If you want to know about poor Maurice, rest his soul, I would have welcomed him as a second son. He would have been perfect for Rosine—amusing, handsome, sophisticated, and with a private fortune. From an old French family, properly educated, completed his military service with distinction, a most able sportsman—what else could one look for in a potential husband? Naturally Jules and I urged Rosine not to miss her opportunity. The silly minx took her time deciding, but girls do sometimes, and she had this loathsome person Morgan doing his best to distract her. She has always had a wild streak and anything vaguely bohemian holds a fascination for her. Gypsy violins, circuses, and sensational novels. When she was just a child she wrote a love letter to a Bretonne onion seller. What I'm saying is that we had to steer her gently in the right direction."

"From what I heard, you had to wrestle with the tiller," said I, "and there were rough seas, too."

"She told you that? She dramatizes everything. What she needs, as I pointed out so often, is a husband who will steady her, not some vagrant painter hoping to live off her money."

"Does she have money?"

"Eighty thousand francs in trust from her late grandfather. She'll inherit on her next birthday. I kept telling her, if Morgan wasn't out to seduce her, he was certainly a fortune hunter."

Bernhardt opened her mouth to speak up for Morgan, but I preempted her, enunciating my words with an emphasis that brooked no interference. "Perhaps you will give us your account of the events leading up to the murder."

"It was supposed to be a celebration," Juliette recalled. "The betrothal was announced on the Saturday after Jules gave his consent. On the Wednesday, the happy couple dined with Maurice's parents at the château and on the Friday we took them to Magny's and the Moulin Rouge. That was at Rosine's insistence—her bohemian streak. I'm sure Maurice would have preferred something more conservative, like a visit to the opera. Our willful daughter had her way, and how calamitous it was!"

"At the beginning, was it an agreeable party?" I asked.

"Perfectly."

"Rosine—"

"Behaved impeccably," said Juliette. "All the tantrums were behind us. She was charming to Maurice and took his arm. I really believed that evening that we could all forget Morgan. It was a blissfully happy family occasion. Tristan was with us, being unusually sociable. Whatever we may say about our son and his moods, he adores his sister. Always has done. And of course it was a great thrill for a boy of his age to be taken to the Moulin Rouge."

"He's a boy no longer," I pointed out.

"To his mother, he is," said she.

"Do you recall any of the conversation over dinner?" said I, knowing that she had dominated it.

"I think we discussed the wedding and what we would all wear. I told them about our own wedding in Nantes Cathedral, waiting behind the beadle in his cocked hat and red sash while he knocked three times with his staff at the great west door and then following him up the aisle to the wedding march from *Lohengrin*. I was dressed in ivory-colored silk with—"

"Was there agreement about the engagement—Rosine's, I mean?"

"Of course. I told you it was harmony from beginning to end."

"No disagreements over anything?"

"None whatsoever. Bertie, I don't know why you keep hinting at misunderstandings. There were none. We all left Magny's together and took a four-wheeler to the Moulin Rouge—a place I shall never set foot in again. I could hardly hear myself speak for the band, and there were scarlet women at the entrance."

"Nonetheless, you went in."

"If it had been up to me, we wouldn't have. What could one say? This was the engagement party. To have objected would have soured the whole occasion. I caught a glance from Jules and I knew he was shocked, but, yes, we refrained from saying anything. Inside, it was pandemonium. So many people of all classes. The dust, the noise, the smell of cheap scent, the drinking. Quite revolting. The whole thing was a terrible mistake, a nightmare."

"You were given a table?"

"Yes, actually on the dance floor at the edge. I made a show of enjoying myself. I'm not in your class as an actress, Madame

Bernhardt, but I can put on an act when necessary. I danced a waltz with Jules—in our coats, if you please, because it was so cold in that barn of a place—and I also took the floor with Maurice. Tristan wouldn't dance—he's at a sensitive age, so I didn't press him. At some point, there was a fanfare or a drumroll or something and the cabaret was announced. I remember thinking, Thank the Lord for that, because when it's over we can all go home. Everyone got up and formed ranks around a small space in the center of the floor. We wouldn't have seen a thing if we'd remained at our table, so we were obliged to join in."

"Now, this is important," said I. "How precisely were you standing in relation to one another?"

" 'Precisely' doesn't come into it," said Juliette. "We were in a seething mob. I've never been so frightened. If I could have escaped, I would have done so at once, but there were people on every side of us. It was vile, finding oneself cheek by jowl with total strangers."

"Where was Rosine?" I persevered.

"Somewhere to the right of me, beside Maurice. I tried to keep hold of her arm, but we got detached in the crush when the dancers appeared."

"And Jules and your son—where were they?"

"On Maurice's other side."

"So you and Rosine were to his left and the two men were to his right?"

"More or less."

"Did you spot Morgan?"

"If I had, I wouldn't have known. I've never met the man. He must have come from behind us. It was all too simple in the melee. That grotesque dancer, the one they call La Goulue, appeared and there was a surge from behind. The next thing, there were two loud bangs and poor Maurice had been shot in the back. After some confusion, the crowd parted enough for it to be obvious that he was collapsing. Jules and another man were holding him up. The dancing stopped and a doctor was found and Maurice was carried to the dressing room, but he was already with his Maker, poor boy."

"Do you remember who was there—in the dressing room?"

"Apart from ourselves, do you mean? The doctor, of course, and a lady I presume was his wife. A disgustingly fat man I took to be the manager. I couldn't tell you his name."

Bernhardt supplied it. "Martineau."

"It means nothing to me. Two policemen arrived and asked us no end of questions. And some of the performers came in to collect their clothes."

"How did your daughter receive the news that her fiancé was dead?"

"Bravely. She went pale, uncommonly pale, but she didn't weep at all. She conducted herself with dignity, as she did at the funeral.'

"The funeral? When did it take place?"

"It was on the Monday after he was shot."

"Was there no postmortem examination?"

"That was on the Saturday morning. They verified that he died from bullet wounds—as if we didn't know!"

"And the funeral?"

"A modest ceremony at the church where the Letissiers worshiped and where the couple would have been married in a few weeks. So tragic!"

"Did Maurice live at the château?"

"No, I believe most of his time was spent in Paris. He had an apartment."

We both hesitated, disturbed by the sound of some creaks as someone descended the stairs and then the rustle of skirts outside the door.

"Do you happen to have the late Monsieur Letissier's address?" I asked Juliette.

"There's no point in going there now. It's probably let to someone else. Good apartments are much sought after."

"Yes, but do you have the address?" My patience was at snapping point.

She went to a writing cabinet, sifted through some papers, and produced a calling card bearing Maurice Letissier's name and an address in the rue Tronchet.

"I am obliged to you, Juliette," I said graciously, "and, unless I am mistaken, your daughter is waiting outside the door to see us. We shall not detain you any longer."

"Oh, I'm quite content to remain," she offered.

"We'll call you back if we require another consultation," I countered.

"Don't you want me here?"

I said, "Juliette, my dear, you and I have known each other long enough to be frank without giving offense."

"You *don't* want me here." She turned scarlet and left the room.

I looked across at Bernhardt. She went to the door and admitted Rosine, still in mourning, in a bombazine dress that made her face appear quite spectral.

"Did you see Glyn?" she asked. "Are they going to release him?"

"We saw him," said I.

"And he will not be released," Bernhardt quickly added, sparing her nothing. "The Sûreté are confident that he will confess."

The rigor of this announcement startled me. I knew that Bernhardt now regarded Rosine as the chief suspect, but the way she said it was almost triumphal. The so-called frail sex can be ruthless with each other when an opportunity beckons.

Understandably, Rosine turned to me, her young face contorted with despair. "Sir, didn't you tell Monsieur Goron that Glyn had no reason to murder Maurice? Didn't you tell him that Glyn doesn't believe in marriage?"

"That was made abundantly clear to Monsieur Goron," I assured her.

Bernhardt said, "Goron has enough evidence to sink a battle-ship—the proof that Morgan was there: a sketch of him standing beside you after the fatal shots were fired."

"That doesn't prove that Glyn fired them," Rosine protested.

"He found Morgan in possession of a gun from the gun room here and he has proof that the murder weapon belonged to the Agincourt family. And if that isn't enough, he is able to demonstrate from a scientific study of criminal anthropology that Morgan has the classic features of a murderer. He showed us Professor Lombroso's book and the resemblance is extraordinary."

Tears streamed from Rosine's eyes. "I don't understand. He's a peaceful man, not a murderer."

"This evidence was not entirely conclusive, my dear," said I, trying to offer some consolation.

Which Bernhardt capped by saying, "But the confession will seal it. The guillotine awaits him."

Rosine covered her face and sobbed. The reason for Bernhardt's pitiless treatment of the young girl was of course apparent to me. She wanted to provoke a confession. But I don't think she is aware that her training for the stage has given her such a devastating force of utterance.

After a while, Rosine managed to say between sobs, "He would have told me if he'd done it. He's completely honest. I've never known anyone so truthful."

"You value the truth, do you?" said Bernhardt, resuming the inquisition. "Are you truthful yourself?"

"I try to be."

"And do you believe in God?"

"Of course."

"Then would you swear before God that you didn't kill Maurice Letissier?"

Chapter 12

All the way back to Paris, I had to listen to a tirade against Rosine d'Agincourt, for, in spite of the repeated denials we had just heard, Sarah Bernhardt remained convinced that we had just been talking to a murderess. The Divine Sarah would blithely have applied the thumbscrews to extract a confession. Call me a cynic if you wish, but I think there was more to this hostility than mere certainty of murder. I couldn't help noting that Bernhardt had lost all sympathy for Rosine since the night we had discovered that winsome young lady in my hotel suite.

"Good Lord, it's almost six already. I'll get you back directly to the boulevard Pereire," I offered, to give myself some respite. "Why don't you join me later for dinner at the Bristol?"

"A night in prison has more to recommend it," said she unkindly, but we were at cross-purposes; she was still proposing ways of persuading Rosine to confess.

I repeated my invitation.

She heard it this time, thanked me, and explained that she was compelled to devote the evening to preparations for her world tour. She said she had never relied so much on her domestic staff as this week.

"May I assist?"

"I'm grateful, Bertie, but packing a trunk requires absolute concentration, don't you find?"

"I don't think I've ever packed a trunk myself," I confessed.

"As I thought," said she, smiling in a superior way. "Perhaps we may meet tomorrow."

"Just as you wish," said I indifferently, and shouted the instruction I had long ago discovered was understood by any cabman in Paris. '*Chez Sarah, s'il vous plaît.* And after that, the rue Tronchet.'

Bernhardt swung around to face me accusingly. "You're going there tonight—to Letissier's lodging?"

"I can't put it off. Not while that poor wretch Morgan is freezing to death in a dungeon."

"Then I shall come with you."

I revised the cabman's instruction.

The rue Tronchet runs between the boulevard Haussmann and the Madeleine, a good address, convenient for the Champs-Elysées and the Opéra and free of the crowds who throng the boulevards. Already the lamplighter had been by and it was becoming obvious that the brass fittings on most of the doors had been polished that day. As is customary in Paris, we let ourselves in and entered the hall. There was an aroma of dried lavender. The concierge, a small, beak-nosed, bespectacled lady in the black merino dress so favored by elderly Parisiennes, came swiftly to inspect us. In no way intimidated when we introduced ourselves, she informed us tartly that she disliked the theater and disapproved of titles.

For this impertinence, Bernhardt was very abrupt with her, but she seemed almost to expect it. These widows who scrape a living by guarding apartment houses are a despised species. You see, the concierge takes in the post and receives visitors and watches the comings and goings of the residents. In short, she knows too much for anyone's comfort except her own. She is a potential spy and informer.

Mindful that we needed the woman's cooperation, I pointed

out jovially that at least we weren't hawking matches or onions. We were calling merely to inquire about her former tenant Monsieur Letissier.

"He is gone," she said.

"We know," said I. "We wish to speak to you, madame."

She melted at the *madame* (I think she *did* have a sneaking respect for rank) and actually invited us through a door, divided like a stable door, to her personal domain, a tiny room equipped with strategically placed mirrors, a single armchair, a reading lamp, a stack of newspapers, and two linnets in a cage. Bernhardt squeezed in there somehow and I remained in the doorway.

I said untruthfully, "What an agreeable room. You have the advantage over us, madame."

"Why is that?"

"We don't know your name."

"Bergeron."

Madame Bergeron went on to inform us that she had told everything she knew to the *chef de la Sûreté*. My hopes plummeted. Would I go anywhere that had not been swept of every clue by Goron?

"Have you come from the Sûreté?" she asked.

"I won't deny that we visited them today, but we have no connection with the police."

"I'm glad to hear that. You should have seen the mess they left."

"Yes, please."

She stared uncomprehendingly.

"We would like to see the mess," I said as if to a child.

"You're too late. The apartment has a new tenant. The elderly lady from the top floor moved down there yesterday. Three flights of stairs are difficult for her these days, so it suited her better."

"What has happened to Letissier's property?"

"Everything the police didn't take was collected. The removal men came two days ago. His father was here to supervise. A charming old gentleman."

"Could we view the apartment?"

"I told you, it isn't convenient."

To avert a sharp riposte from me, Bernhardt said quickly, "There would be nothing to see except an old lady, Bertie."

Reluctantly, I had to agree. "How long was Letissier living here?"

"Three or four years."

"In that time, you must have formed some impressions about him."

A muscle rippled in Madame Bergeron's wrinkled cheek. "I don't gossip about my tenants."

"It wouldn't be gossip, madame. Maurice Letissier was murdered. It is salient information. It will all be made public at the trial."

She brought her hands together nervously. "There is to be a trial?"

"There must be, if they don't release the man they are holding."

"Have they caught someone?"

"The wrong man, we think. We want to prevent them from bringing him to the courts. It's a waste of everyone's time, particularly yours."

"What does it have to do with me?"

"The trial, madame."

She gasped. "Would I have to go before the court?"

"As a witness, almost certainly. Yes, I would bank on it if I were you," said I, watching her eyes bulge. "Let us hope we can arrive at the truth in time to stop it coming before the court. Was Letissier temperate in his habits?"

She was so shaken by the prospect of a trial that she stopped stonewalling. "I wouldn't say so. He had no job so far as I could tell. He was one of the idle rich we had a revolution to get rid of, coming home at all hours of the night, sometimes not at all. He would be away for days on end. Never warned me in advance. Never told me why."

"Women?" suggested Bernhardt.

"You have it in a word, madame."

But we wanted more than a word. "Did you actually see him with women?" I asked.

"Of course. I don't tell lies. He was quite good-looking when he first came. He had more hair then. He lost it very quickly."

"These women . . ." said I.

"Some came here . . . as visitors."

"For immoral purposes?"

She drew in a sharp breath. "I don't permit that. The ones I admitted were proper ladies, to my eye, not demimondaines, or I would have sent them away. But what went on outside these walls was no concern of mine."

"Indeed," said I, confident of hearing more, even if it was no concern of hers.

"Once I saw him in broad daylight leaving the Montyon."

Bernhardt muttered confidentially to me, "Don't ask, Bertie."

The concierge continued, "If he'd worked for a living, he wouldn't have had the energy for that sort of how-d'you-do."

"You seem to have taken a strong dislike to the young man."

"I keep this house respectable, monsieur."

"That is apparent. You mentioned lady visitors. Would you happen to know any of their names?"

"No."

"Would you describe them?"

She removed the glasses from her face and closed her eyes in thought. "The first one he introduced as his sister. She had red hair and a foreign accent, like a Pole. Then there were two dark-haired ones, decently dressed. I can't remember which came first. Good-looking, both of them, but they didn't visit more than twice."

"When was this?"

"I don't know. The first year."

"So this was all some time ago, then?"

She gave a nod. "He kept getting sore throats and headaches last winter and that stopped his philanderings. Migraine, he told me it was, but I think it was jaundice. His skin took on a yellow look. I had to get the doctor to him several times."

"We're interested in the recent past, madame. Did he receive any lady visitors in the past few weeks—since Christmas, let us say?"

"The only one who . . ." Her voice trailed away. She was unwilling to go on.

"Yes, madame."

She replaced the glasses and examined me afresh. "Why do you want to know?"

I reminded her, "We are looking for the truth about your former tenant, madame. We believe the Sûreté may be in error."

She said, "I told the detectives everything I am telling you."

"And they appear to be ignoring it," said Bernhardt smoothly.

"Do you think so?"

"It is obvious to us."

Sucking in her cheeks in a way that didn't enhance her attractions, she said, "I may not have said quite enough to the Sûreté about this young lady. To tell you the truth, I felt rather sorry for her the last time I saw her. I wouldn't like to think she had anything to do with Monsieur Letissier's horrible death."

Bernhardt placed a supportive hand over Madame Bergeron's arm. "We must not suppress anything, madame. What was she like?"

"Quite young, younger than some of the others. No more than twenty, I would say. Good-looking, if not beautiful. Very slim. Dark hair, brown eyes, pale skin. No rouge. An intelligent face. Demurely dressed. A little taller than you, madame."

"How did she wear her hair?" Bernhardt asked with some excitement. "With curls at the front, like mine, in the Greek style?"

"No, more of her forehead was visible. She had a parting at the center and the hair was combed back and fastened behind."

"And it was definitely dark?"

"Chestnut."

Bernhardt turned to me and gripped my arm. "It must be her. Bertie, it must be!" She asked Madame Bergeron, "Did you discover her name?"

"No, madame."

Bernhardt sighed.

The concierge continued. "She must have come four or five times altogether at the beginning of the year before last, on Sunday afternoons. I think they went walking on the boulevards and came back for tea. I'd almost forgotten about her until a few weeks ago and then she reappeared one afternoon, asking to see him. That was when I felt so sorry for her. She had altered. She was pale and tight-lipped and her eyes had gone red at the edges, as if she had suffered. It was a striking change."

"She came alone?"

"That is what I said."

"Did he invite her in?"

"Yes."

"For how long?"

"Half an hour. No more. Then they went out together, I suppose to find a cab, because he came back soon after."

"Did they appear affectionate?"

"Quite the reverse. He was cool toward her. When they came downstairs, they kept a distance from each other as if they'd just had an argument. She controlled her feelings as well as she could when she passed me, but I would say she was burning with resentment."

"Did they speak in your presence?"

"No."

"You could tell her state of mind from her face alone?"

"Her face, her posture, everything about her. Monsieur, she was incensed."

"And you're quite certain that this was the companion he had promenaded with on the boulevards?"

"There's no question. She recognized me, too. It was only because I knew her by sight that I didn't ask her name."

Bernhardt turned and gave me a triumphant look. However, I was not entirely convinced that the mysterious visitor must have been Rosine. True, there were similarities in the description. The color of Rosine's hair and the way she wore it matched what we had just been told and the age was about right. But we had heard nothing until today about the young couple taking walks along the boulevard. Rosine hadn't mentioned it, nor had any of her family. My understanding had been that she had resisted all her parents' attempts at matchmaking until shortly before the betrothal was announced.

I turned back to the concierge. "You said that the visit this young lady made was a few weeks ago. Can you be more precise?"

She gave that tiny movement of the shoulders that in France means a vague dissent.

"In point of fact, it's two weeks since Letissier was murdered," I remarked. "Was that the day she came?"

"No, it was before then—the weekend before." She hesitated. "I think it might have been the Sunday."

"Think carefully, madame."

"Yes, it was Sunday afternoon. I had been to Mass in the morning and I discovered a hole in one of my black lace gloves. I was repairing it when she stepped into the hall. I remember dropping it when I got up to speak to her."

"And she left after a short visit and you haven't seen her since?"

"That is correct."

We seemed to have extracted all that the concierge had to tell about the unhappy young lady. "Did Monsieur Letissier receive any other visitors prior to his unfortunate death?"

"No, monsieur."

"He went out more than once in that last week of his life, I gather?"

"Yes, a number of times. He was often out."

"Dressed for dinner?"

"On the Wednesday and the Friday. He told me he was dining with his parents on the Wednesday. They were having a small party to celebrate the betrothal."

"Yes, we heard about that. He didn't bring his fiancée here that evening?"

"No."

"Nor at any other time?"

"She has never been to this house," Madame Bergeron said as confidently as if it was a response in church.

Bernhardt was quick to take her up. "How can you be certain that the young lady you mentioned just now was not the fiancée, Rosine d'Agincourt?"

"Because she was someone else."

"But you can't be sure!" Bernhardt rounded on her. "How can you know? From the description you gave us, they sounded identical."

If Bernhardt's supposition was right and Rosine, in some distress, had made an unscheduled visit to Letissier on the

Sunday before he met his death and left soon after in a state of burning resentment, we had a fresh insight into the case. It was quite conceivable that by the Friday the anger had formed into a resolve to kill Letissier.

"Mademoiselle d'Agincourt has never set foot inside this house," the concierge insisted.

"If you've never seen her, how can you say that?" cried Bernhardt.

The old woman gave her a glare and selected a newspaper from the neatly stacked collection she had beside her. It was the *Petit Parisien*, one of those gossipy papers so beloved of the masses. She turned the pages until she found what she wanted. "There is Rosine d'Agincourt." She opened the sheet fully to a graphic report of the murder and handed it to Bernhardt. The likenesses of Rosine and Letissier were reproduced side by side halfway down the column. "I tell you that is not the lady who called here."

The artist had caught Rosine rather skillfully. She was portrayed in a dark dress buttoned to the neck and a small hat with a straight brim. Probably the original sketch had been made at a salon, where the prettiest girls are regularly drawn. The *Petit Parisien* would have copied her likeness from some magazine for the beau monde and altered the clothes to fit the solemn character of the report.

"She was thinner in the face and her mouth was quite different," the concierge went on to say. "Her lips were finer than this. And the eyes were not so large, nor so wide apart. This is definitely someone else."

Bernhardt refused to believe her. "But this is only a newspaper. There are pictures of me in the papers that my own mother wouldn't recognize."

"The picture of Monsieur Letissier is exactly like him," declared Madame Bergeron with finality.

"But men are so much easier to portray. Look at Rosine's hair. It is exactly as you just described it."

"The face is somebody else's, madame." She would not be budged.

I had one more card to play. "You informed us earlier that the police left Monsieur Letissier's rooms in an untidy state."

She became animated at this. "Untidy? I should have said disgusting. A pigsty. They tipped everything all over the floor and took what interested them. They put nothing away afterward."

"Did you tidy it yourself before the removal men came?"

"Of course I did. There was nobody else to do it. The tenant was dead."

"What did you do with the rubbish, madame?"

"I threw nothing away. It wasn't mine to dispose of."

"But what did you do with it?"

"I tidied it."

"Put things away, do you mean?"

"Yes, and stacked them together."

"And when the father came with the removal men, did they take everything with them?"

"Yes." From the way she pressed her lips together, it was obvious that she wanted this to be the last word on the matter.

"Absolutely everything?" .

She gave a nod and turned to speak to her birds. "All right, I'll feed you presently."

I said, "I can't believe they took everything. Food, for instance? There must have been stale bread."

"They left nothing of value, monsieur."

"Ah. But they left something?"

"They tossed some rubbish into a tea chest."

"For disposal? Is it destroyed yet?"

"There was nothing of value."

My patience was at an end. "Madame, I know very well that you expect to sell any rags for a few sous. We are not here to deprive you, but we would like to examine the contents of that tea chest. Now, where is it?"

"In the cupboard under the stairs."

"Then we'll pay you a fair sum and take it with us," said I with satisfaction.

She was dubious, and no wonder. You don't expect the Prince of Wales to take away your rubbish. In the end, I had to bribe her with a louis d'or for the privilege. And our driver demanded five francs before he would heave the tea chest on board.

In the carriage, Bernhardt's pent-up anger erupted. "Silly old witch. She'll be laughing her head off now."

"Why?"

"She's a louis better off for a box of stinking rubbish, and what is more, she's sent us on a wild-goose chase."

"If she has, I'm not aware of it," I commented.

"Oh, come on, Bertie! You weren't taken in by all that nonsense about the mysterious woman who visited Letissier?"

"Nonsense?"

"Well, she didn't fool me. It was Rosine, of course."

"Do you really think so?"

"She was protecting Rosine by pretending it was someone else."

"Why would she do that?" I added, not unreasonably, "If she didn't want the truth to come out, why mention the visit at all? No, I'm inclined to believe the old lady. Two years ago, Rosine wouldn't have called once at Letissier's apartment, let alone five times. She wouldn't have been seen dead there."

"They'd been introduced."

"Yes, but she'd already gone dotty over Morgan and she couldn't bear to think of Letissier as a suitor. You're mistaken, Sarah. This mysterious caller must be an entirely different woman. We have a fresh suspect."

"That's it!" said Bernhardt turning her artillery on me. "You can't bear to think that one of the Agincourts is the murderer. You're only too pleased to have someone else to pursue, even if she's a figment of that old woman's imagination."

I answered stiffly, "If that's your opinion, I see no point in discussing this any further. I shall find the young lady without any help from you and you will eat your words."

She laughed mockingly. "Find your Cinderella, then, Prince Charming. Dark, twenty, average height. There can't be more than ten thousand girls like that in Paris. It may take a year or two of trying to fit the slipper, but, knowing you, that will be no hardship."

"Sarah, that's below the belt!"

She said, "A choice of phrase that sums it up exactly."

We parted on frigid terms outside her house. Nothing was said about another meeting.

In case there was any bounce left in me, a strong letter from Alix was waiting for me at the Bristol:

Fredensborg Castle

Beloved Bertie,

My worst fears are confirmed. After all your promises to depart for Cannes, you are still in Paris. How could you mislead me so, knowing that I am half a continent away and helpless to protest? I can think of only two possible circumstances that could detain you. The first, your perennial weakness, I can only trust to the Almighty to control and I pray night and morning that He will help you obey all His Commandments, but especially the one that you find most difficult to keep. The second possibility, this ambition of yours to be a criminal investigator, would be easier for my heart to endure, but it troubles my head, for I can see dreadful danger resulting from it.

Yesterday's French newspapers have reached here and

I am better informed now as to the facts of the Moulin Rouge Murder Case (as it is described). My dearest, I am more than ever seized with the certainty that you should have nothing to do with it. There seems no doubt that this was a crime of passion and that Rosine d'Agincourt is at the heart of it. Whoever killed the young man Letissier was driven by a force we seldom see nakedly revealed in England (and never, I think, in Denmark). It may seem trite to say so, but the French are a passionate people, Bertie. Where your typical English murderer is a doctor who poisons for profit or a wretched wife seeking escape from an unhappy marriage, your Frenchman (or woman) may kill from motives we little understand. Their crime is not calculated; it is not really murder as the English understand it, but slaughter in the heat of passion, vengeful and violent. Stand in their way and you risk being another victim. That is why I urge you with all the love I have to leave the Sûreté to do their own investigating.

The Agincourts are old friends, I know. But you have visited them to express our concern, and in all conscience that is as much as friends can be expected to do.

Believe me, *I fear for your life.*

Ever your loving wife, Alix

I read it twice in my bath. I was mightily pleased to get into a bath after sifting through the rubbish in the tea chest we had brought back from Letissier's lodgings. More of what I discovered anon.

Alix fusses too much, but she is nobody's fool, I told myself as I read the letter a third time. Perhaps she was right. The French may murder from motives that we—the more placid races of Europe—get out of our systems on the grouse moor. I would think afresh about motives.

After dressing for dinner, I found Knollys hovering in my sitting room.

"You found your letter from Her Royal Highness, sir?"

"Thank you, Francis. Yes."

"She is quite well, I hope?"

"Fretting, as usual, that's all."

"About anything in particular, sir?"

"No, it's to be expected after a couple of weeks in that godforsaken castle."

"Ah."

"And now I'm going to dine at the Jockey Club."

"Very good, sir." He gave his diplomatic cough. "Shall we be leaving for Cannes tomorrow?"

"I doubt it, Francis. I have some unfinished business here."

He frowned. I had a strong intuition that he knew the contents of Alix's letter. He wouldn't have opened it. Of that, I am certain, for he is a man of honor. But Alix is perfectly capable of writing to Knollys as well as to me.

Chapter 13

You may wish to cast a discerning eye over the inventory I made of the contents of the tea chest from Letissier's lodgings:

Shirts, linen	3	Cheese, moldy	1
Collars, starched	5	Wine bottles, empty	6
Nightshirts, linen	2	Toupee, brown	1
Vests, cotton	4	Soap, toilet	2
Drawers, men's	3	Soap, shaving	1
Garters, women's	14	Brush, shaving	1
Newspapers, various	7	Razor	1
Magazines, various	9	Medicaments, various	38
Programs, theater	22	Toothbrush	1
Postcards, vulgar	31	Tooth powder, tin	1
Bread, loaf, moldy	1		

The list gives no idea of the unpleasantness of my task, for the decaying food had imparted an odor to everything in the chest. In the interests of the investigation, I persevered to the end, and it was a huge disappointment. I knew, of course, that the Sûreté or Letissier's father must have taken away everything of obvious interest, such as his address book, pocket notebook, photographs, letters, and visiting cards, but I took the view that a detective worth his salt should be able to find clues in the most unpromising material.

The rubbish that remained told me nothing I didn't already know. The collection of naughty postcards testified to his interest in the fair sex and the garters confirmed that his studies had progressed beyond theory, but I had already learned as much from the concierge. Letissier had sown some wild oats, but which young man of spirit has not? The newspapers, magazines, and theater programs were innocuous. That left the clothes, the food, the toiletries, and the medical items. Oh, and the wig. People may poke fun at such things, but you won't hear an unkind word from me. Premature thinning of the hair can cause no end of anxiety, and I can perfectly understand a young man's wish to hide the effect from public view.

The quantity of pills and potions may strike the reader as excessive; Letissier was obviously a man who tried many remedies and persisted with few. Just as well. He had enough laxatives to relieve a constipated elephant: castor oil, black draft, Epsom salts, rhubarb pills, senna pods, cream of tartar, Seidlitz powders, calomel, Glauber's salts, and, in case your stomach hasn't already stopped you reading this list, jalap. I was led to wonder if this was typical of the average Frenchman's medical chest and, if so, what was so binding in the diet. So it was reassuring to find several large bottles of logwood to arrest the laxative effect if necessary. In addition, there were Dr. Clark's pills for headaches; cough mixtures galore; a variety of ointments and poultice mixtures; several sorts of bandages; and—looking to recovery—tonics such as sarsaparilla and camomile. Finally, there was a bottle said to contain Van Swieten's liquor, with no information as to its use.

If it seems wasteful to discard good medicine, ask yourself if you would be willing to take the potions and pills that belonged to a dead man. The inspection complete, I packed everything back in the tea chest and summoned one of the hotel staff to dispose of it at once. You may think my decision premature; you would not if you had smelled the contents.

I was never so glad to get into a bath.

It was too much to expect that I would meet Letissier senior at the Jockey Club that evening. To tell the truth, I had entertained a small hope of finding him there, knowing him to be a member. Instead, I dined with old friends and talked agreeably of other matters.

The evening was not devoid of interest, however. I was looking for a well-placed armchair for a smoke when I spotted Jules d'Agincourt dozing in front of the fireplace. This was no great surprise, for it was his usual haunt. Jules was too much the gentleman ever to say so, but I'm sure the club was his main refuge from Juliette's interminable babble.

I sent for cognacs, occupied the chair opposite, and disturbed his slumbers. Once properly conscious, he greeted me warmly and we soon got down to talking of matters that interested us both. I gave him a résumé of my investigation so far.

He was clearly impressed. "You've left no stone unturned, Bertie."

"Oh, I wouldn't go so far as to say that," I told him. "I haven't questioned the victim's father."

"I doubt if he'll have anything to add," said Jules. "A father is the last person to ask about his son's private life."

"Do you really think so?"

"Well, what is your experience? Do you have the slightest idea what the Duke of Clarence gets up to when he isn't at home? Or George? Young colts will canter, as the saying goes."

I gently rotated the cognac in my glass before answering, "Who am I to read the riot act? I was a fearful trial to my parents."

"I'm a fine one to talk," said Jules. "I don't know what

Tristan gets up to at university. You just have to trust them not to get into trouble."

This seemed a promising avenue to explore. "Tristan strikes me as capable of looking after himself."

"Confident to the point of brashness," said Jules with candor. "I was hoping he would learn more respect for his elders at the Sorbonne."

"He is unfailingly courteous to me," said I.

He appeared not to have listened. "It's a bumptious generation, Bertie. Lord knows what the world will be like when they have charge of it."

I said, "I warmed to your son when we met. And he clearly has a high regard for his sister."

His face lit up. "I think you're right. They've always been close, those two."

"Did Tristan approve of her choice?"

"Morgan?"

"I meant young Letissier, actually."

"*Our* choice, then. I've never discussed it with Tristan. I think he had some sympathy for Rosine when Juliette and I were singing Maurice's praises too loudly and too long. But I'm damned sure he wouldn't have liked Morgan for a brother-in-law."

"That wouldn't have happened, would it?" said I. "Marriage was furthest from Morgan's thoughts."

"I must take your word for that."

"Do you doubt it?"

"The man had a powerful hold over her. Still does. She was ready to go to him whether he married her or not. She's my only daughter, Bertie. I love her dearly. She may doubt it, but I do. I couldn't bear to see her throw away her life on a penniless artist."

"Is that why you championed Letissier so vigorously? A young man of excellent family capable of supporting her, even if she loved another?"

"Bertie, marrying for love is a luxury for the lower classes."

I gave a murmur of assent.

He added bleakly, "One thinks as a parent that one is acting from the best motives."

"Do you blame yourself?"

"For what happened at the Moulin Rouge? Absolutely."

"You shouldn't, you know."

We were silent for an interval, staring at the flames steadily devouring the logs. Neither of us would say outright that the wrong person was sitting in a dungeon in the Ile de la Cité; the alternative was too painful to face.

Finally, Jules said, "If you speak to old Letissier, what do you hope to find out?"

"The identity of the young woman who visited Maurice on the Sunday before he died."

"It's a blind alley, Bertie."

"Why do you say that?"

"He won't know of her existence."

"One thing I have learned about the science of detection is never to make assumptions," I told him, and it sounded an excellent maxim. "I must trace that young woman and question her. And—forgive me, old friend, but you and I know what is troubling you—there is no possibility that she is Rosine. The concierge was adamant that she is someone else."

He sidestepped the mention of his daughter. "A new suspect?"

"Assuredly."

"You seriously believe this woman might be the murderer?"

"Consider the few facts we have," said I. "She visited young Letissier on four or five occasions the year before last. It's reasonable to assume that she believed herself to be his friend, if not his lover."

"You just said you never make assumptions," Jules remarked without his customary tact.

"What I meant is that I never allow them to put me off

the scent," I told him smoothly. "This young woman, as I was about to say, probably had ambitions of becoming the next chatelaine. Maurice's engagement to Rosine must have come as an appalling shock. As Shakespeare said, 'Hell hath no fury like a woman scorned.' "

"Did Shakespeare say that?"

"Actually, my dear fellow, I've no idea."

"It begs a question," said he.

"Perhaps it was Byron, then."

"I'm speaking of the mysterious young woman, Bertie. If she is the murderer, how did she acquire the revolver from my gun room?'

Trying to sound as if the question had been steadily in my thoughts, I answered, "That is one of the matters I intend to explore with her."

"Will you speak of this to the *chef de la Sûreté?*"

"Goron? Not yet."

"You want to present him with a fait accompli, is that it?"

"Nothing less will do, Jules. Goron is convinced that Morgan is the culprit."

I might have added that in either case, the good news was that the Agincourt family was absolved of all suspicion, but Jules wouldn't have drawn much consolation from that. He had seen his name bandied in the popular newspapers for day after day and there was the prospect of a criminal trial to come in which the Agincourts would feature as the principal witnesses. No, there was not much good news for Jules, whatever the outcome.

I changed the subject to horses.

I left before midnight and hailed the first cab that came by, a humble fiacre.

"Do you know the Montyon?"

"You're from England," said the cabman.

"I'm aware of that, thank you."

"But you speak with a German accent."

"The way I speak is no business of yours."

"The Montyon—do you know it?"

"That is the question I just asked you," I told him testily.

He said, "Are you the Prince of Wales, my lord?"

"Yes." It wasn't much of a discovery on his part, seeing that I was standing on the steps of the Jockey Club, where I am so well known.

He said, "The Montyon—that's an introducing house. Do you know what I mean?"

"I should like to be driven there, whatever it is."

"Just as long as you know what to expect, Your Highness."

I got in. Naturally, I had some inkling that the address had a certain notoriety. The concierge had been scandalized at seeing Letissier emerge from its portal "in broad daylight." Anyone like me, who had once sat down to dinner at a private party and been served with a "dish" consisting of the notorious courtesan, Cora Pearl, upon a silver salver, naked except for a deftly placed sprig of parsley, was unlikely to be shocked by anything the Hotel Montyon had to offer.

We clattered across Paris at a canter. I had quite forgotten to ask which district we were to visit and so it was some relief to observe top hats and white shirtfronts on the streets we traveled through. In fact, the Opéra presently came up on the left, so we must have passed close to Letissier's apartment in the rue Tronchet. Turning left, we crossed the boulevard Haussmann, so coming to the rue de Provence.

"Voilà, Your 'Ighness."

The Montyon sign was in elegant lettering illuminated by a gas festoon. I tipped the driver generously, when really I should have saved my money. You can't buy silence from one of his profession. However much I bribed him, he was sure to gossip about his "fare."

I was received cheerfully with the title of monseigneur by

a merry-eyed, Titian-haired young *cocotte* who stepped forward
and took my hat, coat, and cane as if it went without saying
that I had come to stay. She radiated such charm that I am
straining to recall what the surroundings looked like. I have
a fuzzy recollection of a small foyer handsomely decorated in
gilt and white; a chandelier reflected in mirrors on three of
the walls; chairs with striped satin covers; a crimson carpet;
and a piece of marble statuary that would not have been out
of place in a drawing room at Windsor Castle.

"I should like to see the proprietor, if you please," I said.

"But of course, monseigneur," said she. "Do you wish me
to mention your name?"

The way this inquiry was worded was the first indication
that the place was anything but innocent. "You may say that
um . . . Lord Tennyson has called," said I, thinking slyly that
the reputation of the poet laureate could do with pepping up.

She went to a table in the corner and picked up a speaking
tube. A few minutes after, I was shown into a paneled room
furnished with two sofas and some potted ferns. A petite, well-
groomed woman occupied one of the sofas, a sweep's brush
beside her—or so it appeared until the brush barked at me.
The breed I think is known as an affenpinscher, or monkey
dog. This specimen was small, black, and bristly and it yapped
throughout our conversation, simply asking to be stuffed up
a chimney.

"What an honor, Lord Tennyson," the woman said, rising
to shake my hand and steering me toward the vacant sofa. She
was, I suppose, about sixty, although these days I find a lady's
age increasingly hard to judge. This dowager, anyway, made
me feel at least ten years her junior. With her tight gray curls,
lace collar, and rigidly corseted posture, she could have passed
for a headmistress, which I suppose, in a sense, she was. "And
how gracious that you should ask to meet me first. Gentlemen
visiting the Montyon are not always so punctilious."

"Really, madame?"

"They forget the courtesies. Their mind is on other things. Please sit down."

"Thank you."

"Will you be quiet?" She lifted the dog onto her lap in an attempt to calm it down. "We have not had the pleasure of welcoming a man of letters before. Of all English poems, *The Charge of the Light Brigade* is my favorite."

This hit me like a ton of bricks. I had not counted on a madam with a knowledge of English poetry. If she also knew how long ago the thing was written, I was exposed as a charlatan.

"I won't bore you by asking you to recite it," she said with a sweet smile, and I sent up a prayer of thanks for that. "I may ask you to sign the visitors' book later."

I stammered, "Th-that will be a pleasure." This woman knows very well that I am not Tennyson, I thought. She recognized me the moment I came in and is out to enjoy herself.

In a voice pitched high to be heard above the noise from the dog, she said, "We are a famous establishment, patronized by numerous gentlemen of influence and distinction. Politicians, members of the French Academy, men of letters. Guy de Maupassant, the celebrated writer, was often here. You must have heard of his story *La Maison Tellier*, as illustrated by Edgar Degas, the well-known artist. *La Maison Tellier* is the Montyon, thinly disguised."

"Really?" said I.

"Yes, we are part of the great fabric of French literature. If you happened to find the facilities here to your satisfaction and felt inspired to write a few lines of verse in the book, I would, of course, be deeply honored. Monsieur Degas presents me with a pastel drawing each time he visits the house. I have a stack of them now. Strictly between you and me, they're not my idea of art, but the paper is wonderful on wet days for keeping paw marks off the carpets. But you're not here for conversation. . . ."

"On the contrary, madame," I interjected. "It is conversation that I want, a consultation. All I am seeking is information."

She smiled graciously. "Rest assured, my lord. With such a distinguished clientele, we positively encourage conversation. This is not the sort of house that hurries the choice. Ample opportunity will be given for you to arrive at a decision and if—by some mischance—we cannot make an introduction that delights you, you will be at liberty to leave without obligation."

I said, "Madame, you misunderstand me. I am not here for an introduction."

"What is it you want, my lord?"

"I am seeking a certain young lady—"

"So that's it!" she interrupted. "You know whom you want already. Excellent. Who is it?"

The confusion had to end at once. Painstakingly, I explained that I was an English private detective making inquiries into the recent murder at the Moulin Rouge. I admitted that Lord Tennyson was my assumed name and that for reasons of security I was unable at present to reveal my true identity—which was about as frank and open as I could afford to be.

She chose to treat all this as an elaborate excuse. She would not be shaken from the conviction that I had come to sample the wares, even when I made it clear that I was willing to pay as much for information as for intimacy. She wanted more than money. In fact, I was offered the freedom of the house, whatever that involved. It was the honor, she said, the seal of approval. She knew who I was all right.

Finally, I told her straight that when I wanted a tumble, I didn't have to go to a brothel for it. We were talking the same language at last.

She'd read in the papers about Letissier's murder and she

remembered him making use of the Montyon. He'd been a regular at one stage.

"Did he have a regular girl?" I asked.

"Mimi was always his first choice."

"Mimi."

"Yes. She was the favorite. Brunettes appealed to him."

"Is Mimi here? I would like to meet her. To speak to her, that is."

"You're lucky," she said. "She is much in demand. At this minute, she is available." Thrusting the dog to one side, she got up and walked straight toward the wall and pushed a piece of paneling that opened inward. I followed her into a less austere room papered in pink, which, if not exactly homely, was at least reposeful. Here, demimondaines in black stockings, thin peignoirs, and little else lounged on divans. Cheap scent in the air took the harsh edge off the reek of Turkish cigarettes. Nobody looked up. They were not on duty, for this was, in effect, their common room.

Madame clapped her hands for attention. "Where is Mimi?"

"Mimi? Taking a bath," said one, and pointed to a door.

We were back in the part of the hotel that clients were meant to see, a carpeted corridor with gilded lamps and paintings of fruit and poultry. A roar of ecstasy from behind a closed door signaled that one of the team, at least, was gainfully employed. Upstairs we went and along another handsomely furnished corridor. Madame opened a door at the end and I met Mimi.

She was standing naked in a hip bath, with her back to the door, as delightful a spectacle as I'd seen that week, gleaming wet and glowing bright pink from the Plimsoll line down.

"*Mon Dieu*—close the door; it's drafty!" she cried before turning around. Then, hands on hips in a pose of confrontation, with no thought of covering those parts that ladies rarely put on display, she added, "And don't I even get time for a bath now?"

I pulled the door shut and Madame picked a towel off a

chair and handed it to Mimi. "This gentleman isn't a client. He's a detective from England."

"A policeman?" Now Mimi pulled the towel protectively around her shoulders. She had her brown hair tied on top of her head with a white scarf to keep it from getting wet. I noted mentally that it was curly, naturally curly. She was too buxom, anyway, to fit the description of the slender young creature the concierge had seen visiting Letissier. But Mimi was not unattractive. Eyes suddenly turned saintly regarded me from above a mouth just too pert to complete the effect. "I've done nothing criminal."

"You're not in trouble, mademoiselle," I told her. "I want to ask about a gentleman you may remember. Why don't you step out of the water and dry yourself? We don't want you catching your death of cold."

This considerate suggestion was well received by Mimi. She toweled her torso perfunctorily and exited from the bath. "Would you hand me my dressing gown, monsieur? It's hanging on the door behind you."

When I turned back with it, she was naked again and so close to me that I could feel the warmth from her. She flaunted herself shamelessly as she slipped the garment on and tied it loosely around her waist, leaving her Junoesque bosom uncovered until last, like the curtain closing at the end of a good play. Had I been alone with her, the temptation to applaud might have been too strong to resist.

We moved into an adjoining dressing room. Madame came, too, not wanting to miss a word. Mimi took the chair in front of the dressing table and turned it to face us. "Which gentleman?"

"Maurice Letissier."

"I thought so."

"You knew him well?"

"I knew him intimately, and you know it or you wouldn't be here, would you? But I wouldn't say I knew him well. In this profession, monsieur, you get to know the animal in them, not the man. If they say anything at all, it's about the business at hand."

The madam put in quickly, "And that's of no interest to you, monsieur."

"Did he ever speak of other women—other ladies—he knew?"

"No."

That one brief word was a crushing blow. "You're quite sure? It's important."

"I have no reason to lie to you, monsieur. I'd have remembered if he had."

"He was a regular client, I understand."

"For a time—only two or three months, and never more than once a week. He was just another job to me, but I'm sorry he was murdered. If you think I'm going to tell you who did it, I haven't the foggiest idea."

"When did you see him last?"

"It must be a couple of years ago. He'd stopped coming here by then. We met by chance at the Exposition."

She was speaking of the great event of 1889, when for six months the Champ-de-Mars with its awful Eiffel Tower had been the sensation of Europe. "You just happened to spot him there?"

"Yes. I wasn't working at the time. He was with a student. I suppose she was giving him what he wanted, because he didn't pay for it here anymore."

My expectations soared like a skyrocket. "A student? What was she like?"

"Dusky, when I saw her."

As we all know, rockets fizzle out and plunge. "Dusky—like a native, do you mean?"

"Not really." She gave a chuckle. "It was cocoa oil, or something. She was supposed to be a seller of bead necklaces in the bazaar in the Indian Pavilion. They employed students to dress up as foreigners all summer."

"Was she dressed as an Indian?"

"That's what I said."

"Then how can you be certain that she was a student?"

"Because Maurice introduced us."

"He introduced you—his *cocotte?*"

She laughed. "He had no choice. I marched up to him and greeted him. He turned bright pink when he saw me, but I wasn't going to tell her where he'd met me. I'm not mean. She was in her second year at the Ecole de Médecine."

"Her name?"

"Claudine."

"Is that all? No surname?"

"Monsieur, he knew me as Mimi, nothing else. He couldn't introduce one of us with the full name and not the other."

"So she was a medical student by the name of Claudine. Is there anything else you can tell me about this young lady?"

"She didn't need stays. She was as thin as a stem."

This was promising. "How was her hair dressed?"

"In the Indian style when I saw it—combed straight back from the forehead and plaited."

"Unusual," I remarked. "I thought curls were all the rage these days."

"Hers was straight and long."

This fitted the description the concierge had given me. "And dark?"

"Quite brown."

"Any particular shade?"

"Brown is brown to me."

It was too much to hope that she would say chestnut. "What color were her eyes?"

"Brown, if I remember right. I only saw her for a couple of minutes."

"Mimi, this is of the utmost importance. Are you quite certain she was his friend—more than just a passing acquaintance, I mean?"

"Anyone with half an eye could see they were in love, monsieur."

"And you haven't seen her since?"

"No."

I thanked Mimi sincerely. My visit to the Montyon had been well rewarded, and I said so—whereupon the madam informed me that the night was young and once again offered me the freedom of the house, so to speak, before I collected my hat and coat. Politely, I expressed myself more than satisfied already.

I escaped without signing the visitors' book. Madame had to be content with a wink and an *"Au revoir."*

Chapter 14

I ordered an early breakfast—using the English word, which they understand in the Bristol—and was ready to leave by nine. Almost too quick for Francis Knollys, who had expected to find me still in my dressing gown when he came in with the letters.

"Not another blasting from Fredensborg, I hope?"

"No, sir. Some invitations . . ."

"Decline them politely, would you? I haven't a moment to spare, Francis. I'm just off to the Left Bank."

"Before you go, sir, there is something you may wish to cast an eye over." He conveyed disapproval in his tone, as if the casting of the eye would be akin to playing cards on Sunday.

This, of course, intrigued me.

"It is a letter addressed to me as your private secretary, sir. The writer doesn't reveal his or her identity."

"One of those, is it?" said I, less interested. Anonymous letters telling me how to conduct my private life are frequently sent to me at Marlborough House and Sandringham, but in France they are a rarity. "What's the gist, Francis?"

"I think you should read it yourself, sir."

It was inscribed in the sort of immaculate copperplate that betrays no clue as to the writer. The sender gave no address.

The Private Secretary
His Royal Highness the Prince of Wales
Hotel Bristol

Sir,

It has come to my notice that His Royal Highness the Prince of Wales is taking a personal interest in the investigation of the recent death of Monsieur Letissier at the Moulin Rouge. It would oblige me greatly if you would convey to His Royal Highness some information that may expedite the inquiry. I was present at the Moulin Rouge on the evening in question and I can state from personal observation that the man Morgan being investigated by the Sûreté is innocent. At the moment the fatal shots were fired, Monsieur Morgan was outside the hall, in the garden. I swear that this is the truth. Justice will be done if His Royal Highness will use his undoubted influence to secure the release of this unfortunate man.

For reasons of a delicate nature I am unable to divulge my name, but, believe me, sir, this statement is true.

A witness

"This is manna from heaven," said I with some excitement. "Thank you for bringing it to my attention. Damned shame he's so coy. *'Reasons of a delicate nature'* presumably means someone else's wife was with him at the Moulin that night."

"Or someone else's husband, sir. It could have been written by a lady."

"Sharp thinking, Francis."

"Not at all, sir."

"If only you were more sympathetic to my investigative work, we could form a highly effective team."

He gave his diplomatic cough. "I do have other obligations, sir."

"Look, this is too important to delay. You'd better telephone the Sûreté and ask that scoundrel Goron to come here directly. Don't tell him what it's about. Just say we have been handed something pertinent to the case."

"Weren't you leaving for the Left Bank, sir?"

"I was. This is too urgent to put off."

To his credit, Goron responded promptly to the summons and arrived at my suite within half an hour. With his cropped hair and mustache and a brown overcoat reaching almost to the floor, he looked more like the popular idea of an anarchist than the *chef de la Sûreté*. He wouldn't accept my invitation to sit down.

"I assume that Mr. Morgan is still in custody," said I without a hint of reproach.

He answered with caution, "Yes, sir."

"You heard my opinion on the matter yesterday and I didn't invite you here to prove a point, you understand. I'm simply doing what any responsible person would do and handing you a piece of evidence that has come my way."

He took the letter and read it rapidly. Then attempted to hand it back.

"You are welcome to keep it," I offered.

He sniffed. "No, thank you. It's of no interest to the Sûreté." He tossed the letter onto a coffee table.

At this, I'm afraid my cordiality slipped. "What do you mean 'of no interest'? This is independent evidence that Morgan is innocent. I'm sorry if you find it disagreeable, Goron. You've wasted your time on that wretched man Morgan, and you may not care to admit it, but you can't turn your back on the truth."

"It isn't the truth," said he in his uncouth way. "Two letters like this, in the same hand by the look of it, were sent to the Sûreté. They say the same thing."

"This person wrote to you as well?"

"Yes, and it just confirms my opinion that Morgan is the murderer."

"Come now, Goron, you can't duck the truth when it stares you in the face. Someone goes to the trouble of bringing this to your attention, an educated person, judging by the way he expresses himself—"

"Or herself," said Goron.

"I was about to add that. I have an open mind," I told him pointedly. "Someone goes to all this trouble and you disbelieve them?"

"Yes."

"I find that deplorable. I am bound to say that your conduct of this case is irresponsible in the extreme."

He said with a shrug, "I'm sorry you take that view. Good day, sir."

"Don't you dare turn your back on me after all the trouble I've taken to help the Sûreté."

He stopped by the door and half-turned toward me. Then he said with a fish-eyed stare, "That letter must have been written by one of Morgan's friends in a futile attempt to provide him with an alibi. If you remember, Morgan told you himself, and he has told me repeatedly—I have it in a signed statement—that he was in the hall with a glass of beer when the murder took place. He claimed that he kept his distance. He only went into the garden *after* the shots were fired, because he thought some maniac was loose in the hall. The letter contradicts him. Either Morgan is lying or the letter writer is lying. Whichever it is, that letter does him no service at all."

I was speechless. Goron was right, damn him. I remembered now.

He said with a supercilious air, "I'm not ungrateful for the information, sir."

I nodded.

"If there's anything else . . ." he said.

"That was all," I told him curtly, privately resolved that the next time we crossed swords I would have the whole case solved beyond an iota of doubt.

Chapter 15

The sum of all the words I have exchanged in twenty years with the head doorman at the Hotel Bristol wouldn't amount to a conversation. Unfailingly, he wishes me good morning in English and doffs his cockaded blue top hat and thanks me for the coin I press into his gloved hand, but that is the extent of it. If it wasn't for his magnificent cavalry mustache, one wouldn't remember him from year to year. This morning, he surprised me.

"Begging your pardon, Your Royal Highness."

"Did you speak?"

"Begging your pardon . . ."

"Yes?"

"I hesitate to mention it . . ."

"By all means do."

". . . and it may be nothing at all, but you may care to know that there is a man who follows you, sir."

"*Follows* me?"

"Probably you wouldn't have any cause to notice him. The only reason I spotted him is that my duties oblige me to stand here for long hours looking across the street. Do you see the carriage at the front of the cab rank, sir? He is there now, obscured by the horse. If you bend down a little and look under the horse's belly, you can see his legs."

The doorman and I must have presented a curious spectacle, stooping to stare under a horse. However, I saw a pair of brown-trousered legs.

"The minute you step into a carriage, sir, that man will climb aboard the cab and follow you. And when you return, he'll not be far behind. He was there when you returned last night."

"Was he, by George?" I said as I resumed the upright stance.

"I thought it my duty to mention it, sir."

"How right you are!" said I, handing him a louis d'or and trying not to imagine what the more sensational newspapers would make of my visit to the Montyon the previous evening, for who else could my pursuer be but a reporter? "What does this damned jackal look like?"

"Average in height, sir. A youngish man, thickset, bearded, probably under thirty. Wears a brown bowler hat and a black overcoat."

"I'm obliged to you, doorman. He'd better watch his own back in future." I climbed into my carriage and told the driver to take me to the Ecole de Médecine. As soon as we were in motion, I looked for the spy from the press through the small window at the back of the fiacre and saw no more than I expected to see; it is quite impossible to distinguish one cab from another unless one is a horse.

We crossed the river at the Pont des Invalides and started along the Left Bank, eventually reaching the rows of booksellers' stalls where people stand in the cold leafing through dusty tomes. In the most exciting city in Europe, they have their noses in secondhand books! I always feel as if I am venturing into alien territory when I visit the Latin Quarter. I'm unsuited to formal learning, it has to be said. Neither Oxford nor

Cambridge (I attended both) succeeded in convincing me that the academic life has anything to commend it beyond meeting a few like spirits and shirking lectures with them and I've no reason to think that a year at the Sorbonne would have made a scholar of me. The failings were all mine, of course—and would have been all too obvious if I had ever submitted to an examination. The mere sight of the columned portico of the Ecole de Médecine sent a shiver up my back.

Needs must, however, and presently I was in the registrar's office inquiring into students past and present with the name of Claudine. One, I discovered, had left last year and as many as five were currently enrolled. Two in their first year could be eliminated from my investigation, for the young lady I sought had been a student already at the time the Exposition opened in May 1889. I jotted down the addresses of the others: two second-year Claudines, named Lacoste and Pascal, and one third-year, named Collomb.

The easy part was accomplished.

Middle-aged gentlemen inquiring after female students are viewed with extreme suspicion, I learned when I called at Mademoiselle Lacoste's address. Claudine was not at home, the concierge informed me—and that was all she would say in answer to a variety of perfectly civil questions. I fared no better at Claudine Pascal's; in fact, I was threatened with the police.

The treatment I received was dispiriting, not to say humiliating. I didn't trouble with the third address; there had to be another way of contacting the young ladies, I decided, but what was it to be? I had the driver return me to the Ecole de Médecine, where I inquired where the three Claudines would be in attendance for lectures. You would think the registrar would know, but you would be wrong. Students' timetables were subject to modification at short notice, so they might be attending a doctor on his rounds at the hospital, or in the laboratory, or the library, or with a tutor. My best plan, I was told, was to ask another medical student. And the best place to find a student at this minute would be at Père Adolphe's, known as Folies-Cluny, where numbers of the species congregated for lunch.

A noisier, more boisterous hostelry than Père Adolphe's doesn't exist. The racket could be heard from Boul'Miche—and this was some way down a side street. One paid twelve sous at the door and edged in sideways between bodies, at the grave risk of having *le bon bock* poured down one's shirtfront. An unlimited supply of liquor was included in the admission price. The place was an extraordinary shape, scarcely wider than an omnibus, yet three times as long. At the far end was a tiny stage with an upright piano being played robustly while a chanteuse did her damnedest to be heard above the din of several hundred students in earnest conversation.

A glass of bock was thrust into my hand by a serving wench who nudged me laughingly in the stomach. I was on the point of asking her to introduce me to a medical student when someone placed a hand on her derriere and she wheeled around and kissed him. I moved on.

Suddenly, I was eyeball-to-eyeball with a face I knew. Plump around the jowls, clean-shaven, and with ice blue eyes.

"Tristan!"

"God!" he exclaimed.

"Not quite," I remarked, "but not far short."

"I mean, Your Royal—"

I said, "Less of that. I'm incognito here."

"What are you doing in this place, sir?"

"The same as I was doing when I saw you last—investigating. Today I'm looking for medical students."

"You're in the right place, then. We're surrounded by them."

"How does one tell?"

"By the tammy—the tam-o'-shanter. If the border is mauve, he's a medic. Care to meet one?"

Thus it was that I presently found myself bellowing questions in hopes of being heard by Jacques, a personable second-year. Jacques hadn't the foggiest idea that the Bertie he was addressing was of the blood royal. I was just a fish out of water to him. In fact, he took me for a fish looking for tasty bait.

"Claudine? At your age?"

Tristan said, "Careful what you say, Jacques."

"Let him speak freely," said I. "This is too important."

"If you mean Claudine the *poitrine*, she's spoken for," said Jacques. "She goes about with a third-year called Roland."

"Is she dark and slim?"

"You fancy the brunettes, do you, Bertie? No, she's blond and you couldn't by any stretch of the imagination call her slim."

"What is her name?"

"Pascal. The other Claudine in our year is called Lacoste. She's more your type. Dark and slim."

"Does she have straight hair?"

"You *are* hard to please. No, it's curly, very curly."

"Are you being serious?"

"Absolutely. Her mother must have spent some time in Africa."

Tristan said, "Jacques, we are not playing games."

"Neither am I," said he. "Claudine Lacoste has tight black curls. Ask someone else if you like."

I said, "We believe you. I understand there is a third-year student with the name of Claudine."

"She'll be all of twenty," Jacques said, poker-faced. "A little old for your taste. I don't know her name."

"Collomb."

"How is it that you know so much and haven't met her? She's here somewhere. She must be. She always comes in at lunchtimes."

"Is she—"

"Brunette? Yes. Lift me up, will you? I'll have a scout."

Tristan and I put down our tankards and hoisted Jacques above the level of the heads. I was doubtful whether he would see anything through the cigarette smoke, but he announced that he had spotted Claudine Collomb near the piano. In a moment, all three of us were prizing our way through the crush. To add to the din, the pianist was giving a rendering of the "Anvil Chorus" and half the room was joining in.

"This is Bertie, from England. He is quite frantic to meet you, Claudine."

"What?"

"Bertie, from England."

I pumped the limp hand of a young lady who—I was over-joyed to discover—fitted the descriptions I had gotten from the concierge and Mimi, even to the dejected expression last noted at the house in the rue Tronchet. The dejection may have owed something to the discovery that it was I, not Jacques, who wanted the chat. With his dimples and wide eyes, Jacques was just a puppy, but puppies are irresistible to the fair sex.

"May we talk outside, mademoiselle? It's impossible here."

"What do you want?"

Jacques put an arm around Claudine's waist and drew her forward. She came like a lamb. All the way out to the street, I was praying that I'd struck gold this time. I could understand Letissier being attracted to her; she had an air of nunlike melancholy redeemed by remarkable beauty.

Outside, she said, "What is this all about?"

I explained that I was looking for a medical student by the name of Claudine who had sold beads in the Indian Pavilion at the Exposition. For the moment, I kept Letissier's name out of it.

She devastated me by saying, 'I didn't work at the Exposi-tion, monsieur. I come from Grenoble and I go home every summer. You've mistaken me for someone else."

"Have you ever met Maurice Letissier?"

"Who?"

She wasn't bluffing, I was certain. She was genuinely bewildered by the questions. I apologized and let her return to the mayhem. With a shrug and a smile, Jacques went also, his hand on her shoulder. If nothing else, I thought resignedly, I have just played Cupid.

Tristan hauled me out of my brown study. "Sir, what does all this have to do with the murder of Maurice?"

I led him away in search of a quieter place for lunch. The young man had gone to some trouble to assist me, so I would take him into my confidence. The eating house (restaurant would be a misnomer) catered to students. When I tried ordering oysters, I was told curtly by the *patron* that he would tell me what we would eat. It was soup, followed by whiting, followed by *poulet* Henri IV. He was not the sort one argued with.

The advantage of this arrangement was that for once in my experience of eating in France, the courses were served promptly. The soup was a vegetable concoction, piping hot and delicious.

After hearing the gist of my conversations with the concierge and the demimondaine, Tristan commented, "Rather intriguing, sir."

"I would call it highly promising," said I. "Do you see how infuriating it is that not one of these girls in the Ecole appears to be the Claudine who knew Letissier?"

"If she exists—as I am sure she must—what interpretation do you place on her behavior?" he asked.

"It's crystal clear. The friendship between Claudine and Letissier was well established a year ago. He saw her regularly and invited her to his rooms a number of times. She was a young student, less experienced than he. Quite possibly he led her to believe she was his one true love. He took advantage of her innocence and thought little of it. Soon he tired of her. He had a wide circle of women friends. Then Claudine heard

of his engagement to your sister. On the day after the announcement—the Sunday before the murder—she made her
visit to his apartment to express her outrage. Probably he was
dismissive in a way that hurt her deeply. She resolved that if
she could not have him, neither would Rosine. At the Moulin
Rouge the following Friday she shot him.'

After a moment's thought, Tristan said, "It is persuasive,
sir, except for one matter."

"The gun?"

"Yes."

"I have pondered over that and I have an explanation that
may fit the facts. As you know, it was taken from the gun
room at Montroger. Letissier was a sportsman, was he not? A
wildfowler?"

"That is so."

"Did he ever shoot on the Montroger estate?"

His eyes widened. "On several occasions."

"Then he used the gun room, did he not?"

"He borrowed our guns, yes."

"So it was conceivable that if he wanted a revolver—say,
for protection—he may have pocketed one from the drawer in
the gun room at Montroger?"

He hesitated. "Took it deliberately, sir?"

"Let us say borrowed it."

"But Maurice was a gentleman."

"Not quite the gentleman your father took him for, as more
than one young lady could attest."

"That is becoming clear."

"You will accept that under the lax arrangements in the
gun room the gun's absence is unlikely to have been noticed."

"I wouldn't argue with that." His thoughts ran ahead. "You
deduce that he had the revolver in his rooms and that Claudine
found it and resolved to kill him?"

"At the next opportunity."

"My word!"

The soup plates were cleared and the whiting put before us, *en colère*, their tails in their mouths. I was reminded how much one misses by dining in the most-touted Paris restaurants. One is easily deceived into thinking that no other fish are eaten except salmon, turbot, sole, and trout. The delights of herring, conger eel, skate, and *dorade* have to be sought in the small family-run houses in the side streets, the places patronized by priests and students. Helpings are plentiful in cheap restaurants, too. I have always regarded myself as a gourmand rather than a gourmet; it is impossible to like food if you do not have a decent appetite. It was obvious from the way he attacked his plate that Tristan agreed with me.

"Your theory about the murder becomes more persuasive by the minute, sir."

"Or by the glass?" said I as I topped us both up with Chablis. "There is one flaw, unfortunately."

"What is that?"

"This murderer appears not to exist."

"Oh, I don't think you should abandon hope, sir."

"Hope is not enough, Tristan. I must take active steps to find this elusive young lady."

"I'm sure you are right, sir. She is unlikely to come forward."

"But who is she? I was convinced that the girl we spoke to, Claudine Collomb, was telling the truth. When I mentioned Letissier's name, she had no idea what I was talking about. And if Jacques was to be believed, the others, Pascal and Lacoste, have to be dismissed because they look nothing like the descriptions I was given."

"You are certain she was at the Ecole de Médecine?"

"Mimi was certain, and I'd lay money on Mimi's memory."

We continued in this vein for some time, relishing the excellence of the meal and deploring our inability to solve my problem. The chicken was served and eaten, then cheese, fruit, and coffee.

"What is the time, sir? I should be going to my lecture."

"Half past two."

"I wish I could have been of more help, if only for Rosine's sake."

"Why, precisely?"

He flushed.

I added rather deviously, "I know you have a brother's concern, but she isn't under suspicion, is she?"

He said, "She thinks of Morgan all the time. I hate to see her suffering."

He left me at the table smoking and reflecting that Morgan ought to be on my conscience, too, after the hopes we'd raised in his prison cell. It was not impossible that the poor wretch had been persuaded to sign a confession by this time. I finished the cigar in a pessimistic mood.

I tipped the *patron* more than he expected and asked if by some chance he knew of a medical student called Claudine. He shook his head. I got up to go. As I rose from the table, so did a young man across the room. He picked a brown bowler hat off a chair.

"Who is the young man over there?"

"I have never seen him before, monsieur," said the *patron*. "He came in just after you did. He is one of those who sit for two hours over a *consommation*. I wish I could afford to be so idle."

"I'm sure he wasn't idle," said I.

"What is he, then, a poet?"

"Probably not a poet, but a writer of sorts."

On my way out, I gave the fellow a penetrating stare, leaving him in no doubt of my disapproval. If he wasn't the reporter following me, there was no great harm done. If he was, I would know his coarse features, the thick brown eyebrows and the great trough of a mouth, the next time.

I strolled the streets of the Latin Quarter in the thin spring sunshine for a while, stopping occasionally to look behind me.

If my pursuer was there, he was being less obvious about it. Eventually, my steps took me for the third time to the Ecole de Médecine.

"Not one of those students by the name of Claudine is the one I seek," I told the clerk in the registrar's office. "I have checked them all."

"When did you say she was in attendance, monsieur?"

"Two years ago. She took a job at the Exposition in May 1889."

"In term time?" He snapped his fingers. "You should have mentioned this before. She must be the one who had to give up her studies, stupid girl."

"Named Claudine?"

"Or was it Cloette?" He tapped his chin. "No, Claudine, I'm sure."

"You said she was stupid. Did she fall behind with her work?"

"No, monsieur. She was pregnant."

"Pregnant?"

It was a shock that left me speechless for some time after that. If this was really Letissier's lover, the case took on a dimension I had never considered until now.

The clerk was running his finger down a list. "Voilà! And it *was* Claudine—Claudine Jaume."

"Jaume. Would you kindly write it down for me?"

"Perhaps I was unkind to call her stupid," said the clerk, reaching for a pen. "They only have to make one mistake, and she was a charming girl, not the sort you'd expect to get into trouble. Others I could name give their favors at the drop of a hat and get away with it."

"Did she have the child?" I asked.

He didn't know. The Ecole had lost touch with her.

I asked if he had Claudine Jaume's address. Upon checking, he was able to tell me that during her time as a student she had lodged in the rue du Chemin-Vert, across the river, but he was uncertain where she had gone after giving up the course.

I must have betrayed signs of exasperation, because he asked me to wait while he made inquiries of one of his colleagues. The consensus was that Claudine Jaume still lived at the same address.

I took a cab there directly.

The district was northeast of the place de la Bastille and might as well have been Timbuktu. I suppose it afforded cheap lodgings within a mile's walk of the Ecole de Médecine. Frankly, it was shabby, if not a slum.

After instructing the driver to be sure to wait, I ventured across to a door that stood open. No concierge here; simply some crudely scribbled names on scraps of paper pinned to the newel post at the foot of the stairs. I was profoundly pleased to see that one of them was Jaume. She occupied room eight.

Up the uncarpeted stairs I went, taking care to keep my gloves off the grimy banister rail. Behind one of the doors on the ground floor, a dog was howling. This was not a comforting place in which to find oneself. I stepped up sharply to the second floor and the third. Just as I reached the top stair, a door opened and an old crone in a black shawl with a face like a walnut looked out and said, "Who do you want?"

"Mademoiselle Jaume, if you please. Which is number eight?"

"She's gone."

"Gone out, do you mean?"

"Done a moonlight flit with her bastard child a couple of weeks ago. I'm not sorry. It was a miserable brat, forever crying."

My spirits plunged again. My murderer was on the run. "Are you sure of this? Did you speak to her?"

"People don't speak much here. It's obvious, isn't it? And by the way, if you think I took any of her stuff, you're mistaken. It was that gang downstairs and their friends. Filthy scavengers."

I moved past her to the room at the end. A figure eight was marked in chalk on the wall. The door was ajar, so I stepped inside.

The scavenging had been thorough. Not a stick of furniture remained. The garret Claudine Jaume had occupied was a mess of broken china and paper, as if a mob had fought over her possessions. Threads of torn fabric hung from the rings on the curtain rod. There were sheets of what I took to be lecture notes, apparently ripped from exercise books for the blank paper remaining. Scattered among them were nutshells, cabbage stalks, and hardened orange peels.

I said to the old woman, "Who are the people downstairs who did this? Which room?"

She said, "The one with the dog. You'd be a fool to go in. It's a vicious tyke, and they're not at home. They have a barrow in Les Halles."

"I suppose you have no information where Mademoiselle Jaume went?"

"She'd be a fool to tell me, wouldn't she?"

I returned downstairs and this time the dog registered my approach by a low growling that made my blood run cold. I knew the likely result if I tried the door.

Instead of going out through the front, I turned the other way along the passage, past a stone sink that probably serviced the entire house and through a door into a small yard. My idea, if possible, was to peer through the window of the room so ably guarded by the dog. The window was shuttered and bolted. However, I made an interesting discovery in the yard. A number of items had been heaped against a wall, among them some medical textbooks in too tattered a state to have been worth selling, a moth-eaten shawl, and a collection of pots and bottles. My contention, made earlier, that nobody has any use for other people's medicines, was borne out here. I found a well-known cough mixture, some liver salts, and a number of jars, among them one of green glass with a black

lid and an Ecole de Médecine label. The powder this jar con-
tained was white and gritty. I didn't care to taste it. Unhelp-
fully, someone had gone to some trouble to scratch away the
part of the label that would have named the contents. At least
it appeared to confirm that I had found Claudine Jaume's
lodgings, so I pocketed the jar.

But the trail was cold.

Chapter 16

"Bertie, what was the powder in the jar?"

"Arsenic."

Sarah Bernhardt and I were in a café just off the Champs-Elysées near the Arc de Triomphe—neutral ground. We both had some pride at stake. She had declined to come to my hotel and I had refused to set foot inside her house. It was that efficacious modern instrument, the telephone, that had restored communication between us, a call from Knollys to milady's servant Pitou. I knew that she would be unable to suppress her curiosity if I dangled the bait of a vital clue in the Letissier case. After some token reluctance, she had consented to meet me for no more than a drink.

This was *l'heure verte*, the absinthe hour, in Paris, when business has ceased and the businessman sets aside his troubles at work and makes an interlude before facing the troubles at home. He buys his evening paper in the kiosk and takes it to the café, orders the French national drink, and enjoys an hour of quiet contemplation.

Without wishing to denigrate the French palate, I dislike the licorice flavor of absinthe and prefer a glass of cognac, and had ordered one. Bernhardt was supplied with a thimbleful of Madeira. Diplomatically, I didn't refer to her wounding remarks the last time we had spoken. The account I gave her of my latest discoveries made the point far more effectively. What a blunder to have doubted the existence of Claudine Jaume!

"Arsenic? Are you certain, Bertie?"

"As night follows day, my dear. I had it analyzed by the best chemist in town, at the pharmacy in the rue Washington. He described it as a compound of arsenic. He was appalled that it was not labeled as a poison."

"Why would Claudine Jaume possess such a dangerous substance?"

I smiled cryptically. "It is not impossible that she used it to put down rats or mice. I'm sure vermin are common in the area where she lived."

"Does one buy rat poison in that form?"

"She didn't buy it. She was a medical student. She took it from the laboratory."

"To put down for rats?"

"Don't ask me. I am not an expert. If rat poison is required at the royal residences, someone else looks after it and says nothing to me."

"You don't really believe she kept the arsenic to kill rats, do you?"

"That isn't the point, Sarah. The fact that she possessed the stuff at all is what matters. Thank heaven I had the good sense to pick it out of the rubbish heap in that yard."

She traced a gloved finger pensively around the rim of her wineglass. "Do you think she was a poisoner?"

"What I *think* is of no importance," said I mischievously, for I meant to make the most of this. "A detective assembles evidence and makes deductions."

She said with her sledgehammer tact, "Oh, Bertie, don't be so blessed pompous. What was she up to?"

"Consider her situation—a poor student living in a tenement slum. Because she is pretty, she was befriended by Letissier, and there's no disputing that he was a rake and a seducer, charming by all accounts, but utterly unscrupulous. Unbeknown to her, he had a string of females in tow and—as if that was not enough—frequented an introducing house. He toyed with young Claudine for a time, brought her home to his elegant rooms in the rue Tronchet, impressed her with his wealth and breeding. Then came the day when she was obliged to tell him he had made her pregnant. Precisely how the fellow reacted, we cannot say for certain, except that he declined to do the gentlemanly thing."

"You mean marry her?"

"Of course. Is this a reasonable thesis up to now?"

"Go on," said she impatiently.

"As we saw for ourselves, Letissier was a copious taker of medicines."

"He had a large supply, but we don't know how many he took," she corrected me.

"Sarah, do you want me to go on?"

"Very well."

"Quite soon, he became rather unwell. Last winter, he complained to his concierge of sore throats and migraines. He filled his medical chest with laxatives and tonics. Moreover"— I raised a finger—"his hair was falling out."

"Is that indicative?"

"Most certainly."

"Of poisoning?"

"According to the chemist I consulted, the classic symptoms of chronic arsenical poisoning include general malaise, headaches, dryness of the throat, diarrhea alternating with constipation, jaundice, and falling hair." I paused and gave her a steady look.

"The concierge mentioned jaundice."

"And loss of hair," said I.

She frowned, taking in the implications. She believed me now. "How would she have administered the arsenic?"

"She could have added it to anything he took regularly—sugar, salt. Or she could have tipped some into a liquid. There was that stuff in a medicine bottle."

"Van Swieten's liquor."

"Yes, it was practically empty. If that was some kind of tonic he took each day . . ."

She leaned forward, an expression of awe written over her features. "Bertie, did you work this out yourself? I'm going to need another drink."

I called the waiter, and when it was ordered, I rested my case for an interval. The café was filling and most eyes were on us; people find it hard to believe that in Paris I behave as others do—although I suppose not many others share a table with Sarah Bernhardt. Then my attention was taken by someone who had just come in. He appeared to be distributing folded pieces of paper, placing one on the corner of each table. I watched this procedure curiously. Some picked up the paper, unfolded it, and read what was written inside, but the majority conspicuously ignored the gift, even if they had nothing else to distract them.

"You mentioned chronic poisoning," said Sarah. "By that, you mean steady doses rather than one lethal amount?"

I nodded. "That way, it is less likely to be detected by the victim. He just assumes he is ill. All she had to do was tip some arsenic into one of the preparations he took."

"But in the end, it wasn't the arsenic that killed him; it was two bullets."

"Granted," I admitted serenely. "All I am asking you to believe is that Claudine Jaume intended to kill Letissier. She possessed the arsenic and he exhibited the symptoms. In the end, she lost patience and shot him."

"Bertie, it wasn't a question of losing patience," Bernhardt said in some excitement. "She was bitterly angry in the end."

"Angry?"

"Yes—at the news of his engagement to Rosine. We know

she made one more visit to his apartment on the Sunday before the murder, obviously to appeal to him to acknowledge the child he had sired."

I nodded. Of course I had deduced this already, but I can be generous when others talk sense. However, it was my dogged persistence that had led us to the truth, and I didn't want Bernhardt stealing this scene from me, so I said firmly, "She found a revolver there, a revolver Letissier himself had acquired from the gun room at Montroger. Let us say borrowed. She secreted it in her handbag, took it away with her, and shot him at the next opportunity, at the Moulin Rouge."

"Oh no."

I glared at her. "What is wrong now?"

She stared back defiantly. "Claudine didn't shoot him. That's far too fanciful. You've been amazingly clever up to now, Bertie. Don't spoil it."

"What are you saying—that after all this, you don't believe she did it?" said I, flabbergasted.

"This complicated theory about the gun," said she. "It contains some doubtful assumptions, to put it mildly. First he steals the thing and then she does—really stretching credibility. You don't understand women at all."

"That's rather sweeping."

"I withdraw it, then. I'll rephrase it. You have overlooked the explanation that I, as a woman, find transparently obvious."

I greeted this with the frigid silence it deserved.

"What happened is this," she told me. "Claudine appealed to Letissier to do the gentlemanly thing and marry her and found him unsympathetic. Her remedy was not to shoot him, but to expose him. If he wouldn't disclose to his fiancée that he had fathered a child, she would. She went to Montroger and told Rosine the truth about the man she was to marry. As I have maintained from the beginning, it was Rosine who shot Letissier, and for very good reason. You have supplied the motive, Bertie. I salute you." She gave me a sweet smile. "Between us, we have arrived at the truth."

"Whoa there," I said. "I can't agree with that."

"Why not? If Rosine is the murderer, you don't have to explain how the fatal weapon came into her possession. It was already there, in the house where she lives."

"But she didn't do it, Sarah."

The drinks came. To our left, the fellow distributing pieces of paper was still going diligently about his business, not missing a table. A few people unfolded the papers and looked at the contents. The majority did not trouble.

Bernhardt would not be subdued. She had to wring an admission from me. "Bertie, don't be so dense. You must see that Rosine's motive is overwhelming now. Not only was she being forced to marry the man she didn't love; she'd learned that he'd fathered someone else's child."

"I may be naïve where women are concerned," I said with heavy irony, "but if your theory is true, isn't it far more likely that she would appeal to her parents to call off the engagement? She had just been handed a very persuasive reason not to marry Letissier."

"Appeal to her parents, after all that had gone before?" said she with a sharp note of scorn.

"Wouldn't Jules and Juliette support her?"

"No."

"Why not?"

"Because they are not bourgeois, Bertie. In the circles the Agincourts move in, they take a more tolerant view of a young man's indiscretions. They wouldn't see his conduct as an obstacle to marriage. To make an issue of it would be a social gaffe. It would neither be understood nor supported by the people they fraternize with."

"That must be debatable," said I.

"It isn't. Jules d'Agincourt is an old-fashioned aristocrat. His promise had been given to the Letissier family. He would see it as his duty, a matter of family honor, to insist that the marriage took place. Privately, he might have had strong words with the young man and insisted that he make Claudine some kind of settlement and would never repeat the adventure, but that is the most he would do. The engagement would stand."

I was about to insist that Claudine Jaume had a stronger motive than Rosine, but I was in imminent danger of being overheard, so I took a sip of cognac instead and watched the man with the folded papers approach our table, put one down for us, and move on.

Just as I started to put my hand out, Bernhardt grabbed my wrist. "If you do," she warned me, "he'll demand two sous. Only the tourists fall for it."

"But what is it?"

"A form of begging. He's dumb, or pretending to be. This paper has printed on it the key to the deaf-and-dumb language. If you are curious enough to touch it, he'll notice and take that as consent. Watch him now. He'll visit all the tables again collecting the papers, and his dues."

It was a new form of enterprise to me. Habitués of the cafés are regularly approached by sellers of parakeets, puppies, toffee apples, roses, plaster figurines, walking sticks, and sexual favors. In most cases, one may examine the goods, more or less. In this instance, you paid to have your curiosity satisfied. You were unlikely to keep the paper, for who wants to study sign language? So it was nearly all profit.

Therefore, we ignored the piece of paper.

Rather than debating Claudine Jaume's behavior any longer and provoking another argument, I switched to a less controversial matter and informed Bernhardt about the anonymous letter that had come that morning and my conversation with Goron. "I really believed it to be the proof of Morgan's innocence," I said. "You may imagine my mortification when

Goron pointed out that it didn't square with the statement Morgan himself made to us."

"Who would have sent it?" she asked.

"Some well-meaning friend of Morgan's, according to Goron."

Her eyes narrowed and she drummed her fingers on the table. "Rosine, perhaps."

"Oh, I shouldn't think so."

"Bertie, she went to the length of visiting you at the Bristol to protest his innocence, so she certainly wouldn't stop at writing you a letter."

"But unsigned?"

"Without question, if she felt it would lead to his release. It was a decently written letter, you said, an educated letter?"

"Yes."

"It wouldn't have been written by one of his artist friends, then. Most artists are practically illiterate. I would be fascinated to compare it with Rosine's handwriting. Do you still have it?"

"At the hotel."

"Keep it, Bertie. It could be a vital clue."

"Goron doesn't think so."

"Goron is an idiot."

On that, at least, we were in accord. Pensively, we sipped our drinks. I remarked in the spirit of cooperation that even though our theories on the murder differed, we would both dearly like to speak to Claudine Jaume.

"Perhaps the landlord has a forwarding address," Bernhardt suggested.

"I wish it were so," said I. "Unfortunately, all the evidence is that she did a flit. She left her possessions behind."

"Perhaps she couldn't pay the rent. It would be due soon. All rents must be paid by April eighth, the next quarter day."

"Sarah, she is on the run because she is a murderess."

The dumb man was on his round for the second time, and

I took a franc from my pocket. Thanks to Bernhardt, I hadn't
fallen for the trick, but I admired the poor fellow's enterprise.
He deserved a tip.

"That's too much," Bernhardt scolded me.

"This is his lucky day, then. I never carry sous."

The man gave me a nod for my generosity. Instead of picking
up the paper, he placed a finger on it and slid it across the
table toward me. Then he moved on.

"My, you're honored!" said Bernhardt. "They don't usually
let you keep it."

"May I look at it now?" said I, unfolding it. And then I
frowned.

"What is it?" she asked.

"Not sign language, for sure." I turned to look for the
dumb man, but he had left the café.

A message was inscribed in pencil:

> 7 *rue Alexis*
> 8 P.M.
> *Claudine Jaume*

I handed it to Bernhardt and said, "Where's the rue Alexis?"

"Across the river."

"Do you think I should go? It may be a trap."

"Of course we must go," she said, slipping smoothly into
the plural. "She wants to prove to us that she is innocent."

"But she isn't innocent. How did she know we were here?
I don't care for this, Sarah. I don't like the way it was done.
I don't care for it at all."

Chapter 17

I was deeply suspicious of the message. A strong, almost-supernatural impulse urged me to ignore it. I was hearing another message, the words my own wife had written to me: "I can see dreadful danger . . . Believe me, *I fear for your life.*" My dear, devoted Alix was speaking to me as passionately as if she was sitting at the table.

Whatever my failings (and I admit to plenty), I am no coward. It wasn't a blue funk that made me hesitate, it was loyalty to Alix. And there were also practical reasons for caution. There was the knowledge that if I took up Claudine Jaume's invitation, she would have the advantage over me. Up to now, every action of mine had been my own choice; she couldn't possibly have predicted where I would go next or what I would discover about her. Now the advantage would swing to her. She had named the time and place.

There was, of course, another consideration. I had been handed a matchless opportunity of catching up with her. To reject it was to throw in the towel.

Bernhardt, seeing me of two minds, said, "If you like, I'll go and meet her by myself. She doesn't frighten me in the least."

Ignoring the barb, I said, "Where exactly is the rue Alexis?"

"Near the Champ-de-Mars, where the Exposition was."

"We'll go together. I think there's time for another cognac first."

"Dutch courage?"

I preserved a dignified silence while pinching her under the table.

A little after half past seven, we hired a closed coupé. Paris was about its business as gaily as ever in the lighted streets and boulevards, the strains of violin and harmonium from the restaurants and brasseries competing with the clink of harness and the clatter of hooves along the roadways. Beside me, Bernhardt behaved as if we were blithely out for an evening of food and fun like everyone else. Leaning half out of the window, she gave me a commentary on everything outside, mocking the stuffed-bird trimmings on other women's hats, urging me to sniff the appetizing odors wafting from open doors or to wave to friends she spotted in other carriages.

I was silent, unmoved, a coiled spring.

What was Claudine Jaume's game? I kept wondering. Why risk a confrontation with me when she knew—she surely knew—I suspected her of murder? And I was at a loss to understand how she had discovered precisely where to reach me with the message—and recruited the dumb man to deliver it. The whole thing was mysterious and extremely unnerving.

Somewhere along the avenue Kléber between the Arc de Triomphe and the Trocadéro Palace, Bernhardt said, "Chin up, Bertie. Even if Claudine did it, which I dispute, I don't think she'll kill you."

"You forget something. I am the only person in Paris who believes she is a murderess. My life is definitely at risk."

"Then I shall make it very clear that I don't share your opinion," said she, unable to take anything seriously that night.

Our carriage swung around the terraces of the Trocadéro and crossed the Pont d'Iéna. I was so preoccupied that I failed even to comment on the ugliness of the Eiffel Tower when it loomed up, fully illuminated and soaring to the stars. We veered left and skirted the Champ-de-Mars for a few minutes before venturing up a short unlighted street.

"You said rue Alexis, monsieur?" our cabman called down.

"Number seven. And be sure to wait for us if you want the fare."

They were tall tenement buildings. The darkness may have restricted my observation, but it seemed to me that Mademoiselle Jaume's new address was even less desirable than the last. Most of the houses were boarded up and one end of the street was just a heap of rubble, left over, I guessed, from the Exposition.

"I should have armed myself," said I.

"To meet a woman with a baby?" said Bernhardt.

"A murderess who shot a man in the back."

"Allegedly," said she.

"It's not a risk that one should take."

"But she doesn't have the gun any longer."

"She is also a poisoner."

"Don't drink the coffee, then."

We got out. Boards had been nailed across the windows of number seven, not just on the ground level but to the roof. It looked most unlike a domestic habitation. The front door was solid wood apart from a small recess halfway down that was protected by an iron grille. I knocked boldly. After some delay, a hatch behind the grille slid open and a pair of dark eyes inspected us.

Stooping, I said, "We are here at the invitation of Mademoiselle Jaume." I had no intention of announcing our identities, not to a pair of goggling eyes.

The scrutiny continued.

"Jaume," I repeated. "Mademoiselle Claudine Jaume."

The hatch closed, the door opened a short way, and I had my first shock of the night. Behind it was a dwarf, a proper dwarf about a foot shorter than Toulouse-Lautrec and with a head too large for his body. He was dressed in a cockaded red turban, white shirt, black suede waistcoat, pink satin pantaloons, white stockings, and red Turkish slippers with pointed, curling toes.

"How many cognacs did I get through?" I muttered to Bernhardt. Then I told the little man, "I think we must be mistaken. We wanted a young lady."

He piped, "Claudine Jaume?"

"Well, yes."

Then he beckoned me inside. Naturally, I stepped back to let the lady pass through the door first, but Bernhardt had an extraordinary effect on the dwarf. He raised both hands to bar her entry and jabbered something excitedly in his own language, which was neither Bernhardt's nor mine.

"The lady is with me," said I in a civil tone calculated not to excite him more. "We are together."

He shook his head vigorously and wagged a finger at Bernhardt, who said, "This is utterly absurd."

"For some occult reason, he doesn't wish you to enter," I said superfluously.

"Who the devil is he?" said she.

"By his dimensions, he appears to go with the door," said I. "The peephole is exactly his height."

"He can't be the concierge, can he? Well," she said, articulating her words as if she was on the stage, "it's apparent that *Sarah Bernhardt* is persona non grata here."

But the dwarf didn't exactly jump to attention at the sound of Bernhardt's name. He continued to stand in her way, scowling ferociously.

She said, "You'd better go in without me, Bertie."

"That's out of the question."

She said, "I shall wait in the cab. You go in."

I was reluctant to leave her outside, for my own convenience as well as hers. I'd counted on her support in extracting the

truth from Claudine Jaume. I made one more attempt to
communicate our intentions to the dwarf, this time introducing myself as the Prince of Wales and my companion as the
celebrated Madame Sarah Bernhardt.

I might as well have said she was Medusa. He shook his
head so hard that the turban swiveled.

Sarah told me, "You're wasting your breath, Bertie. You'll
have to go in alone. If it's a misunderstanding, you can send
for me, but don't send him. If he wags his little finger at me
once more, I'll pick him up by the seat of his pink satin pants
and toss him in the river." She strutted back to the waiting
cab.

I called out to her, "I have an uncommonly nasty feeling
about this."

She retorted, "Oh, get on with it, Bertie! I shan't wait out
here forever."

The dwarf pulled the door fully open. With a troubled sigh,
I stepped inside. He shut out Paris with a thud.

At least the hall was carpeted, which was an improvement
on Claudine's previous address. A miserly light gave me little
chance to inspect the interior. It was as much as I could do
to follow the bobbing turban along a passage that eventually
led completely through the house, down a couple of steps,
and into what looked like a conservatory but turned out to be
a glass-sided corridor that evidently connected number seven
rue Alexis with another building.

"Where are you taking me?" I demanded without any expectation of being understood.

Of course I was given no answer.

The dwarf opened a door at the end and gestured to me to
go ahead. Having begun this bizarre adventure, I was obliged
to continue it. Greatly to my surprise, I stepped into a spa-
cious, well-lit octagonal room with a tiled floor and a fountain
playing in the center. An ornate wooden screen exquisitely
carved in an Ottoman design formed the surround. Four arch-

ways were incorporated in the screen. A number of marble benches provided the only furniture. Looking up, I saw that this elegant place was sited under a large cupola painted deep blue and intricately decorated with stars, crescents, and lozenges.

Behind me, the door shut, and to my disquiet, I heard a bolt forced home with vigor by the dwarf on the other side. I was abandoned in this alien place. I stood uncertainly, extremely doubtful now that Claudine Jaume would materialize. I could think of no possible connection between an unmarried mother and this vestibule of what appeared to be a Moorish palace. I had never heard of such a building in Paris. One could only speculate that it was one of the many exotic pavilions put up for the Exposition. I thought they had all been dismantled except Monsieur Eiffel's enormous offense to good taste, but obviously this place, too, had been reprieved.

The Exposition must be the connection, I thought. Claudine was employed here. Mimi, the demimondaine, had told me of meeting Claudine with Letissier in the Indian Pavilion. Obviously, she had come to know this building while she was working at Champ-de-Mars. I felt a little easier in my mind at having worked this out for myself. That wretched dwarf had undermined my confidence.

Then a naked man walked in.

I had better qualify that. He was wearing sandals. He also carried a towel. Regrettably, he carried it without the slightest concession to decency. He was an unprepossessing sight, too, pink as a flamingo, corpulent, hirsute, and without any attribute that I would have thought worthy of putting so flagrantly on display.

I cleared my throat to attract his attention or he would have walked straight past, I am certain. "Do you speak French, monsieur?"

He hesitated, stared at me as if *I* were the naked man, gave a Gallic shrug, crossed the floor to the archway opposite, and disappeared from my view.

I am not used to such rudeness.

I followed him. Through the archway on the other side of the screen was a tiled passageway with latticed half doors to a series of cubicles that I took to be changing rooms. The man's head and torso were visible in the nearest of these. He turned and stared at me over the half door with the expression of a horse reluctant to be saddled.

I said with such deference as I could muster, "You must excuse me. I am a visitor. Do you happen to have seen Mademoiselle Jaume?"

He said in a squawk of outrage, "Mademoiselle? Where?"

"That is my difficulty. I don't know where. I was brought here."

"Brought? Who brought you?"

"A Turkish dwarf."

"Oh?"

"Before that," I went on, "I received a message, but that needn't concern you." I was beginning to sound as confused as I felt.

"A message?" said he dubiously.

"To come here and meet Claudine Jaume."

"You came to this place to meet a woman? How did she get in?"

"I haven't the faintest idea."

He said, "Well, who are you?"

"The Prince of Wales."

This was the last straw as far as he was concerned. He said firmly, "Just move away from me, will you? I'm sure somebody will come for you."

Crushed, I gave up. I would be better employed making a tour of the cubicles in search of somebody who would help me. And so it turned out. I had not gone more than a few steps when a figure—a clothed figure—approached from the opposite direction. My rising hopes dived again when I saw what clothes they were. He was dressed like the dwarf in baggy trousers and a turban. However, I could now be reasonably certain of one thing that had gradually been dawning on me: I was in a Turkish bath and this was an attendant. Make of it what you will, reader, and you will probably be as mystified as I was.

Ever the optimist, I said in French, "Good evening, can you help me? I am the Prince of Wales and I was directed here in the expectation of meeting a young lady, Mademoiselle Jaume."

The attendant smiled, nodded, pushed open the door of the nearest cubicle, and ushered me inside.

"I don't think you understand," said I.

He pointed to a towel hanging over the door, as if that explained everything.

"But I haven't come for a bath."

He folded his arms in a way that I could easily have taken as menacing. They are muscular fellows, these Turkish bath attendants.

My beleaguered brain struggled to make sense of this pantomime. There had to be some logic to it, some reason why I had been led or lured here. Clearly, I was in the gentlemen's section of the baths. Perhaps Claudine had sought sanctuary in the ladies' half—if such a facility existed. I had once been shown a postcard of a French painting in the Louvre of twenty or more ladies in a state of nature disporting themselves in a Turkish bath (presumably in Paris), drinking tea, playing a mandolin, and passing time in other ways I shan't go into, except to state that it wasn't the sort of place where a man would have been welcomed. It made me curious how the artist (a man) had obtained permission to set up his canvas. I remembered noticing an unusual feature, and that was that the painting had been circular, giving the impression of a view through a window, or peephole. Knowing mankind's insatiable curiosity, it would not surprise me to know that there were secret arrangements between the attendants of both sides of the baths. No, I would not abandon hope of meeting Claudine Jaume.

There remained the matter of my clothes. Clearly, I couldn't walk around a Turkish bath in a silk hat and overcoat. On the other hand, one feels so vulnerable with only a towel for protection. An English gentleman is not comfortable in the buff. In London, I occasionally visit the Jermyn Street Turkish bath, which is conveniently close to my club. There, bathing drawers are de rigueur. The likelihood of obtaining a pair in this place was negligible. The French are shameless in their attitude to the human form.

I came to the reluctant decision to remove all my clothes, reflecting, as I stepped out of my trousers, that the dwarf, after all, had acted properly to exclude Sarah Bernhardt from this baring of the flesh. I'm not coy where Sarah is concerned and I can't believe she would object to parading au naturel, but who could say what sights lurked in the inner sanctum of the baths?

Taking care to tuck the towel securely around my middle, I slipped my feet into the sandals provided. Only then did my attendant unfold his arms and allow me out of the cubicle.

"Now will I have your cooperation?" said I with a withering stare.

He took a step back and pointed to a set of swing doors, making it patently clear that he would not be coming with me. Wisps of steam were escaping through the slot at the center.

I pushed open the doors and entered a white vault. The heat inside was palpable. The modern Turkish bath is supposed to function with hot, dry air, but they are always full of vapor and it was far from easy to see anything. It took some time before my vision adjusted sufficiently to show me another set

of doors ahead, streaming with condensation. The idea is that
one progresses through a series of rooms of increasing tempera-
ture. This was merely an antechamber. Staunchly, I persevered.
The second chamber was so hot that I felt the moisture rolling
steadily down my torso. It was necessary to remain some minutes there before even thinking of moving on, so I sat for a
while on one of the marble benches provided. No one else was
present. If I had come here from choice, I would have endured
the sensations in the happy knowledge that I was purifying
my blood, protecting myself against scrofulous diseases, gout,
sciatica, rheumatism, corpulence, baldness, and ennui. Because it was involuntary, I resented every second of it. I was
beginning to suspect that I had made myself a laughingstock.
Bernhardt would think this risible if I emerged pink-faced to
announce that I'd been through a Turkish bath and learned
absolutely nothing.

Passing swiftly through another sweltering room, I penetrated to the steam room itself. There, I was obliged to halt.
It was the nearest thing to hell that I am ever likely to encounter. I held the door open a moment and the steam rushed past
me as if I was in a railway tunnel—traveling *outside* the train.
I couldn't see much at all. There was no other way through,
so I took a deep breath and stepped into this inferno and out
by the opposite door as swiftly as possible.

Then, by contrast, blissful cool air. I pushed open the doors
to a grander room, in fact an atrium, a place of classical pillars
and tall arches, the very center of the Hammam. Immediately
in front of me was a huge temptation, a pool of water that I
could tell at a glance was ice-cold. Had I been totally confident
of privacy, I would have discarded the towel, stepped out of
the sandals, and plunged in. However, one has one's standards
of decorum. Through the vaporous air (it was still tropically
warm in here), I had spotted two fellow creatures, and one
doesn't parade naked in front of strangers, even though these
two were inert. They were lying facedown on the vast marble

platform at the center of the room that is used for massage. So far as I could tell in the conditions, they were not female.

A third figure, a boy of Eastern features in a blue loincloth, appeared from behind a column and gestured to me to join the others on the platform. One is frightfully vulnerable facedown; however, I submitted. I don't know if the heat saps one's resistance, but at that minute the prospect of being horizontal was peculiarly appealing.

When the boy eased the towel from underneath me, I didn't even murmur. I lay there like a beached porpoise. He commenced to massage me by pressing lightly with his fingertips on my neck and shoulders, working downward to my feet, which he chafed assiduously to remove hard skin from the soles.

I was lulled into a state approaching sleep when the second, more vigorous stage of the massage began. Unknown to me until this moment, a second masseur had arrived, an adult. I opened my eyes and saw him, huge, solemn, and silent, in loincloth and turban and with a black beard, just as he grasped my wrists and jerked them suddenly from under my head to engage in what felt to me like a tug-of-war with the boy, who gripped my ankles. My spine stretched and my limbs ached. Not satisfied with that, the man immediately tried another maneuver, pressing his knee into the small of my back and pulling hard on my shoulders until the joints cracked. I've had Turkish massages before and I know about the joint cracking, but this was more like the Inquisition. Of course, the manipulations are well founded, subscribing to a ritual universal in the Muslim world, differing only in the degree of energy expended by the masseur. This fellow was herculean. Ignoring my groans of protest, he attacked every joint in my body from the toes to the fingertips with sudden twists and savage jerks, the sole purpose of which was to achieve the audible crack of bone and gristle that signals success. He was inexhaustible, and turned me over like an omelette several times. At one stage, he was standing on my chest, kneading my ribs with his bare feet. The next, he grabbed my arm to raise me up while he pressed his foot against the opposite thigh.

I have no idea how long this torture persisted. He signaled the end of it, as they invariably do, with a sharp slap across my buttocks. To me at that stage of the process, any indignity was welcome if it brought respite. I felt as if my entire body had been taken apart and reassembled. I swear that no muscle, ligament, or nerve had escaped his attention.

I flopped on the marble, panting.

As if from another world, a voice said in French, "Your Royal Highness?"

I remained supine.

"Mustafa is unequaled at his trade. You will feel the benefits later, Your Royal Highness."

I wouldn't have troubled to raise my head if the voice had not sounded familiar. I couldn't trust my ears alone. I hauled myself onto an elbow and stared across the marble surface at the naked form of the *chef de la Sûreté*.

Chapter 18

My first thought was that the dreadful mauling I had just received had affected my brain. With my blood in its parboiled and turbulent state, was it any wonder that I should experience hallucinations? I blinked twice, fully expecting to remove Marie-François Goron from my field of vision. But when I looked again, he appeared more substantial than before. His cropped hair glistened with sweat and his fat face was crimson. The wax had melted from his mustache and the tufts at each end had sprouted and sagged.

He raised himself to his hands and knees and crawled toward me across the massage dais like a large naked baby—a spectacle too ludicrous to be a figment of my imagination.

The squelch of his potbelly coming to rest beside me on the marble removed any lingering doubt. I won't say I was reassured; I preferred the illusion.

I sat up and said, "This can't be a coincidence."

He grinned sheepishly.

I was incensed. "I came here in the expectation of meeting someone else. Instead, I am the victim of an ambush. I have been forced to strip, then pummeled, mauled, and beaten. Every joint in my body has been tugged out of its socket—and now I know exactly whom to blame."

He raised his shaggy eyebrows in pretense of innocence and two beads of moisture rolled down his cheeks. "May I respectfully suggest that you lie still and relax, Your Royal Highness? Mustafa would like to complete the shampoo."

"Shampoo?"

He nodded.

The effrontery of this charmless clown took my breath away. Nobody on this earth, not even my mother, the Queen, refers to my receding hair, however obliquely. When I managed to find words, I told him, "This is beyond belief! Who do you think you are to make offensive remarks about my appearance?"

"Sir, I think you misunderstand me. *Shampoo* as the Turks understand it is a massage of the entire body, not merely the head. You have just had the manipulation and it can be rather nerve-racking to hear one's joints cracking, but that is the way they do it. The embrocation is the next stage. I think you will find it more agreeable. While Mustafa does his work, we can talk."

"Never mind Mustafa. I demand to know why I was lured here."

"Understandably," said Goron. "It was a necessary stratagem and I apologize for it. I needed as a matter of urgency to speak to you in private, without Madame Bernhardt in attendance."

"Bernhardt? All this because of Bernhardt? It's preposterous. If you wanted a word in private, you should have asked."

"Ah, but she would have taken it as a challenge," said he. "She hates being excluded from anything. This is one place where I can be assured of meeting you alone. At this time of the day, the bath is hardly used. Actually, I come here several times a week. It is the most discreet location for a meeting between gentlemen."

"*Discreet* is hardly the word I would use," I commented. "Parading in the buff is not my idea of discretion. Couldn't we have met in a club?" By declining to answer this, except with a sigh and a shake of the head, he intimated that his reason for bringing me here was too compelling to delay any longer. Making it plain that I was seething over what had happened, I resumed the prone position beside him—only because I was immensely curious to learn why he had tricked me into coming here. "Well, if this is the way the Sûreté conducts itself, I'm glad your methods haven't crossed the Channel. I take it that the message I was handed in the café was from you?"

"That is so. The man distributing the notes was one of my officers."

"How did he find me?"

"Another of my men has been following you for the past two days."

"I was not unaware of him," said I smoothly, quick to remember the fellow in the brown bowler hat. The fact that I had taken him for a newspaper reporter was of no importance. "You should teach him to be less obvious."

Goron sidestepped the criticism. "I became concerned about your activities. There was serious danger that you would undermine my investigation."

"By finding out the truth, do you mean?"

"No, sir. If I thought you were likely to find out the truth, I would have no cause for concern."

"Except the trifling inconvenience that you arrested the wrong man," said I with a shaft of irony that was deflected by Mustafa planting a blob of cold cream between my shoulder blades. "Jerusalem!"

Goron said, "Morgan is guilty."

To which I retorted, "That's the fallacy of French justice. You presume a man is guilty when he's innocent and has no chance of proving it. Is he still rotting in your prison?"

"He is still being questioned, yes."

"Hasn't he confessed yet? He must have a will of iron."

"I can vouch for that," he said with feeling.

Mustafa had smeared the cream liberally across my shoulders and was kneading my flesh with his fingertips, and I have to say that he was producing quite tolerable sensations.

I told Goron, "You are completely wrong about Morgan. The murder was committed by a woman."

His response was to yawn without even covering his mouth. "You mean Claudine Jaume? That is impossible."

"It most certainly is not. She was Letissier's lover before he met the Agincourt family. She bore his child and when he rejected her, she understandably became incensed. She visited him on the Sunday before the murder to beg him not to marry Rosine. All this is indisputable."

"I don't dispute it," said Goron, yawning again.

I would not allow his want of manners to deter me. "It was a classic French crime, the rejected mistress driven to a desperate act, a *crime passionnel.* I would have told you everything in time to arrest her, but I was hot in pursuit. If you had not inveigled me here under false pretenses, I would certainly have caught her. She must be up and away by now."

He said indifferently, "Up and away? Yes."

I hesitated. "Do you know this for a fact?"

"Yes, sir."

"Then in the name of justice, why didn't you detain her?"

He said flatly, "Because she is dead."

"Dead?" I stared at him, aghast. "How do you know?"

"I have seen the body. When you remarked that she is up and away, I could not disagree. It is true in a metaphysical sense. Whether she is up or down, it is difficult to say, but she is certainly away."

Only a French detective could have talked metaphysics at a moment like this. "How did she die?" I asked, still unwilling to believe him.

"Suicide, we believe. Her body was recovered from the Seine, near the Pont des Arts. A child's body was also found. Both have been identified."

"Already?"

"Already."

He gave the information in such a colorless way that I was beginning, after all, to accept it as fact.

"If this is true," I commented, "it's dreadful. She took the child's life as well as her own?"

"No, sir. The evidence suggests that the child was dead before entering the water. The most likely explanation is that Claudine killed herself from grief and had the dead baby in her arms when she jumped from the bridge."

"Grief, you say. Let's not exclude guilt."

"I'm not excluding it, sir. She was a tormented young woman."

As if by mutual consent, a silence descended. We respected the gravity of death, regardless that the deceased had sinned more than most. For an interval, the only sound was the rubbing of Mustafa's hands across my back.

I was dumbfounded by Goron's statement and, if the truth be told, crushingly disappointed. After so much diligent detective work, I had looked forward to unmasking the murderer myself. Was that too much to have hoped?

"I suppose she didn't leave a note, a confession?"

"No note," said Goron.

"It's so unsatisfactory this way."

"Yes."

Mustafa grasped me firmly by the hip and shoulder and turned me face upward, this time dropping the towel strategically over what an intimate friend of mine once called the crown jewels.

"Anyway, her suicide is tantamount to a confession of murder," said I.

"No, sir," said he flatly.

I gasped at his obtuseness. "You're not still insisting that Morgan did it, not after this?"

"I am more certain than ever," he insisted. "Claudine couldn't have murdered Letissier."

"Why ever not?"

"Because her body was found six hours before he was shot."

I sat bolt upright and pushed Mustafa away. "That's impossible."

Goron also heaved himself up. "I don't tell lies, sir."

"That's rich! What do you call it when you inveigle me here with a note supposedly from a woman who turns out to be dead?"

"I'd call it deception—in the interest of justice."

"Don't talk to me about justice, Monsieur Goron. You've deceived me from the outset," said I. "This is the first I've heard of her death. You didn't mention it when I came to see you at the Sûreté headquarters."

"I was unaware of it then. The bodies lay in the morgue unidentified for a fortnight. The girl's father, Felix Jaume, an hotelier, came up from Nantes yesterday because she hadn't written. She always wrote two letters a week to her family. After he'd described her to me, he was shown the body. He recognized his daughter at once, her face, her clothes, her crucifix, the comb she wore in her hair."

I shook my head. It is painful to reject an explanation one has firmly believed to be the truth. I would have staked my reputation on Claudine. Yet now that I cast my thoughts back to the conversation I'd had with the old woman who was her neighbor in the house in the rue du Chemin-Vert, she had told me that Claudine had done a moonlight flit with the baby two weeks previously. Two weeks—the interval matched Goron's information.

I said, "It would appear that I may be in error."

Goron gave a magnanimous shrug (which looks odd when given by a naked man).

I said, "I suppose I should thank you for mentioning it in private."

"You need not," said he, adding, after a significant pause, "All I would ask, sir, is that you now leave the Sûreté to complete its work."

This I did not particularly care for. I said, "I see no reason to abandon the case, if that is what you mean."

He frowned.

"I'm damned if I'll give up," said I. "The tragic death of this young woman must have a bearing. It can't be coincidence."

"She killed herself because her baby died," said Goron.

"It was also Letissier's baby, remember."

He pressed his hand to his head and gave a sigh like the ebb tide. "Sir, I wouldn't have brought you here—wouldn't have gone to such lengths—unless there were overriding reasons to ask for your cooperation. This unhappy episode can only inflict more grief and distress on those already mourning the death of young Letissier. I am thinking of his parents in particular, decent elderly people who have not the slightest idea that their son fathered an illegitimate child. If you had met them and seen their suffering already, as I have, you would not wish them to be dealt this additional blow. Without wanting to be overdramatic, I fear that a further tragedy might be the result."

I said, "I shan't trouble the Letissiers unless it becomes absolutely necessary. My suspicions point me in another direction."

"And which is that?"

"Back to the Agincourts, I'm afraid. I say that with a heavy heart, Monsieur Goron. I am a family friend."

A look sprang into his eyes that I had not seen before, and it was akin to the look of a child caught raiding the pantry.

"The Agincourts? They are just as vulnerable," he said quickly. "Surely you can see that? The daughter, Rosine, was engaged to Letissier. The parents welcomed him as a future son-in-law. In recent days, they have had to endure repeated interrogation by the police and the press, not to mention you. They have seen their name bandied in the cheapest newspapers and they have borne it all with dignity. To heap this fresh infliction on them would be to invite more press sensations, more wagging tongues in the cafés and on the boulevards. We can spare them that, Your Royal Highness."

"Spare the Agincourts—or spare the Sûreté?" said I. "You nailed your colors to the mast when you took in Morgan as your prime suspect, didn't you?"

He said, "That is immaterial."

"On the contrary, it's so material, you could make a convict suit out of it, my friend, and it might not fit Mr. Morgan. If the news of this tragedy gets to the ears of the examining magistrate, he may not be so impressed by a forced confession."

He said with vitriol, "You exceed yourself, sir."

"We shall see. I have not the slightest intention of surrendering the case to you. I may have been mistaken over Mademoiselle Jaume, but no more mistaken than you are over Morgan. I shall persist in pursuing the truth, Goron, whatever the cost to people's sensibilities. If necessary—who's that?"

My attention was distracted by a movement at the other end of the massage dais. Someone had stood up and was creeping away. I couldn't see him clearly through the vaporous atmosphere and he was swallowed altogether by steam billowing from a door he went through, but I can tell when a man's movements are furtive.

"Just another bather," said Goron.

"That's the steam room," I pointed out. "He's gone the wrong way."

"That's his choice," said he.

But I wasn't satisfied. I remembered taking note of two

recumbent figures when I had entered this place. The shock of meeting Goron had dismissed the second from my mind. That mysterious person, whoever he was, had been well placed to eavesdrop on our conversation.

"I'm going after him."

Goron said, "Don't."

That galvanized me.

I swung my legs off the dais and dashed across the atrium, past the cold pool, skidding dangerously on the wet tiles and just staying upright. When I tugged open the door, steam fairly rushed out and hit me like a solid mass. It was a lunatic act to subject oneself to the experience without first becoming inured to heat in the purgatory of the other heat chambers. But if the man I was following was so keen to escape, then I was keener still to follow. Inside, the shock of the heat made me stagger. With eyeballs popping, heart thumping, and my entire body streaming, I groped toward a stone bench supposedly provided for the patrons to disport themselves upon—if their physiques could endure the experience. No one was there, so I shuffled to the other side. There I found a set of steps. The ventilators belching out the heat were high above me, near the ceiling, and it was a test of bulldog courage to mount the steps, increasing the agony. The only reason I submitted to it was that I had glimpsed through the billowing steam a pair of legs about four steps above me. Whoever was up there, he would be blistered all over if he stayed for long.

I braced myself and ascended two steps. The legs above me became sharper to my vision. I could see the calves, dark where the hair was flat to the skin, and the thighs, slender yet solid. As I watched, the muscles tensed.

I should have been more wary. I hadn't expected violence. One of the feet swung at me and caught me in the chest, pitching me backward. I might have been thrust on the tiled floor and seriously injured. However, my instinctive reaction to the attack was to grab the foot. I held on. I *did* fall backward, but slowly, tugging my assailant with me. We ended together in an ignominious heap at the bottom of the steps.

We were soon back on our feet, both of us, because the heat of the tiles was searingly painful against delicate areas of flesh. Before I could get a look at him, the man mounted the steps again—on the principle, I suppose, that the high ground was tactically easier to defend, but this time I was close behind. He was slight in stature; I'd gleaned that much from our encounter. I'm no Eugene Sandow, but I reckoned with my superior weight I could subdue him.

The problem was that the higher one went up the steps, the closer were the ventilators belching out the steam. I got almost to his level and grasped an elbow that he tried jabbing into my midriff. I held on as well as I could with the steam gusting into my face. He was a doughty antagonist, because he twisted one of his legs behind my own and forced me to relax my grip under the threat of losing my balance. Then, before I was steady again, he secured an armlock around my neck.

My face was forced down brutally. Below the ventilators at the top of the steps was a large semicircular cistern half-filled with steaming water and lined with sediments of gray clay. My head was being inched toward it and the searing sensation on my skin made me cry out. To come into contact with the enamel edge would result in terrible burns. I was so close and the heat so terrific that I could not tell whether I was already being scalded.

The Marquis of Queensberry's Rules weren't written for people in the process of being casseroled. My only hope of escape was to go below the belt, so to speak. Groping like a blind man at a door, I found his most vulnerable point, squeezed with all my strength, and twisted. He emitted a roar of pain and relaxed the armlock. But you are right: I did not relax the hold I had on him. Holding tight, I braced and drew back from the wicked heat. My efforts toppled us both off the top step. We slithered down the steps together, staying upright only because we held on to each other. At ground level, I let go and pushed him away. I was practically expiring from the heat and the exertion. The only thing in the world I wanted was to get out of the steam room. I staggered to the door, pushed it open, and took a running jump into the cold pool.

Sinking thankfully under the surface, I thought, I shall never order a cooked lobster again.

I came up for air in time to see a pink blur at the edge of the pool, followed by a mighty splash. My antagonist had taken the same escape route. I rubbed water from my eyes and waited for him to surface.

I blinked. "You?"

He groaned, gave me a long look across the rippling water, and said, "For pity's sake, keep away from me, Bertie. I can't take any more."

He was Jules d'Agincourt.

You may imagine my confusion. I said, "I had no idea it was you."

"I won't make a run for it, I give you my word," said Jules. "I'm not even sure if I can walk after what you did to me. Just let me stay in this water."

When Goron, the far-famed *chef de la Sûreté*, came to the side of the pool and offered to help me out, I declined. I said in a dignified way, "You'll be better employed attending to your confederate."

I won't say Goron's shamefaced look was worth the indignity I had suffered. But it was some consolation.

Dressed again, the three of us met over mint tea and *keblahs* in the tearoom of the Hammam, a blessedly cool, secluded place with a fountain playing.

Goron had taken time to marshal his defense. "Your Royal

Highness, allow me to explain why I invited the comte to be present when I met you in the bath," he said in an emollient tone.

"To eavesdrop," said I. "I understand now why you chose this place. It's ideal for eavesdropping."

"That wasn't the spirit in which it was done, sir. The comte was deeply troubled about the distress your, um, investigation was capable of inflicting on innocent people like the Letissiers and his own family."

"*Distress?*"

"In all innocence, of course. But I shared his concern. We at the Sûreté had serious worries that your activities might interfere with the process of the law."

"This is really too absurd," said I.

He continued doggedly, "I agreed to arrange a meeting with you. And you're correct in suggesting that this place seemed the ideal choice, because it enabled the comte to be present but unseen. He would be well placed to come forward, if necessary, and use his influence—"

"You don't have to go on," I cut in. "It's all transparently clear. Frankly, Monsieur Goron, I am more interested to know why my old friend the comte crept away like a thief in the night—or tried to."

"Because you impugned his family, sir," said Goron. "No sooner had I convinced you that Claudine Jaume could not have committed the crime than you pointed your finger at the Agincourts."

"Are you suggesting that he beat a retreat rather than defend his family's good name?"

"He avoided an unpleasant scene."

"I think you are mistaken." I glanced in the direction of Jules, who had stayed conspicuously silent. "That isn't the conduct of a gentleman and Jules is a gentleman through and through, regardless of the dustup we had this evening. Isn't that so, Jules?"

My old friend looked at me bleakly and, to my astonishment, said nothing. Now, I'm as prone to error as anyone else
(some would say more prone), but I know the ways of the
aristocracy of Europe. Jules would defend his family like a
tiger, whatever their failings.

"Jules?"

His silence was a revelation. In that moment of scintillating
clarity, I understood.

Reader, I rumbled him.

"You killed Letissier."

After a moment's stunned silence, Jules said, "Yes, I admit
it."

"What?" said Goron, jerking upright as if his name had
been called by Saint Peter.

Jules said in a tone drained of all emotion, "Bertie is right.
I shot Maurice Letissier. I have behaved abominably. You must
release that poor man Morgan. He is innocent."

"When did you discover this?" Goron demanded of me as
if *I* was the guilty man.

I ignored him. Addressing Jules, I said, "You were the
sender of that anonymous letter—the one insisting that Morgan was innocent."

"Yes—and the others to the Sûreté. I did everything I
could, short of confessing, but this man took no notice."

Goron reddened. "The information you gave us was flawed.
Morgan wasn't in the garden when the shots were fired. He
was in the hall."

"Jules didn't know that," said I. "All he knew was that
Morgan didn't fire the shots. As a man of honor, he couldn't
allow an innocent man to be accused, so he invented what he
thought was a watertight alibi for him. He didn't know that
Morgan's own statement contradicted it."

Goron's hands were clasped in front of him and his knuckles
were white. "If this is true, it's astonishing."

"You dismissed those letters as unimportant," said I. "A

more alert investigator recognized them as clues." (The attentive reader may recall that this was Bernhardt. I would have given her the credit if she had been present, but the distinction would have been lost on Goron.) "Jules, you had better explain what made you into a murderer."

The word unsettled him. He shuddered and ran his hand through his hair. "The immediate cause, I suppose, was meeting Claudine Jaume."

"By chance?"

"No, she came to me. I knew nothing of her existence until the Wednesday before. She wrote a letter asking to meet me in front of the Madeleine at noon the following day. It was a simple letter in an educated hand and I decided to act on it. I took her to a quiet café and she told me the story that you know, of her *affaire de coeur* with Maurice, about the love child and her attempts to persuade Maurice to acknowledge the child and come to some arrangement for its upkeep. Over the last days, the child had become sick to the point of death. In desperation, Claudine went to Maurice's apartment to make one more appeal for money, to pay for a doctor's attention. He sent her off without a sou and now she was appealing to me. Of course I did what I could to help. Tragically, the help came too late."

"Did you confront Letissier?" Goron asked.

"Maurice? Of course. I did it discreetly, on the Friday. I told him frankly that I thought he should have the decency to help the girl. One might forgive his peccadillo with Claudine, if that was all it had been, but as a gentleman he was in honor bound to make provision for the child. His reaction was to tell me that Claudine was lying, that he had never been intimate with her. I didn't believe him. The girl had been convincing—utterly convincing—and Maurice was not. And if he was prepared to lie to me over this matter, I didn't want him marrying my daughter."

"What was his answer?"

"He challenged me to break off the engagement. He said if I muddied his reputation, he would be justified in muddying Rosine's and he went on to allege deplorable things about her."

"With Morgan?"

"Yes—and I am sure they were untrue, but you know how scandal is spread in society. He fully intended to ruin her life if I intervened. What could I do as a father? Throw my daughter to a jackal like that—or risk her being slandered as a slut? I couldn't allow it, Bertie. I had to remove the threat. I decided to kill him."

I nodded. "The rest we know. You don't need to tell us how it was done, except one thing. After shooting him, whatever possessed you to put the gun into Valentin's overcoat pocket?"

He gave a shrug. "Incompetence. I didn't think ahead. After I shot him and he was carried to the dressing room, I realized that the police would be called and that any of us might be searched for a weapon. The coat pocket was the only hiding place I could find. It didn't occur to me that the owner of the coat would collect it while we were still in the room. I was in no state to think clearly."

We became silent. Each of us, I suppose, was imagining the devastation this would wreak in the Agincourt family and in the larger family of Parisian society. I almost wished I had left the Sûreté floundering in its own incompetence. But then an innocent man would have been executed.

Chapter 19

There is a postscript to this case.

More than a year later, Sarah Bernhardt arrived in London to fulfill the latest engagements of her world tour, and naturally I attended a performance and visited her dressing room. Capricious as ever, she declined my offer of supper at the Savoy and instead proposed tea the following afternoon. She said tea would be more discreet. I suggested breakfast as a compromise and got a ticking-off. She was most anxious not to cause offense to Alix while in London, and I am sure on reflection that she was right. Those two formidable ladies have always respected each other.

A world tour can be tedious in the telling, and I was resigned to hearing how the Bernhardt troupe had been received at every stop from Amsterdam to Zanzibar, but to my relief, Sarah had called at Paris en route to London, so she had more intriguing news to impart when we met at a quiet corner table toward the back of Elphinstone's, the tea shop in Regent Street.

"That dreadful Rosine d'Agincourt, Bertie!"

"Rosine? What has she done?"

"Married an American millionaire."

"Good Lord! I thought she'd sworn undying love to the painter—what was his name?—Morgan, the fellow I saved from the guillotine."

"I told you she was not to be trusted. It appears that she was wrong about the undying love. It was puppy love."

"Well, I don't suppose Morgan is brokenhearted. All that passion was too much for him to handle. He'll have to find someone more his own age."

"He has," said she. "The gossip is that he's living at Montroger now."

"On the estate?"

"In the house, as Juliette's lover."

I choked on a cucumber sandwich. "Did you say Juliette?"

"She is more his age."

"Yes, but she hated him. She called him a parasite."

"A lady can change her mind, Bertie."

"He's not her type."

"Who can tell? With Jules gone, she needs someone else to talk to. I'm sure he'll earn his keep."

When I'd adjusted to the shock, I nodded. "It still seems insensitive, not to say callous. Poor old Jules. He deserved better from his family after the dignity he showed, and right to the end. I read about his execution in *The Times*. I gather he went bravely."

"Nobly."

"I think about him often," I added. "That a decent man like that should feel driven to murder—quite appalling. It occurred to me that there could have been a much more satisfactory outcome to this wretched business."

She leaned forward eagerly. "What is that?"

"Well, we know that Claudine Jaume did her best to poison Letissier with arsenic."

"Do we?" said she archly.

"My dear Sarah, I thought your memory was better than

that. She possessed a jar of the stuff. I took it to the chemist for analysis, remember? And Letissier displayed the classic symptoms of slow poisoning—gastric problems, headaches, loss of hair, and jaundice. Now, this is the point: If only the poisoning had succeeded, Jules need not have shot him. Claudine would have taken her own life, anyway, after the baby died. And Jules would still be alive to this day!"

The corners of her mouth twitched. I thought for a moment she was deeply moved, but she scolded me instead. "Bertie, that's the silliest nonsense. After all these months, I can't believe you still don't know the truth of it. The arsenic wasn't for poisoning. It was medicinal."

I shook my head. "Sarah, this is no joking matter."

"I mean it. I'm serious. Claudine was taking it for her condition."

"Taking arsenic?" I was utterly skeptical.

"Yes."

"For her condition? You do mean when she was, um"—I cleared my throat—"expecting the child?"

"No, Bertie. She had the pox."

"Good Lord!" I looked about me. "Keep your voice down. Do you mean . . . syphilis?"

She gave a nod. "I am not conversant with the condition, but the treatment is well known. You take arsenic or mercury in tiny amounts."

"Sarah, how can you possibly advance such an unedifying theory?"

"Bertie, she caught it from Letissier. He was a roué. He went to whores."

I winced, certain that the entire tea shop was listening. "I don't dispute that, but it was never suggested that he contracted a disease."

"He did," she insisted. "And I'll tell you how I know. Do you remember the medicines you found in his lodgings at the rue Tronchet? Among them was a bottle of Van Swieten's liquor. I made inquiries. It is a preparation made from sublimate of mercury dissolved in alcohol and water and it is the standard remedy for chronic syphilis."

"Oh."

"She favored arsenic—I suppose because she found it easy to acquire—and he used Van Swieten's."

"Really?"

"And what is more," she said, "all those symptoms you described for arsenic poisoning are characteristic of the pox in its secondary stage. The stomach upsets, the sore throats, the headaches—what else?"

"Loss of hair."

"Alopecia."

"Jaundice."

"Hepatitis."

"And they are . . ."

"Characteristic of the second stage. It lasts up to three years."

I took a sip of tea. I'd lost my appetite for the sandwiches. The cakes would not be eaten, either. 'If this is true—and I admit you make a strong case—why didn't Jules speak of it when he confessed? Wasn't he aware of the truth?"

"I'm sure he knew," said she. "What happened is this. When Claudine met him in the last days of her life, she was in despair. She showed him her dying baby, another victim of the disease."

"He didn't mention it to me."

"Bertie, he wouldn't," said Bernhardt with such an outpouring of feeling that I was quite subdued. "Jules was a gentleman to the last. He regarded what that poor girl told him as confidential. But he was appalled that Letissier—having infected Claudine and her child and ruined their lives—should still insist on marrying his daughter. When he saw Letissier and heard his lies, his absolute denials, he felt he had no choice but to shoot him. That was the real motive. But he went to the guillotine without mentioning it once."

I needed no more convincing.

She said, "Do you believe me now?"

I nodded. "I am a father myself, and, I hope, a man of honor. I understand why Jules acted as he did."

I wouldn't have added anything else, but Bernhardt, being Bernhardt, couldn't let an opportunity go by. "So it was, after all, a crime of passion, as I always insisted."

"I don't agree," said I. "Jules wasn't driven by passion."

"No, but the source of it all was one man's promiscuity."

"Well, if you put it like that, yes."

"Thank you."

"But you chose the wrong suspect. You kept telling me quite mistakenly that Rosine was the guilty party." I softened my expression. "However . . . I could be persuaded to forgive you, my dear. We have at least two hours before the play begins."

She missed my drift entirely, she was so indignant. "Who are you to talk about mistakes? You suspected Claudine. You were just as much at fault as I."

"Very well," I said, wanting a truce. "We were both mistaken."

"But I was right in saying it was a crime of passion, wasn't I?"

"Yes, I already said so."

She gave a faraway look. "Love is dangerous. It isn't worth it, Bertie."

"What do you mean dangerous? It's perfectly safe with me, I assure you."

She smiled. "It isn't you, Bertie. It's the hat."

"Which hat?"

"The hat that just came in. Unless I'm mistaken, it belongs to my dear friend the Princess of Wales."

And it did.

FICTION   Lovesey, Peter.
Lov
             Bertie & the crime of
             passion.

DATE		
MAR 2 9 '95		
AP 28 '95		
AUG 1 1 1995		
AUG 2 2 ...		
OCT 3 1 1995		